One-Eyed Jack

OTHER BOOKS BY LAWRENCE WATT-EVANS

The Nightmare People
Among the Powers
Shining Steel

THE FALL OF THE SORCERERS
A Young Man Without Magic
Above His Proper Station

THE ANNALS OF THE CHOSEN
The Wizard Lord
The Ninth Talisman
The Summer Palace

THE OBSIDIAN CHRONICLES
Dragon Weather
The Dragon Society
Dragon Venom

LEGENDS OF ETHSHAR
The Misenchanted Sword
With A Single Spell
The Unwilling Warlord
Taking Flight
The Blood of a Dragon
The Spell of the Black Dagger
Night of Madness
Ithanalin's Restoration
The Spriggan Mirror
The Vondish Ambassador
The Unwelcome Warlock

Lawrence Watt-Evans

One-Eyed Jack

Misenchanted Press
Takoma Park

This is a work of fiction. None of the characters and events portrayed in this novel are intended to represent actual person living or dead.

One-Eyed Jack

Copyright © 2011 by Lawrence Watt Evans
All rights reserved

Published by Misenchanted Press
www.misenchantedpress.com

Cover art by Kyrith Evans

Dedicated to
Roger MacBride Allen
for convincing me that
publishing wasn't that hard.

Chapter One

It started with a dream. It usually does.

There was a street, broad and straight, with sidewalks on both sides, and wide green lawns, and tidy little houses set back behind those lawns. A bright summer sun was setting behind the houses on one side, and shadows were stretching out across the lawns. The sunlight sparkled from drops of water flung up by sprinklers in the shadows, and the sidewalks were turning orange in the sunset. A dog was barking somewhere, and a hammer was thumping; kids were riding bikes along the sidewalks, the shadows of the spokes flickering across the grass.

A family was gathering for supper on a glassed-in porch; a white-haired couple sat side by side on the porch next door. The unnatural colors of TV screens flickered behind a dozen windows.

I didn't recognize the street; it wasn't anywhere I had seen before, either sleeping or awake.

And then, as the sun dropped out of sight, I was watching a particular house, one where the paint on the garage door was starting to peel, and where a man's voice was shouting inside closed windows. I listened, and I could make out the words.

"...worthless little creep," he said. "You, too, missy – you aren't any better. I see the way you look at me, you think your old man's a drunken loser, but whose fault is that, huh? I was doing *fine* until you two were born! Then all of a sudden your mother didn't have any time for me, she had to spend all her time cleaning up after *you* two. Couldn't keep a job, either – she had to keep running home to wipe your noses. Couple of little retards!"

I was looking in the window then, where a big man gone soft was leaning over a boy of twelve or so, jabbing his finger at the kid. The boy was sitting in a chair by a kitchen table that held three empty beer bottles. A little girl was curled up in the corner beside the refrigerator, staring up at the man, and a woman in a cheap house-dress was standing at the kitchen sink ignoring it all, her shoulders hunched.

The boy was glaring up at his father defiantly.

"You want to say something to me, Jack? You got something you want to say, Jackie-boy?" the man bellowed.

The boy didn't speak.

"What's the matter, you can't talk? Can't remember how to speak English?" The man straightened up.

"I don't have anything to say to you," the boy whispered.

"No? You can't be civil to your own father?"

The boy didn't reply.

"Get out of here, then! Get out of my face, and stop reminding me I'm saddled with your useless little butt!" He gestured wildly.

The kid got out of his chair and fled, out of the kitchen, through the living room, into the hallway, where he glanced at the stairs, then turned the other way and stormed out the front door.

He didn't slam it, though. He started to swing it hard, then looked back toward the kitchen and caught himself. He stopped the door, then pulled it gently closed until the latch clicked.

Then he paused on the front steps – no porch on this house – and looked around at the twilight, at the looming black shapes of trees and the glowing squares of windows and the fading gray lawns and sidewalks. A streetlight buzzed and lit, and yellow light chased the darkness away from half a dozen yards.

The boy turned the other way and walked out into the darkness, and that was when I woke up in my own bed, in my seventh-floor apartment, staring at the ancient stain on the ceiling while the clock-radio played a Jordin Sparks song.

I sighed, turned off the alarm, got up, and headed for the bathroom.

I didn't know what the dream was about. I didn't know who the kid was, or where the street was, or why I was seeing it. I didn't know, and really, I didn't particularly *want* to – but it was a safe bet I was going to find out. Maybe not right away, but eventually that kid would become my business. The people I dreamed about like this always did, one way or another.

It had been awhile since I'd had one of those dreams, but I could tell this was one, that it wasn't just my subconscious messing with me. I can't explain how I knew, but I knew.

These dreams were one of my special little talents. I had a couple of others, but we'll get to those.

I liked it better when I had normal dreams, where I was flying around like Superman, or standing naked at the chalkboard back in high school, or falling into bed with Catherine Zeta-Jones. I liked it better when my dreams didn't make any sense. Those dreams might be scary or frustrating or confusing, but they were just dreams.

The dreams about strangers doing ordinary things, though, those were more. Those were real. I was seeing things that were actually happening, or had actually happened, or were going to actually happen. The strangers were real people, and sooner or later I was going to meet them in real life. That was when the dreams would stop, when I met the person I had dreamed about and had to deal with him in the waking world. We were going to be associated in some way that would make a connection between us, something more than a casual greeting. That stranger was going to change my life somehow – or at least, that was how it had worked the half-dozen times I'd had dreams like this before.

The nature of that connection, that change, might be anything, good or bad, and I didn't really know why I had the dreams days, or months, or even years in advance, but I had a theory. My guess was that whatever was going to happen between us would create a psychic event that resonated backward through time to my sleeping brain.

It was all part of what my history teacher had done to me in eleventh grade, what she had called her four additions to my education, and I could have just said it was magic, but I kept trying to make some sense of it, to figure out how the magic worked, and resonances from my future self seemed more reasonable than just calling it prophetic visions.

Why this stuff didn't resonate forward as well I didn't know, but it didn't – or at least, it never had yet. Once I met someone I'd dreamed about, met him in the waking world, that was it, I was on my own, with no more supernatural knowledge, no more visions or premonitions or clairvoyance. Oh, I would still see those things normal people don't see, the things I'd rather not see; that part of Mrs. Reinholt's gift was permanent. But I wouldn't have any more dreams about a particular individual after I'd met him face to face.

I just wished that whoever or whatever sent me these dreams would make them a little more informative. All these rules I've just explained were things I'd worked out or guessed at from the half-dozen example I had; no one had ever told me what was happening, or how any of this worked. It was entirely possible that I had some of the rules wrong, or that they could change without warning. I just didn't know.

I was grumbling about it while I shaved and dressed. Every previous round of dreams had meant a change in my life, usually a change for the worse, and I didn't feel any need for more changes. My life sucked quite enough as it was.

I tried to remember more details of the dream; was there anything in there that might tell me where it happened, or when, or who Jack was? The whole thing had taken place on a pleasant suburban street, but not too fancy – no McMansions, no gated community, just a bunch of tidy little ranch houses and Cape Cods. It wasn't anywhere I recognized. From the architecture I'd say the neighborhood was built in the 1950s, but that didn't narrow it down much.

If it was in the Washington metro area, where I was, it was a part I'd never seen. There were a few streets in Arlington and Silver Spring that were roughly similar, but I knew it wasn't an exact match for any of them. The terrain was flatter than most of the older Maryland suburbs, for one thing. I didn't think it was local.

That left a lot of possibilities.

I was pretty sure from how green the lawns were, and how big the trees were, that it wasn't in a desert anywhere – Phoenix and El Paso were not among my top candidates. The houses didn't look quite right for New England, either. It *felt* like someplace in the east, not California or Hawaii or Colorado, but I couldn't be sure of that. There were no palm trees, no pines. The cars – was there anything useful about the cars? Could I get the state from the license plates?

I didn't remember seeing cars. Suburbs always had cars, but I hadn't noticed any. I growled at how useless my dream-self could be, rinsed my razor, toweled off my face and hands, and headed for the kitchen.

Kitchenette, really. I wasn't exactly living in the lap of luxury. I had a decent little apartment on Maple Avenue, about a mile from the District line and the Takoma Metro station, but the key word is "little."

Ever since the disasters back in high school I try to tell the appropriate people when I have one of my special dreams – police, social workers, parole officers, whoever. Not that it does any good. This time, though, I couldn't think who to call, other than my friend Mel, who always wants to know when I'm dreaming this stuff. A kid named Jack, a kid with a verbally abusive father, took off; who should I call about *that*? I didn't have a last name, didn't have a location, didn't have a date, didn't know whether the kid had already come back.

I'd just have to wait until I had more to go on, and in the meantime I had a long day at the store ahead of me. The dream had distracted me from hitting the snooze button the way I usually do, so I had time for a real breakfast, for once, and I concentrated on that, not on this mysterious Jack who was destined to change my life.

That afternoon I dozed off on my break. I don't usually do that. I dozed off, and I dreamed again.

It wasn't clear and detailed this time, maybe because I was sitting at a battered Formica table in an ugly room lit with cheap fluorescents instead of safely tucked in my own bed, or maybe because something else was interfering somehow. It was night in the dream, beneath a clear and starry sky, but Jack was lying under a tree with his head in a woman's lap. I couldn't tell whether this was on that same street, or nearby, or the other side of the world, but it was definitely Jack lying there.

I couldn't see the woman's face; she was leaning forward, and her long black hair had tumbled forward and hidden her features from me. She was wearing a white dress – or maybe it was just a slip, not a dress at all. She was thin, thin and bony – not model-thin, more like Auschwitz thin.

I wasn't sure she was human. I suspected she wasn't. There was something ever so slightly off about her, even in a dream.

Don't listen to him, she murmured into Jack's ear. I didn't hear the words exactly, there was something strange about her and how she spoke, but I knew what she had said. *Don't pay him any mind*, she told him. *You're my friend. You're a good boy, a smart boy, worth two of him any day, and I love you, even if he doesn't.* She closed her left hand over Jack's left, and lifted it up.

He didn't resist; he let her lift his hand, pull it up toward her face...

And then Fred the assistant manager was grabbing my shoulder, saying, "Hey, Greg, break's over. Time to earn your pay."

"Right," I said, straightening up in my chair. My head had fallen back; I'd probably been snoring like a goddamned Boeing. I tugged my stupid red vest into place and got to my feet.

My body went back to work just fine, but my mind needed a few minutes to review that tiny fragment of a dream.

Jack was with a woman, one older than he was, and he was friendly enough with her to put his head in her lap and hold her hand. I got that. I didn't know who she was, though, or *what* she was – I've seen enough supernatural beings, in my dreams or awake, to know that some of them can look almost entirely human, and this woman had looked and sounded "off" enough that I was pretty sure she was one of those creatures. I didn't know where they had been talking, or what she wanted with Jack. I didn't know why Jack could see and hear her when most kids his age can't see anything supernatural at all. I didn't know why I was supposed to care about any of this.

I *was* supposed to care, though. I knew that. The dreams always mattered.

My best guess, I swear, is that my own future self's unconscious mind sends these dreams back in time to me. If it was under conscious control, or if some outside power, God or an angel or a demon, or some goddamn aliens, or some future humans messing around with time travel, or some mysterious cosmic force, sent them, I'd expect them to be either more useful, or *less* useful.

They weren't completely random, the way they might be if it was a purely natural phenomenon; I never got anything about Chinese peasants or gun-runners in Mozambique, it was always someone I might have met someday even without trying. It wasn't just someone I was going to meet, though; it was someone who was involved in something that would mess up my life. He was going to be in trouble of some kind, or was going to *cause* trouble of some kind. Usually, but not always, supernatural trouble.

Assuming, of course, that the rules weren't about to change on me.

I hated that. I know it probably sounds crazy coming from someone you'd consider a psychic, but I didn't like the supernatural. I never had.

My Dad never believed in the supernatural at all; it used to drive him nuts that Mom bought into a lot of New Age crap, crystals and vibrations and all that stuff. I was on Dad's side, back in the day, but then Mrs. Reinholt took an interest in me and I started to see things, and the dreams began, and...

Well, if it was any comfort, Mom was mostly wrong, too. Not that I ever got a chance to tell her. It isn't auras and meditation and astrology; most of it is obsession and darkness and blood and fear. It's things living in the dark that have no right to exist, doing things that don't make sense. I'd really rather not know that stuff is out there, but I can't pretend, not anymore, not since high school.

Dad still *can* pretend; he hasn't seen the things I have. That's one reason we don't talk much. If we talked more, I'd eventually tell him things he doesn't want to hear, and he'd try to explain them away, and I'd get pissed at him about it.

So we don't talk.

I got through the rest of the day at the store without breaking any merchandise or insulting any customers, and some days that's all I can ask.

And I knew it probably didn't matter. I was probably going to get fired. When I get the dreams it usually leads to trouble that takes over my life for awhile, and the sort of job I take generally doesn't tolerate people who miss a week or two of work without a decent explanation.

I keep meaning to take classes, maybe even go for a degree from Montgomery College, so I can look for something better, maybe something that would lead to an actual career instead of just a small, steady paycheck, but something always happens to interfere, so I just get one crappy wage-slave position after another.

This one wasn't a bad job, though, all things considered, so at the end of my shift I stopped in the manager's office and told him there were some personal issues brewing, family problems, and I might need some time off soon. I figured it couldn't hurt to lay the groundwork.

"What sort of problems?" he asked.

I stammered and coughed and told him I'd rather not say.

He stared at me for a moment, then said, "I can't make any promises, Greg. Keep me posted."

"Yes sir, Mr. Sanchez."

Then I was out of there, headed for the bus stop, eager to be home before the summer sun set. I don't like being out after dark. When the sun's up, I don't see the various phantoms and apparitions prowling the streets of Takoma Park; when it's down, I see them all too well. It doesn't exactly do wonders for my social life, but I try hard to get home while the sky's still light.

I managed it that night, and was safely in my apartment well before dark. I didn't want to be around people, and I didn't feel like cooking, so dinner was a ham sandwich, and I spent the evening channel-surfing or browsing the web. The Nationals beat the Pirates for once, and every episode of "Friends" ended the way I remembered it, and there wasn't anything on any news I could find about a twelve-year-old runaway.

I was pretty sure what would happen when I went to bed. Sometimes the dreams are spaced out, spread over weeks or months, but getting the second one during a nap like that made me think that this time there weren't going to be any gaps. Half of me wanted to put it off, give myself that much more time before I got caught up in whatever this was, and the other half wanted to get it over with so I could get on with my life, and the result was that I packed it in about my usual time – turned the TV off around 11:30, brushed my teeth, and dropped into bed a little before midnight.

And sure enough, I dreamed.

I was back in Jack's house, a silent, invisible observer as the woman I'd seen standing at the sink before, and who I took to be Jack's mother, trudged upstairs, leaving Jack's father sprawled in front of the TV. "Sports Center" was on; whoever these people were, they got ESPN. Not that that narrowed anything down much;

pretty much everyone with cable gets ESPN. Half a dozen empty beer bottles – well, five empties and one about half gone – stood on the table in front of the sofa.

Cable TV and beer, a house in the suburbs somewhere, a wife and kids – what was this guy griping about? He lived better than I did.

The woman shuffled along the upstairs hall, then stopped by a closed door and slowly, carefully, opened it and looked in.

She froze, her head in the door. She opened it farther, stepped into the room, looked around at a cluttered desk, and a bookcase overflowing with books and toys and junk, and a bureau with three drawers closed and a half-open one with a pair of jeans sticking out, and a bed.

An empty bed. A bed that appeared to have been hastily made up that morning, and not touched since.

"Jack?" she called quietly, as she flicked on the ceiling light.

No one answered, and the light revealed nothing she hadn't seen in the light from the door, so she glanced in the closet, then looked around the room again, then went back out into the hallway and down the passage to the open door of the dark, unoccupied bathroom.

Then she tried the other closed door, as quietly as she could, and found the little girl asleep with her thumb in her mouth. There was no sign of Jack.

The woman's manner as she approached the master bedroom made me think the idea that Jack could be in there was a strange and unpleasant one for her, but I didn't really find out, because he wasn't there, either.

She went back downstairs and stood by the family room couch, and when "Sports Center" cut to a commercial she said, "Jack's not here. I looked everywhere."

Her husband looked up blearily. "What do you mean, he's not here? Isn't he in bed?"

"No, he isn't. His room's empty. He isn't anywhere in the house."

"That's... that's ridiculous." He pushed himself into an upright sitting position. "Where is he?"

"He's missing. He's run off."

"He wouldn't dare!"

"Well, I can't find him!"

The man on the couch glowered at her, then at the TV. Reluctantly, he picked up the remote and turned the set off, then got to his feet, swaying slightly. He headed for the stairs. "Jack?" he roared. "You up there?"

"You'll wake Katie!" his wife protested.

He glared at her over his shoulder. "That's too damn bad. *Jack!*"

He stormed up the stairs and tore through the rooms, flinging doors open, turning on lights, and shouting; he paid no attention to Katie as she cowered against the wall, her blanket pulled up to her chin.

Finally, he marched down the stairs. "The little son of a bitch isn't up there," he said. "You looked in the kitchen? And the basement?"

The woman nodded, and I think she might have been about to say something, but then the latch on the front door clicked, and both of them turned to stare.

The door swung open, and there was Jack, standing in the doorway.

He looked awful – pale and unsteady. He had the expression of someone trying not to vomit. Something dark was smeared on the front of his shirt. His right hand was on the door, his left was stuffed in his pocket, and something about his pose was horribly uncomfortable.

"Jack!" his mother cried.

"*There* you are, you little bastard!" his father bellowed.

He looked at them, but didn't say anything.

"Get your ass in here!" his father demanded, and Jack stepped into the house.

"Where have you *been*?" his mother asked.

"I took a walk," he said, his voice husky.

"At *this* hour?"

"I... lost track of time," he said.

"What's on your shirt?" his father asked, and his voice was lower than it had been for several minutes.

The stain on Jack's shirt, which had looked dark brown out on the stoop, was dark red in the foyer light. His mother's hand flew to her mouth as she gasped.

"It looks like blood," his father said.

Jack looked down, and brushed at the stain with his right hand. His left stayed in his pocket, and I knew that wasn't natural.

So did his father. "Let me see your hands," he said. "Both of them."

Jack did not argue, did not protest; he held out his right hand, and then pulled his left from his pocket, wincing as he did. He held it out.

His father looked at Jack's hands and slumped against the foyer wall; his mother looked at them and started screaming.

I looked at the boy's hands, and I woke up.

But before I woke, I saw that the little finger on his left hand was gone, the side of his ring finger was scraped raw, and a bit of blood-soaked rag had been plastered over the wound as a bandage.

Chapter Two

I didn't have much of an appetite that morning. Oh, I've seen much worse than a missing finger, but it still wasn't exactly my favorite way to start the day. Breakfast was a bowl of Cheerios, and I didn't bother with milk, or with a spoon; I ate them with one hand while my other worked the mouse on my old Dell, searching for any news stories about a kid losing a finger.

I didn't find any, at least nothing recent, or about a boy the right age.

Whatever had happened to his finger, it was a safe bet that was just the beginning of something, and that I was going to get dragged into it.

And since I was dreaming about it, and it was happening to people I didn't know in a place I didn't recognize, it was another safe bet that the supernatural was involved. If a spook chopped off his finger, that was bad. That was *really* bad. Ordinarily the things I see at night can't actually hurt anyone; they aren't substantial enough. When they *can* hurt people, it's bad, because how do you stop a phantom? Worrying about that killed the idea of a big breakfast.

Another reason for the weak appetite, if I even needed another reason with the image of that kid's hand still in my head, was that I knew I needed to call Mel soon. It was about time to talk to her anyway, just to stay in touch, and the dreams made it more urgent – she always wanted to know about it when I had the dreams.

But it was too early; she wouldn't be up for hours. I'd have to wait until evening. Which meant a whole day with that hanging over me.

I didn't really think she would know anything, but no matter how unpleasant the conversation might be, it would be comforting, in a way, to talk to the one friend I had who totally accepted the reality of my dreams, and who was accustomed to dealing with things that didn't belong in the natural world.

Of course, in other ways it wouldn't be comforting at all. Talking to Mel was not fun. That wasn't her fault, but it was true. Quite aside from the hours Mel kept, if I ever called before work there were likely to be after-effects that would not help me keep my job. Trembling hands are not good when stocking shelves, and customers don't like people who jump at the slightest surprise.

Instead of calling her I shut down the computer, went downstairs, and caught the bus to work. That meant not talking to anyone about the kid, or doing any more research, for an eight-hour shift. Selling hardware and building supplies is about as far from dealing with psychic phenomena as it's possible to get, which is one reason I liked the job there; I'd never told anyone at the store about my little involuntary hobby.

That was another reason I didn't have much of a social life, on top of not going out after dark; I had to constantly watch what I said if I didn't want people thinking I was completely insane. Most of the people I'd known as a kid had drifted out of my life because I'd stopped talking openly with them. Most of my neighbors in the apartment building kept to themselves, and a lot of them didn't want to hang around with a white guy in any case – I think they considered me creepy, and I didn't blame them. I was friendly enough with some of my co-workers, but none of them were exactly close.

Some education Mrs. Reinholt gave me. Some gift.

I didn't nap during my break this time. I didn't lose any customers, either – in fact, I had a pretty good day, moved a lot of merchandise, did a little harmless flirting with a cute brunette. The only bad moment was when I was showing someone a power saw, and my imagination made an unwelcome connection with the sight of Jack's left hand.

Not that I really thought a power saw was involved; the gash on his ring finger didn't look right for that. Still, I had to stop talking for a few seconds and regroup. I told the customer I'd rushed my lunch and probably ate something I shouldn't have, when I hadn't actually eaten lunch yet at that point.

I gave Mr. Sanchez another heads-up about my imaginary family problems, said something about my Dad's health getting bad, before I left.

I didn't like doing that; so far as I knew, Dad's health was fine, and I didn't want to jinx that, but it was the only thing I could think of at the time.

When I was a kid I didn't worry about jinxes. Hell, I felt superior to the other kids about that – I knew better, I knew that stuff was all crap. When they were worrying about stepping on cracks or walking under ladders, I laughed at them and did whatever I wanted.

Now I don't know one way or the other. Maybe there really *are* jinxes. There are sure as hell actual curses. Mel was living proof of that. Some people might say I am, too.

I wished I knew the rules – not just the bits I thought I'd figured out about how my dreams worked, but about all of it. I wished I knew there actually *were* rules; the more I dealt with the dreams and portents and visions and monsters, the more I believed that there weren't. In all the stories I'd ever read as a kid, or seen on TV, the monsters followed rules – werewolves change on the full moon and can be killed with silver, vampires suck blood and fear the sun, magic takes careful preparation and specific rituals. From what I'd seen, it didn't work that way. The things that went bump in the night generally didn't have tidy little labels like "werewolf" and "vampire," so far as I could see. Each one was different. And magic, when it worked at all, could happen spontaneously, and couldn't always be controlled. I don't think Mrs. Reinholt *intended* the curse she put on Mel to do what it did. I *know* she didn't intend *all* of what her spells did. She certainly hadn't *looked* suicidal.

I called Mel pretty much as soon as I walked in the front door of my apartment; I wanted to get it over with. I punched her number on my cell and held it to my ear.

She answered on the third ring, and an ominous feeling, a sensation of foreboding, came over me. I grimaced. The curse was still there.

Of course it was. It had been there for eight years; it wasn't going to just spontaneously vanish.

"Yes?" Her voice was cold, almost threatening, and I shivered at the sound of it. A sensation of emptiness sucked the strength out of me; I turned my back to the wall and braced myself.

"Hey, Mel, it's Greg," I said.

It seemed as if she paused before answering, and a feeling of dread, a certainty of looming disaster, crept up my back at that. The phone felt like ice in my hand, and I began to think that calling her had been a very, very bad idea.

But that was just the curse, I told myself. Talking to Mel was always like this.

"Gregory! How *are* you, dear boy?"

She's a month younger than I am; "dear boy" was an affectation, part of her act. I knew that. She didn't need to keep up the act with me, but sometimes she kept it going out of habit. I knew she didn't mean anything by it, but I couldn't help hearing it as vicious sarcasm. The sound of her voice sucked the life out of me, all the hope and light; the apartment that was my refuge from the world suddenly felt like a stark, empty prison. "I've..." I swallowed. "I've been better," I said. "I had a dream."

"You're dreaming again?" The words were harmless enough, and I knew she didn't intend them to be threatening, but they sounded like an accusation. Dreaming suddenly seemed like the worst thing I could do, a crime against nature and a betrayal of... well, everything.

"Yes," I managed. It came out in a whisper.

"I'm so sorry! Is it bad?"

"It's..." I couldn't finish the sentence; the words caught in my throat. I didn't know whether she meant the dreams or her curse, and I didn't dare give a wrong answer. I didn't dare question her.

"Strong as ever, isn't it?" she said.

She meant the curse, then. "Maybe stronger," I said.

"Maybe," she said. "It didn't used to be so bad over the phone. It's brave of you to call me then, Greg; I appreciate it."

I made a noise.

For a moment we were silent, a horrible ominous silence. "I'll tell you what, Greg," she said after a few seconds. "I'm going to be quiet now, and you're going to tell me all about your dreams. I want to hear it *all*, and I'll be very displeased if you leave anything out. And when you're done telling me, then you can end the call. How's that sound?"

"I love you, Mel," I told her, and a wave of sheer terror washed over me at the thought that she might take that as an invitation to meet in person, to spend time together.

But I meant it; I did love her, I had since high school – not romantic love, but as a friend. Even the curse hadn't been able to change that. The way she dealt with the curse, the way she refused to let it destroy her, made me love her all the more; she called me brave, but she was the one who lived every day with what that old woman had done to her, and *used* it, instead of letting it rule her.

I might not always agree with how she used it, but I admired her strength.

And she had stayed my friend, when the other people we knew from high school avoided both of us. She had *power*, she had money and influence, and I had nothing. She had turned her curse into an identity and a career, while I had let my "gifts" ruin my life, but we had stayed friends.

She laughed. "You're sweet, Greg," she said. "Now, tell me your dreams."

I told her. I talked for several minutes, and she didn't say anything. Talking to her wasn't so bad; it was when I was *listening* to her that the curse really hit.

"His finger was gone?" she asked, when I finished, and I shuddered so badly at the sound of her voice I almost dropped the phone. "I mean, he didn't have it in his pocket? It wasn't just severed?"

I felt like a fool for not even considering that possibility, and despaired at my own stupidity and incompetence. "I don't know," I admitted. "I didn't see it anywhere."

"You think that woman cut it off?"

"Maybe," I said. "I don't know."

"What did she look like?"

"I couldn't see her face. She was thin, pale, with long dark hair – "

I stopped, as I suddenly realized that description could more or less fit Mel, too.

Mel realized the same thing. "Gregory Kraft, you didn't think she was *me*, did you?"

"No!" I shouted. My voice cracked. "No, of course not! Please." I was crying. She was angry with me, and I couldn't face that.

Well, really, she probably wasn't, but I couldn't think straight enough to believe that. I had been stressed by the dreams to begin with, and talking to Mel was hard enough when I was calm.

"Greg, are you all right?" she asked, and on one level I knew she was genuinely concerned, but the curse changed it; she was mocking me, taunting me, berating me for my weakness. I pushed the button to end the call, and then fell into an armchair and sat trembling.

The phone rang.

It was her; I knew it was her. Part of me wanted to fling the phone aside, but I pressed the "send" button, and put the phone to my ear. I didn't say anything; I didn't need to.

"Gregory, you *hung up* on me!" she said.

"I know," I said miserably.

"You *hung up* on Madame Melisandra, Dread Mistress of Fear and Queen of Despair, when you knew I didn't want you to?"

"Yes," I croaked.

"My God, you've got balls!" She laughed.

"You scared the *shit* out of me!" I said, shivering uncontrollably.

The laugh cut off abruptly. "Well, yes," she said. "That's what I *do*." She sounded sad, almost wistful.

That wasn't the curse. Sad and wistful wasn't a misinterpretation that would fit the curse. That was her real feeling.

"You said that when I was done telling you my dream I could end the call," I reminded her.

"Yes, I did. But I hoped you wouldn't. And you weren't *done*, dear boy – we were still discussing how closely this woman resembled me."

I tried to remember the woman from my second dream, and match her against Mel – or rather, against Madame Melisandra de Cheverley, the Dark Lady, Queen of Despair and Mistress of Fear. Mel was the girl I'd known in high school, and Madame Melisandra was what she had become to accommodate the curse Mrs. Reinholt put on her.

"Madame" was also technically a lie, since she had never married, but Mademoiselle didn't sound right.

"I didn't really see her face," I said. "She was thinner than you..."

"Oh, thank you so *very* much!"

I jerked in a spasm of terror, and I must have screamed, because next thing I knew the voice from the phone was calling desperately, "It's okay, Greg! It's all right! I'm not mad! Gregory, are you there?"

"I'm here," I said. I didn't say more than that; I didn't need to. Mel knew what a sarcastic rejoinder like that could do to me.

"I'm so sorry! You just describe her, and I won't say another *word*, I promise, until you're done."

"Thank you." I took a deep breath, and then I said, "You know, I think it may be *worse* over the phone now. Next time I'll come out there and we can talk in person."

"I'd like that very much. Now, tell me about the woman in your dream."

I told her everything I could, which wasn't much. She had been very thin, bony, hunched over, with long, unkempt black hair that hung straight down like rope, hiding her face. She wore a simple white dress or slip. Her nails were long but unpainted. I hadn't seen her feet, but her hands were pale and gaunt. She was definitely female, but had nothing like Mel's curves.

When I was done there were a few seconds of uncomfortable silence – at least, they were uncomfortable for me – and then Mel said, "I'm sorry, Greg, I can't think of a thing that would help. I have no idea who or what she is. She isn't anyone I know, or that I've seen around here. Do you think she was human, or something else?"

"I don't know for sure," I said. "Could be either one." I didn't have the confidence to say any more than that, but given her appearance, I didn't really think she was human. What would a woman that thin, and dressed like that, be doing sitting under a tree at night, comforting someone else's kid?

"Then I don't know, either. Do you think you'll dream more tonight?"

"Probably." I let out a long, shuddering breath.

"Well, that will probably tell you more. If it's exciting, you'll tell me, won't you?"

"Of course."

"Then I'll let you go. But honestly, Gregory dear, thank you *so* much for calling! It's lovely to hear from you, and just to listen to your voice. Seriously. And I'd love a visit – I could send a car, if you like. I'm so sorry your dreams are troubling you, and I wish I could be more help."

"Thanks, Mel. I'm sorry the curse is still so strong, and that I can't resist it better."

"You do fine," she said. "You do better than anyone else." I think she wanted to sound reassuring, but it came out more like a veiled threat.

"Good night, Mel," I said.

"Good night, Greg."

And that was that.

I sat in the armchair with the phone in my hand for about ten minutes before I dared to get up.

Poor Mel. She was so lonely. She did her best to hide it, from herself more than anyone else, but I could still tell. She was completely alone in that big house of hers; no one else could bear to stay that close to her.

When we first met, back in high school, I don't think she was lonely. That was before Mrs. Reinholt cursed her, of course. Back then we didn't believe in curses. We didn't believe in witches. We didn't believe in prophetic dreams, or ghosts, or monsters. We believed in changing the world, and brushing after meals, and happy endings, and the health benefits of dark chocolate.

Kids always believe in lies.

I wondered what lies that kid Jack had believed that cost him his finger.

Well, I told myself that maybe I'd find out later, but it was too early for bed. I settled at the computer and did more searching for news items about a boy losing a finger.

I still didn't find any. I found some other interesting links, and chased around the net for awhile, reading this and that, but there wasn't anything about a runaway named Jack who came home short a finger.

I tried to see if I could find something about the skinny black-haired woman in white, but all *that* got me was porn, some of it pretty strange stuff. It's amazing what turns some people on.

I checked a few other things while I was there. My little stock portfolio was up a little, the Nationals were losing, Congress was still being stupid. My e-mail was all spam; I hadn't heard from Dad for three months, so I sent him a quick hello, just to remind him he'd had another family before he married Nancy and she started popping out daughters.

On a whim, I looked at some real estate listings. A lot of the houses around Mel's place were for sale. Not a surprise.

Poor Mel.

I did make a quick supper somewhere in there, and watched some TV, and finally I packed it in and went to bed.

And there was Jack's mother, in an office somewhere, talking to a nice man in an expensive suit who was explaining that Jack was suffering from severely low self-esteem, and that from a psychological point of view it was not impossible that the wound might be self-inflicted.

"He says it was an accident," she said.

"He wouldn't *admit* he did it himself," the psychologist replied. "It may be that he meant to do something far less drastic, and the knife slipped; that would be a kind of an accident, after all."

I tried to look around the office, to see if I could see a name, or some other evidence of where this was happening.

Jack's mother did not look convinced. She stood up. "Thank you, Doctor," she said. She walked out of the office, carefully closing the door behind her, and I could see that the name on the door was Dr. Brown, which was astonishingly unhelpful. There must be thousands of Dr. Browns out there. She walked down a hospital corridor to a waiting area where Jack's father was talking to a man in a white coat – another doctor, presumably. The two men looked up at her approach.

"Dr. Brown thinks he cut it off himself," she said.

Jack's father started to say something, but the man in the white coat spoke first.

"That's impossible," he said.

"It's what Dr. Brown – "

"Dr. Brown may be a fine doctor in his own field, but I'm telling you, your son did not cut off his own finger," the man interrupted.

"Why – "

"Even saying it was cut off is misleading," the man continued, ignoring the father's attempt to speak. "I looked at the wounds when I sewed them up. Those weren't nice, tidy cuts made with a good sharp knife; if they were made with a knife at all, which I *very* much doubt, it had a very dull blade."

"Then what *did* happen?" Jack's mother demanded.

"Was it a dog?" Jack's father asked.

The doctor shook his head. "I do think something bit it off, Mr. Wilson, but it wasn't a dog. The teeth-marks, if that's what they are, aren't right for any breed of dog I'm familiar with."

Jack's mother went pale, and I took note of the name, Wilson. I was looking for Jack Wilson, a kid with nine fingers.

"Then what... if it wasn't a dog, what the hell *was* it?" the father demanded.

"I don't know," the doctor said. "But it wasn't a sharp bite, like a dog or a wolf or a cougar; something *gnawed* that finger off. Or if it wasn't teeth after all, then someone hacked it off, little by little – it wasn't chopped off with a single whack."

Jack's mother made a small, half-strangled noise; her hand flew to her mouth.

"*No* child, no matter how disturbed he is, could have done that to himself," the doctor continued. "Dr. Brown is simply wrong about this."

And then a cop appeared, and I could see the patch on his uniform that read Lexington Fayette Urban County, and I had the clue I needed. The three of them all turned to look at him.

"Mr. And Mrs. Wilson? You can see Jack now."

And with that, both parents hurried into an examination room, where Jack was perched on the end of the examining table.

His mother hugged him, while his father hung back, looking uncertain. Jack didn't move; he accepted the embrace, but he didn't hug her back. He didn't look at his father at all.

"Jack, what *happened*?" his mother asked. "The doctor says... he says your finger..." She couldn't finish the question.

"Jack, did a dog bite it off?" his father asked. "Because if there's a dog out there that's attacking kids, it has to be found and put down."

Jack's head slowly turned to face his father, but he still didn't say anything.

"Was it a dog?" Mr. Wilson persisted.

"I don't remember," Jack said. He looked down at his bandaged, four-fingered hand. "I don't know what happened."

I wanted to say something. I wanted to ask about the hunched-over woman. I couldn't, though – I wasn't really there, I was just seeing this. I didn't even know whether it was past, present, or future.

At that thought I tried to look around the examining room for a calendar, but I didn't see one. So I still didn't know when this was, but that patch on the cop's sleeve would tell me where, I was pretty sure.

That didn't tell me what I should *do* about it. I didn't really know what was going on. I knew Jack had met a thin woman who comforted him, and that he came home missing a finger, but had the woman cut it off? If that doctor was right, had she *bitten* it off? Or was there more to it? There might be any number of things I didn't know yet.

I watched and listened for awhile longer, as Jack's parents questioned him, as the police questioned them, but I didn't learn anything useful. Jack wasn't talking; he never mentioned the woman in the white dress, but just kept insisting he didn't know what had happened to him, how he had lost his finger. He did say it was an accident, but nothing more; when asked how he knew it was an accident, he shut up completely.

The dream dragged on for what seemed like hours, going nowhere so far as I could tell, but that wasn't unusual for my visions, or psychic experiences, or whatever you want to call them.

I sometimes think my mysterious powers, whatever they are, could use a good editor.

Finally, though, it was over.

No, Jack didn't go home. He didn't talk. No one solved any mysteries. I just woke up.

And when I awoke I lay there in bed, staring at the stained ceiling.

I was at that difficult point where I had to decide what to do. If I tracked Jack down while I was awake, what would I do? What could I say to him? I couldn't put his finger back. I couldn't make him talk to his parents or the doctors. *I* couldn't talk to them; they'd think I was crazy. I wouldn't have any idea how to go about finding the thin woman. I didn't know enough to be useful.

If I waited, I might dream more, and learn more – but something terrible might happen. I had no idea what that might be, but *something* might. Something had caused a strong enough psychic disturbance to send me these dreams. It might just be having a finger gnawed off, but it might be something far worse. I didn't know.

That something was chewing off a kid's finger was really, really not a good thing, as it probably meant that there was a creature out there with a taste for human flesh and the ability to take it. There was no telling where that might go.

And whatever was going to happen, it presumably involved me somehow – maybe not directly, but *somehow*.

If I waited, I might find out more of what was going on, but I also might be too late to stop whatever it was from becoming an outright nightmare.

If I went now, if I found Jack and talked to him, I wouldn't dream about him anymore – but I might never find out what had happened to his finger.

I didn't think that was enough. I needed to know more.

I wasn't going to get back to sleep and dream anything more that morning, I could tell that, so with a sigh I got out of bed.

I didn't get my breakfast right away, though. First I went to the computer and searched on "Lexington," "Fayette," and "Urban."

That got me a nice clear answer: Kentucky. The Wilsons lived in Lexington, in Fayette County, Kentucky.

I'd never been to Kentucky, and I didn't know anything about Lexington.

I had an idea, though, that I was going to learn a few things pretty soon, whether I wanted to or not.

And I thought that maybe it was time I paid a visit to the Bluegrass State.

Chapter Three

I could get a flight out of Baltimore for $353. National or Dulles would be $500-plus. Amtrak didn't go to Lexington, and I hate long-distance buses even more than I hate flying.

Renting a car and driving wasn't totally out of the question, but flying would be faster.

But there was the question of what I would do when I got there. Wilson was a common name, and I didn't know the parents' first names, so finding the right family might take awhile, and when I found them, what would I say? "Hi, I've been dreaming about your son, and I think his finger was bitten off by a mysterious woman in white, who might be a supernatural creature of some sort, not really human at all. No, I don't know who she is, or where to find her, or why she would bite off a kid's finger. Yes, I dreamed this, I have no actual evidence. Yes, I guess I'm a psychic, but not one you ever heard of. I've never been on TV, I've never worked with the police or anyone official, and I don't know a thing about your town. I've lived pretty much my entire life in Maryland."

Yeah, that would go over well.

But I couldn't sit home and do nothing, either. I'd tried that. It didn't end well. I had dreamed about the man who killed my mother, and I didn't do anything because I thought they were just nightmares. I had dreamed about the cop who decided I must have killed Mrs. Reinholt, and if I'd paid more attention I might have avoided some of that mess and graduated high school.

Or maybe I wouldn't have avoided a thing; I doubt I could have ever convinced him of the truth. I saw the thing that killed Mrs. Reinholt – I didn't dream about that, since I already knew her, but I saw that thing, and even spoke with it, after a fashion, but how would I have ever made anyone else believe me? *They* couldn't see it, even if it had hung around.

I hadn't known what to do. I wasn't even completely sure yet that what I saw was real; I thought I might be hallucinating.

I wish I *had* been hallucinating. I wish those dreams *had* just been nightmares. And I wish I had *done* something. My mother might still be alive. Mrs. Reinholt might still be alive. Mel might not be calling herself the queen of despair, and she and I might have graduated with the rest of our class.

I didn't ignore the dreams again, ever. They weren't always about terrible things – I saw Nancy in my dreams before Dad even met her, and she's not a bad person – but they were always important. If I hadn't had dreams to warn me, I might have handled Dad's new girlfriend even worse than I did. The dreams I had about the guy who used to own Mel's house had helped me deal with that mess, and might have kept Mel out of jail – or kept her from unleashing several kinds of Hell on the cops. So I didn't ignore the dreams.

For the most part I did ignore the things I saw that other people didn't – there were just too many of them, and most of them were harmless, and anyway I didn't know any way to stop the ones that weren't. If they were really determined to hurt someone, and they were able to do it, there was nothing I could do. Usually, the night-things couldn't touch humans any more than humans could touch them – but there were exceptions. When I spotted the exceptions, I would try to chase them off. Sometimes just letting them know they'd been seen was enough to drive them away.

Sometimes it wasn't. The thing that killed Mrs. Reinholt knew I saw it, and it hadn't cared. It didn't think I could stop it. It didn't think I could hurt it.

It had been right – but maybe if I'd done something sooner, I could have frightened it away. Maybe if I'd warned Mrs, Reinholt, *she* could have stopped it.

But I didn't, and she died.

So now, if one of the creatures looked dangerous, I'd try to do something. Oh, I didn't go out looking for them, in fact I tended to stay indoors after dark as much as possible, but when I *did* see one trying to hurt someone, I didn't ignore it.

I didn't know if I could stop whatever had chewed off Jack's finger, but I intended to try.

But first I had to find it, and the only link to it that I had was Jack Wilson, who was in Kentucky and who didn't seem eager to talk, but who I could watch in my dreams.

I was going to meet Jack eventually; I knew he was the one because he was the only one who was in all my recent dreams. The rest of the family had been in most of them, but in the one during my break room nap there had only been Jack and the mystery woman, so Jack had to be the key. I was going to meet him, and if my previous dreams were anything to go by, that meeting was going to change my life somehow. Everyone I had dreamed about this way had precipitated some major alteration in my circumstances.

So I was going to meet Jack, and when I did, the dreams would stop. I grimaced at that. If I couldn't get Jack to talk – well, maybe I didn't want to rush off to Kentucky just yet. I didn't really know what was going on; maybe once I did I would know what to do.

But then, if I stayed home I would probably keep dreaming – and if I went to Kentucky, I would probably keep dreaming. It was only when I met Jack that it would stop. In Kentucky I could talk to other people, look for the thin woman, and generally get involved without meeting Jack. I didn't know just what I would do, but there would be *something*.

I booked a flight for Sunday – there weren't any decent fares for anything sooner, and that would give me time to prepare. The return flight was trickier, but I could always change it; I went for Thursday. I thought three days should be enough to get a handle on the situation. I booked a rental car, too, and made sure they had GPS available, since I didn't know Lexington.

This was going to come out of savings, of course, out of the little investment portfolio that Mom had called my college fund. When she was alive everyone assumed I would go to college, even if it was just Montgomery; it was only after she died that everything fell apart. I got my GED a couple of years later, when things were a little less chaotic, but college? Maybe someday.

I tried not to use the college fund for everyday expenses, but I didn't go flying off to Kentucky every day.

I told Mr. Sanchez that I had to leave town for a few days, I didn't know how long but I hoped it would be less than a week, and that I hoped I'd still have a job when I got back. He said I probably would, but that it better not be more than a week, which I thought was fair.

I called Mel again and told her what I was doing.

I packed a bag – underwear and jeans and a toothbrush and a couple of shirts. No amulets or magic swords or spell books; I wish I had stuff like that, and that it worked, but I didn't and I don't.

Mrs. Reinholt hadn't seemed to need any books or talismans, anyway.

I dreamed again every time I slept, even just a catnap, and in my dreams I saw Jack being held in the hospital or youth center or whatever it was, being questioned by doctors and cops, talking to psychiatrists and counselors – or really, *not* talking to them, as he stuck to his story of not knowing what happened to his finger. He insisted nothing was wrong. His parents were fine, he said, they never hit him, though his Dad did yell sometimes. He and his kid sister got along. School was okay; he was going into seventh grade. Everything was fine.

They didn't believe him. Neither did I. But they were going to release him on Monday anyway, because there wasn't anything they could do if he didn't cooperate. I got a look at a calendar in one office, and that was this coming Monday, the day after I would arrive.

Kentucky's school year was starting on Wednesday, a couple of weeks earlier than Maryland's. I had no idea whether that would complicate matters or not.

Sunday came, and I took the 25 bus down to the Takoma Metro, rode out to Greenbelt, and got the B30 bus to the airport. I changed planes in Cincinnati, and then I was landing at Blue Grass Airport, looking out the plane's window at horse farms and trees.

The rental car was a gray PT Cruiser. I didn't much care, so long as it ran and the GPS worked. I hadn't booked a room anywhere; I figured I could sleep in the car if I had to.

I didn't know where I was going, but I got in the car and started it up. I hadn't driven in months, but it came back quickly enough; I got out of the airport and turned right onto the main drag into town, Versailles Road.

I got supper at a sub shop, and while I sat there eating my ham and cheese I thought about what I should do next.

There were hundreds of Wilsons in town, and I had no way of knowing which family was Jack's; I still hadn't gotten his father's first name for certain, though I thought it might be Bill. I knew what the street where they lived looked like, but not where it was. I thought that if I could find the neighborhood, I might be able to find the mystery woman. I didn't know any street names or anything, but it wasn't downtown, and it wasn't new. I might be able to find it just by driving around; Lexington wasn't *that* big, and I could skip any areas that were recently built, and any areas that were too old.

Versailles Road went straight east into downtown, and I didn't want that, so instead I turned onto Alexandria Road and started driving.

Even as I did it, I knew it was a stupid idea, but I just didn't know what else to do. I didn't really know what I was doing there at all. Some kid had his finger bitten off, and I had come to do something about it – but what?

I didn't really know.

I couldn't put his finger back; about the best I could do would be to prevent whatever it was from biting any other pieces off kids. Which was a worthwhile goal, but I had no clue how to go about it.

So I drove randomly through the streets, looking for anything familiar, anything I had seen in my dreams, as the sun settled toward the western horizon. If night fell before I found it, I didn't know what I would do; I wasn't sure I would recognize it in the dark.

And there would be other things out there in the dark, distracting me.

I turned south on a road called Clay's Mill Road, but that started getting into housing developments that were too new, so I turned east and began winding my way through residential streets.

I had more light than I had expected; I hadn't taken into account that I was a few hundred miles west of home. Lexington was still on Eastern time, but it must be on the edge of the time zone or something, because sunset was definitely later than back home in Takoma Park. I was able to get through a dozen neighborhoods, all around the southern half of the city, before the light really began to fade.

There was a stretch where the neighborhoods were *too* old, maybe a hundred years old, but then I got back into the postwar areas, and finally I turned a corner onto a wide, straight street where sprinklers were hissing on green lawns and trees shaded the sidewalks, and if it wasn't exactly the right street it was close. I slowed the car to a crawl.

The architecture was right. The trees were the right size and spacing. But it wasn't the street I wanted.

I turned left at the next corner, and then left again onto the street paralleling the first, and that was it. That was the place. I saw Jack's house; his sister Katie was sitting on the front steps with a woman I didn't recognize, presumably an aunt or a neighbor who was looking after her while her parents were with her brother, talking to doctors and social workers.

I didn't stop; I just kept the car moving slowly up the block, and turned right at the next intersection.

I had the neighborhood, and the street, and I programmed it into the GPS. Now I began studying the trees, looking for the one where Jack had laid his head on the mystery woman's lap.

If I were a twelve-year-old boy taking an unauthorized evening walk to get away from a verbally abusive father, I asked myself, which way would I go?

I tried to remember what I had seen in my dreams; which way had Jack gone when he walked out the door?

I drove down to the end of the block, and on into the dead end beyond.

The houses here weren't quite as well maintained, and the trees somehow seemed a little wilder. At the very end the street didn't have a round court, or become someone's driveway; it just stopped, the sidewalks blending into the grass on either side, as if the builder had intended to extend it someday, but had never managed it. The little bit of undeveloped land where the next block would have gone wasn't tidy enough to call a park, but it wasn't wilderness, either; it was just an empty place, with trees and tall grass.

I stopped the car by the curb and killed the engine; with the air conditioning off it seemed to instantly turn hot and stuffy.

The sun was below the horizon in the west, and the light was beginning to fade; the sky overhead was not as blue anymore, and the golden sunset was tarnishing. I opened the car door, stuck my head out in the fresh air, and listened.

I could hear traffic in the distance – maybe on Winchester Road, if I remembered the map correctly, or maybe on that beltway thing they called New Circle Road. I could hear children shouting somewhere in the distance, but not on *this* block. Leaves rustled, and I smelled something on the wind, something sweet.

It smelled like a carnival, like popcorn and cotton candy and funnel cake.

Well, maybe there *was* a carnival somewhere nearby. I peered into the shadows beneath the trees at the end of the street.

Under the biggest tree, a big tulip poplar, something moved. Something white.

"Hello?" I called.

The white thing froze.

"I can see you, you know," I said, in a conversational tone.

That was only partially true; I could see something, but not what it was, there in the shadows of twilight. Dead leaves were scattered around it, and a lot of the leaves still on the tree were turning yellow; it seemed awfully early in the year for that, but I didn't know whether to blame that on the weather, or the thing I was talking to.

No, something said. It wasn't exactly sound; it was more like a memory of sound, as if I knew what had been said, but didn't actually hear it. *No*, it said. *You're too old. You're a grown man.*

I didn't like that.

"I'm only twenty-five," I said, stepping out of the car and carefully, quietly closing the door. "I'm just a kid." I tried to get a better look at the thing. It was hunched over at the foot of the tree, pressing up against the trunk. I thought it was probably the thin woman, but I couldn't be sure; even though it was still daylight, whatever I was talking to was faded and dim.

Supernatural, almost certainly. Even without the soundless voice, I would have guessed it wasn't anything normal.

In the dream where the mystery woman comforted Jack I had noticed something strange about her voice, but in dreams you aren't hearing with your ears in the first place, so I hadn't been sure. Now I was – whatever I was talking to, it wasn't human.

I was assuming this really was the same person, or the same thing, that I had seen in my dreams, but I couldn't be absolutely sure of that at first.

I could see it a little more clearly now, though; it had long black hair and the white was almost certainly a garment. It had to be the woman.

No, it said again. *Go away. Leave me alone.*

"My name's Greg," I said. "Gregory Kraft. Kraft with a K, like the cheese."

Go away.

"Why?"

It turned its face toward me, but I couldn't make out any features; the shadows and the long hair concealed them. *How can you see me?* it demanded. *How can you hear me? Only children can. Only some children. Only special children.*

That wasn't really what I wanted to discuss, but I didn't want to antagonize it, not when I'd been lucky enough to find it like this. "I... am special," I said. "Something happened to me when I was seventeen. I see everything now." I mentally added, but did not say aloud, *Whether I want to or not.*

I didn't tell it that there were other adults who could see night-creatures, either. There are, though. Not very many; it's not one person in a hundred, probably not one in a thousand. It's more common in kids, but still not exactly common.

I can spot the people with the ability – that's another part of the nasty little gift Mrs. Reinholt gave me, another part of the "everything" I see. It's a little hard to explain how I recognize them; it's not an aura or anything like that. Instead, they have a sort of *otherness*, as if they aren't quite part of the natural world; it looks almost as if they were photoshopped into our reality, rather than belonging in it, and whoever did it didn't get it exactly right. They just don't quite fit with their surroundings.

Some of them have it more than others. Mrs. Reinholt had looked like a bad cut-and-paste job where no one had tried to match the light – she was always brighter than the world around her, never fitting in.

Mel doesn't have it, despite the curse. Her wrongness is completely different, more like darkness seeping out into her surroundings.

One funny thing is that it doesn't show in my dreams; if any of the Wilsons or the cops or doctors or social workers were psychic, I didn't know about it yet.

And another peculiar feature of my talent was that the supernatural creatures themselves don't have that oddness, even though most of them can see one another. Most of them are pretty clearly not human anyway, though. The thin woman might have passed for human under the right circumstances, but most of them, no.

Go away.

"Why?" I repeated. "Aren't you lonely out here? Wouldn't you like someone to talk to?"

Go away.

It didn't seem to be interested in conversation, or at least, not in talking about itself, or about me. Well, I thought I knew a subject that would get its attention.

"If you're waiting for Jack," I said, "they're releasing him in the morning."

It seemed suddenly attentive. *Jack?*

"Yes."

Jack is coming back to me?

"Jack is coming home tomorrow," I said. "I don't know if he'll want anything more to do with *you*, though. After all..."

I was interrupted by the sound of a storm door latch; the front door of the nearest house, the last house on the left, was open, and a fiftyish woman was staring out at me.

"After all," I finished, a little more quietly, "aren't you the one who bit his finger off?" I realized I had been almost shouting.

"Who are you talking to, Mister?" the woman called from the door.

"No one, Ma'am," I answered. "Just practicing lines."

She stared at me thoughtfully for a moment, and moved her hands enough to let me see that she was holding a long gun behind the skirt of her house-dress – a shotgun by the look of it, but I'm not an expert. It might have been a rifle of some kind.

"Well, go do it somewhere else," she said.

"I just wanted somewhere quiet," I said.

"Well, we like it quiet around here," she said, pulling the gun out of concealment and holding it across her chest, "and that means we don't like strangers shouting to themselves on the sidewalk."

It only had one barrel, but it definitely looked like a shotgun, the kind you pump.

I raised my hands – not high, not as if I felt threatened, just enough to show her that they were empty. "Sorry, Ma'am," I said. "I didn't mean to disturb you."

"Then don't disturb me. Go away."

"Ma'am, I don't think that's called for. I just wanted a quiet place to practice, and this street seemed perfect. I didn't mean to bother anyone. I'll try not to be so loud."

"I think you should try it somewhere else."

"Honestly, Ma'am, I think you're overreacting. Do you always answer the door with a gun?"

She glowered at me. "A boy was attacked a few days ago, a kid from just up the street. Whoever did it hasn't been caught."

"Well, it wasn't me. A few days ago I was in Maryland."

"I don't know that."

I sighed. "I don't want any trouble, Ma'am."

"Then go away, before I call the police."

"Ma'am, I'm on a public sidewalk."

"In a neighborhood where you've got no business."

"I was looking at the trees," I said, gesturing toward the end of the street. I turned my head and pretended to start. "Did you see that?"

"See what?" She followed my gaze, keeping the gun pointed harmlessly down and to the side. That made me think she knew how to use it. Someone who wasn't familiar with guns would have brought it up automatically, and might be waving it around wildly, maybe pointing it at my face; she wasn't doing that. She was handling it properly.

I wondered what it was loaded with. From what little I knew about shotguns, it could be anything from rock salt to solid slugs.

"There," I said, pointing at the white-clad thing. "Under that tree; I thought I saw something move."

She looked. "I don't see anything," she said. "Light's going, anyway. You go on about your business, young man; if you want to look at trees there are some beauties on East Main, and if you want to recite lines you can find a theater somewhere. Around here you're a public nuisance."

The white figure was definitely supernatural, beyond any possible question, because I could still see it just fine; in fact, it had turned to glare at me with dark eyes set in a deathly pale face.

It was the woman from my dream, no doubt about it, and now that I got a good look at those eyes I knew I hadn't needed the woman with the shotgun to confirm anything.

I couldn't talk to it with the homeowner standing there, and it didn't want to talk to me anyway. The time had come to retreat and regroup.

"Sorry to have bothered you, Ma'am, and I hope they catch whoever hurt that kid." I nodded to her, gave the thing under the tree a final glance, then climbed back into my rental car.

Daylight was fading rapidly now, and I could see other things besides the one I had been talking to; there was something that looked like an old woman in a dark robe crouched on the sidewalk, hunched over and motionless. There was a pale, offensively male shape, stark naked and somewhat larger than a human, stalking through a nearby back yard.

Three big obvious apparitions – that was a fairly typical concentration for a quiet neighborhood like this. Maybe a little less than average, really. There were some smaller, less distinct ones around, too; I didn't bother counting them before closing the door and fumbling the key into the ignition. Those fuzzy little ones turn up everywhere, and I've never yet found one that could talk, or that was even remotely dangerous.

I was leaving but I wasn't giving up. I had found the neighborhood in just a couple of hours, and I had found the mystery woman, the creature in white, right away, which was much better progress than I expected. A few setbacks were to be expected.

I would come back later, when Mrs. Armed Homeowner was asleep in her bed, and talk to the thing under the tree again.

I started the engine and turned the car around.

Chapter Four

I still didn't know what was going on. I knew there was a manifestation of the supernatural lurking under a tree at the end of Jack's street, I knew Jack had visited it, and I knew something had gnawed off Jack's finger, but that was about it. The obvious theory was that the creature in white had bitten the finger off, but I didn't know that; in fact, the mystery woman might be protecting Jack from some worse menace, and the lost finger might have happened when she let her guard down for a moment. There were lots of possibilities.

The only two who were likely to know what was really going on were Jack and the woman under the tree, and neither of them seemed eager to tell anyone about it. In my dreams Jack had insisted that he didn't know what had happened to his finger, and I couldn't rule out the possibility that he was telling the truth, but I didn't think so. A kid who found himself missing a finger, with no idea what happened to it, would have been screaming and crying and demanding an explanation, wouldn't he? He wouldn't have been calmly telling everyone it was an accident, and that he didn't remember what kind of accident. Maybe at first, while he was still in shock, but those dreams had dragged on and on and on, and Jack had stuck to his story for hours, maybe for *days*, without ever getting upset. That wasn't shock, that was lying.

He knew, and he wasn't telling.

And the woman under the tree didn't want to talk to me because I was an adult – but she had wanted to talk about Jack.

I wished the homeowner hadn't interrupted; I might have gotten something out of the creature.

I still might, if I went back about 2:00 a.m.

I drove out of the neighborhood onto a major street called Winchester Road. As long as I was in Lexington, I figured I might as well look around; I didn't have anything *better* to do until midnight or so.

It wasn't a bad-looking city, from what I saw of it. Lots of tree-lined streets in the older residential areas. Some nice buildings downtown. Some not so nice industrial areas along Winchester Road, too, but that's normal.

There were things lurking in the dark, though. There was something shapeless and dark gray that was perpetually falling from one of the towers on High Street. Thin blue blurs slithered along Water Street. One block on West Main had a line of phantom storefronts laid across the modern facade of an office building, a phenomenon I'd never seen before.

I didn't see these things in daylight, but at night they were almost everywhere. When I got away from downtown again I saw black things with scalloped wings flittering through the trees, and pale shapes moving in the gutters, and a hundred other varieties.

I was fairly sure they were there in the daytime, too, at least most of them, but I couldn't *see* them in sunlight. And they were weaker by daylight, I think. Most of them were weak to begin with, and harmless, and the sun seemed to weigh them down into complete invisible impotence.

That thing under the tree, the woman Jack had talked to – well, first off, it wasn't a woman, because the lady with the shotgun hadn't been able to see it. Beyond that, though, it was unusually powerful; I had been able to see it when the sky was still light, and Jack had apparently been able to treat it as a material being. *How* powerful, or what form that power might take, I didn't know.

On TV, the psychics and witches and detectives can look this stuff up; they'll haul out musty old books and flip through them until they find the particular monster they're fighting, or they'll google stuff up on the web. There might be a mentor figure who's an expert on the six hundred and forty-seven kinds of demons, or a friendly magician who can cast a spell that explains everything.

I wish I had something like that. I don't. I have my dreams, I can spot people with some sort of second sight or psychic power, and at night I can see the ghosts and monsters, and that's it – Mrs. Reinholt said she'd given me four gifts, but I only count those three. Practically the only two people I've ever talked to about the stuff that I can see are Mel and Mrs. Reinholt; Mel doesn't know any more than I do, and Mrs. Reinholt has been dead for years.

I used to visit psychic advisors and wiccan priestesses and that sort of thing, but none of them knew anything useful. Most of them were outright frauds. A few had fooled themselves, as well as their customers. A couple might have really been seeing something, as they maybe had a faint trace of that psychic otherness, but they were pretty vague about it, and from what they told me they didn't see the night creatures the same way I did. They couldn't help me much.

I'd met a few kids who could see some of the night creatures, but they generally knew even less than I did, and the ones I'd known longest all grew out of it. Most of them didn't even remember that they used to see things in the dark.

The few real psychic adults I'd spotted and managed to talk to over the past eight years – well, most of them denied knowing what I was talking about, at least at first, and if I did convince them that I wasn't crazy and I didn't think *they* were crazy, it always turned out that just like the kids, they didn't know any more than I did. None of them had the dreams, or the ability to spot other psychics, the way I did; they only saw the things that came out at night. And they'd all had the talent for as long as they could remember, they didn't get it thrust on them by a history teacher turned witch.

They'd all learned to ignore it as children. I'd had some interesting conversations about that, but none of them had led anywhere useful.

At least I knew those people were seeing more or less the same things I saw. On the other hand, the books on the occult that I'd read were just plain wrong. Everything in them was nonsense. It didn't matter if it was the old ones about vampires and witches, or the New Age stuff about crystals and vibrations – their explanations of the supernatural didn't match what I saw, or what the other psychics saw. They didn't even come close.

So for eight years, whenever I left the safety of my apartment at night, I'd been winging it, making it up as I went along.

I'd have given anything for a watcher, a teacher, or a *sensei*.

After awhile the stores closed, and then the restaurants, and when the bars started shutting their doors and turning off their neon signs I headed back out Winchester Road toward that quiet little 1950s development, trying not to look at the night-things scampering and scurrying in the corners of my vision.

At that, though, Lexington didn't seem quite as densely populated with shadows and monsters as back home in the Washington area. I don't know whether that was because there were fewer people in the area, or because it hadn't been settled as long, or what.

Once I turned off the main drag into the residential areas I drove slowly and carefully; I didn't want the sound of the car's engine to disturb anyone or attract attention. If someone *did* see me, I hoped they'd just think I was one of their neighbors coming home late.

The streets were deserted. The houses were dark. Not a single window was lit. This was clearly not a place with any nightlife. Yes, it was well after midnight, but still, I wasn't used to seeing anywhere *this* quiet.

I coasted to a stop at the end of the street, killed the headlights, rolled down the window, and sat for a moment, looking and listening and smelling the air.

That carnival scent I'd noticed earlier was gone; I could smell trees, and mown lawns, and engine fumes. The air was cool, but so humid it felt clammy. I could hear wind rustling in the leaves, and a faint hum of insects.

There were things moving out there, lots of them. Some of them were making noises, or at least doing something I seemed to hear, though I knew pretty much no one else over the age of puberty would hear a thing; I was aware of giggling and whispering and stifled little shrieks. I couldn't see much in the dark; the nearest streetlight was out, and the glow from the rest didn't penetrate this far very well.

And under the big tulip poplar crouched something white.

I got out of the car, and slowly, carefully closed the door, making sure that it latched and making sure that the key was safely in my pocket. I glanced at the last house on the street, the home of the shotgun-wielding woman, but it was as dark and quiet as any other.

I walked forward cautiously. I remembered that the tulip poplar had been dropping leaves, so I watched where I put my feet; I didn't want to rustle like a damned newspaper.

"I'm back," I whispered.

Where's Jack?

"In the hospital. For another few hours, anyway."

He's coming back to me?

"I don't know about that, but he's coming home."

He'll come to me. He loves me.

I stopped walking to consider that. "Does he?" I asked at last.

He does love me. He cares for me, and I care for him. I take care of him when his own mother won't.

I didn't have an immediate answer for that. I took another cautious step forward. "He cares for you?"

He feeds me. I'm so hungry, so very hungry, and Jack is good to me.

I shuddered. "He feeds you? Feeds you what?" I had a horrible suspicion I already knew the answer.

He feeds me flesh. I can't eat anything else.

"What flesh?"

It didn't answer at first, but just as I was about to suggest that it had eaten Jack's own finger, it said, *He brought me a cat once, but I couldn't eat it. My teeth wouldn't touch it.*

I felt slightly ill. "Whose cat?"

Jack brought it to me.

"You don't know where he got it?"

He brought it to me.

Whatever this thing was, it clearly didn't worry about details. "Was it alive?"

Of course. Jack knew I can't eat dead things. He had brought me meat, meat from his father's table, but I couldn't touch it.

That was something, anyway. I had been afraid the kid was killing neighborhood pets even before he brought the cat. I hoped it was just a stray he'd caught, and not one he'd kidnaped.

If the thing *could* eat cats, of course, then bringing that live one might have been even worse.

Have you brought me food?

I stepped back involuntarily. "No," I said, a little more vehemently than I intended. I paused and glanced back at the house, but there was no sign my little outburst had roused anyone.

Go away, then. Let me wait for Jack.

"I want to know more about you," I said. "Do you have a name?"

It turned its head toward me; I could just barely make that out in the dark. *A name?*

"Yes, a name."

I did once. I was called Jenny. Jack calls me Jenny now.

"Jenny?"

Yes.

"Any last name?"

It shook his head. *Not any more.*

That implied it had a last name once, and *that* meant it might have been human once, or at least passed for human. This might be a ghost; I'd met ghosts before, or at least I'd met things that claimed to be ghosts. "What happened?" I asked.

Go away. I don't want to talk to you.

"I'm not going anywhere until I know more about you."

I'm hungry.

"I don't have any food for you."

Then go away. I'm so hungry! I could feel its hunger now, a gnawing emptiness. This wasn't anything as natural as an empty belly.

"Jenny, tell me what happened," I coaxed. "Why are you hungry? Why are you here, under this tree? Where were you before, when you had a last name?"

Go away.

I wasn't about to leave, but I thought a change of subject might help. "Why is Jack good to you?"

He loves me. Jack is a good boy. He loves me.

"Why?"

His mother doesn't comfort him. His mother doesn't speak up for him. I do.

"You aren't his mother."

I could be his mother.

"He *has* a mother."

I could do better. Not like with my other children.

That was interesting. "What other children?"

Its first response wasn't words, but a wave of anguish. I stumbled back involuntarily.

Then the words came.

My lost ones my loves my babies, dead dead dead, I lost them, I starved them, I killed them, how could I? How could I? What did I do? What have I done? No no no no no... The thing was curled up into a ball, its hands wrapped around its head, and I thought I heard an actual sound, a low moaning, as it bewailed its loss.

Something looked odd about its hands as it pressed them against its skull. The nails were very, very long, the hands were very bony – except for the little finger of the left hand, which didn't seem to match.

That finger was shorter, thicker, the skin a little darker than the horrible pale complexion of the others, the nail trimmed back.

I didn't think I would need to concoct any elaborate explanations or look for any other creatures, after all. I was pretty sure I knew where that finger came from.

"You love Jack?" I called quietly. "Then why did you chew off his finger?"

The hands sprang open and the head jerked up to glare at me with dark, dark eyes, eyes that looked, in the midnight gloom, more like holes than like eyes.

Go away! You hateful evil man, GO AWAY! I love Jack.

"You call *me* evil? *You're* the one who ate your friend's flesh!"

Hungry, I was so hungry! He did it for love, and I love him for it. Go away!

"I don't think..." I began.

Then it stood up, like a marionette unfolding out of its box, rising up on bone-white, bone-thin legs, and pointed at me with one of those long, white fingers.

GO. AWAY.

It didn't just use words, either; a wave of revulsion swept over me, and again I stepped back without meaning to.

The thing took a step toward me, then paused, and then took another step, its gaze fixed on me, its finger pointing.

I hadn't been sure it could move away from the tree, but it did. It was advancing toward me, obviously furious. I didn't know what it was capable of, but it had bitten off a boy's finger, so I knew it wasn't completely harmless.

"I'm going," I said, "but I'll be back. You stay away from Jack, and from the other kids on this street."

Go!

I went; I got back in my car, being careful to never turn my back on the creature, and closed the door. I fumbled the key into the lock, started the engine, and flicked on the lights.

The thing flung up its hands to shield its eyes, but it didn't retreat.

I turned the car around and drove away, heading nowhere in particular.

I didn't know where I was going. I didn't know what I was going to do. At least now, though, I had some idea what I was up against.

Not that I was happy about it. Child-eating monsters – what sort of sense does that make? I hate the supernatural. It isn't logical. You can't figure out how it works.

Or at least, *I* can't.

I looked at the hunched old woman on the sidewalk, and a fluttering thing in the trees, and a dozen other creatures as I drove, hating them. They were, so far as I knew, completely harmless, but why were they *there*?

And why was that bony woman lurking at the end of that street?

I didn't really know where that ghost, if that's what she was, came from, or how long it had been around, or why it was under that particular tree instead of somewhere else, but I didn't think it mattered. All I wanted was to make sure it didn't hurt anyone else.

I had no idea how to do that. Somehow, I didn't think a stern talking-to was going to cut it. My warning to stay away from Jack didn't seem to impress it.

Going by what it had said, it had been a woman once, or thought it had – a woman who blamed herself for her children's deaths. Why did that result in something that wanted to *eat* children? Shouldn't it want to *protect* them, to make up for failing to protect its own?

And plenty of people blamed themselves for unwanted deaths; why did *this* one wind up a sort of ghoul?

Maybe I should have tried harder to find out what its last name had been when it was human – assuming it really had been; for all I knew, it had eaten the original Jenny and absorbed her memories, and it hadn't ever been human at all. Still, with a last name I could have poked around online, maybe found out what happened to her kids, maybe found some way to use that.

I turned left, and considered going around the block and heading back to talk to it again.

What the hell, why not?

I drove back to the end of the street and killed the lights. I leaned out the window and called softly, "Jenny?"

No answer. I waited for my eyes to adjust to the darkness, then looked under the big tulip poplar.

Nothing there.

I scanned to either side, but I didn't see that white dress anywhere.

In fact, I realized I didn't see *anything* unnatural there. I looked up in the trees, as well as along the ground.

Nothing. Nothing flittering, fluttering, or flapping, nothing slinking or slithering. For a moment I wondered if I'd lost my... my special ability, my second sight, or whatever you want to call it.

But no, when I turned around I could see the usual night-things in the yards and walks along the street, and something unpleasant was hovering in the air above a house just past the corner. It was only the little grove at the end of the street that was strangely free of any supernatural infestation.

I was sure I'd seen and heard things in those trees before, but they were gone now.

I didn't understand it. I found it creepy. I mean, the night-things were creepy to begin with, but I was used to them, and somehow *not* seeing them, when they'd been there just a little while earlier, was even creepier.

It had to be related to Jenny's disappearance somehow, but I didn't know how.

I waited for awhile to see whether anything would reappear – I mean, it's not as if I had anything better to do – but eventually I gave up. I intended to find a quiet place to park and sleep in the car, but I didn't want to sleep *here*, because having Ms. Shotgun find me snoozing out front in the morning would not be good for my situation, so when I found myself starting to doze off I started the car and headed back out of the dead end. I eventually settled in a quiet corner of a shopping mall parking lot, curled up, and went to sleep.

Chapter Five

I did dream about Jack, but nothing that seemed significant. I saw him lying in his hospital bed, inspecting the bandage where his finger had been; I saw him eating ice cream the nurses brought, and watching TV.

And then I saw him waking up, and getting dressed, and waiting for his parents, who arrived, and helped him pack up, and took him downstairs and loaded him in the car and drove away.

I'd had a long day, so I suppose I shouldn't have been surprised that I slept later than I intended to. I'd expected the noise of the mall's Monday-morning business to wake me up no later than nine, but apparently business wasn't booming, or I'd picked too quiet a corner, or I'd been more tired than I thought, because when I was finally awake enough to look at it my watch said half-past ten.

"Damn," I said. Jack was probably already home. My dreams had probably been in real time, not visions of past or future.

I wasn't ready to meet him yet; I was still hoping the dreams would show me more about Jenny, and about Jack, and about why she was preying on him, and why he hadn't told anyone what happened.

Of course, maybe that was just common sense – "My finger was gnawed off by a skinny woman in a white dress who lives under a tree" would probably not have gone over well with the cops and psychologists.

Still, I thought there was more to be learned from my dreams.

I didn't know just how much contact it would take to make the dreams stop; it hadn't been an issue in the half-dozen previous instances, because in every case I met the person directly. I spoke to him or her, and usually shook hands, the first time I ever saw him in person.

If I saw Jack from a distance, would that be enough? If he saw me, would that do it? I didn't know.

I didn't know what to do about any of this.

If Jenny had been human it would have been simple – call the cops, let *them* deal with her. If she were a vicious animal, once again, there were people to call, people who dealt with such things.

Most people couldn't even *see* ghouls like Jenny, though – or ghosts, or whatever she was. There wasn't anyone I could call.

If Jenny had been a live person, and attacking children, and for some reason I couldn't call the cops, again, there would be a simple solution – get a gun and shoot her. Killing a beast in self-defense, or defense of innocents, wasn't a crime. But shooting a ghost wouldn't do any good. Bullets wouldn't hurt her.

Well, actually, I'd never tried shooting, but I knew a blade wouldn't cut a ghost, and running a car into one didn't hurt it. I *had* tried *those*. I didn't think bullets would do any better, and I didn't have a gun, or particularly want one.

I didn't know any way to kill a ghost. Exorcism didn't work; I'd tried it. It was just words, and it didn't do anything.

I had a moment of existential despair sitting there in the mall parking lot – what was I *doing* here? What did I hope to accomplish? Why hadn't I ignored my dreams and left Jack and his family to their own devices? I wasn't doing anything here but wasting my pitiful inheritance, putting my job at risk, and wishing I'd gotten a hotel room so I could take a shower.

This wasn't my responsibility. My life was already pretty crummy, yet I'd risked my job and burned off part of my savings to come here – for what? What had I expected to accomplish?

I could put an end to the dreams by walking up to Jack and introducing myself. Then I could go home, and let Jenny get him or not, however it worked out. It wasn't *my* fault she was after him; I was just an observer. I didn't have any way to stop her; I wasn't sure there *was* any way to stop her.

But giving up and going home now wouldn't make sense. I was here, and my return ticket wasn't good until Thursday. I'd had the dreams because Jack was going to be important to me somehow. At least, that was how the dreams had always worked before. I had dreamed about the man who killed my mother, and I had dreamed about the guy Mel ruined, and I had dreamed about my stepmother, and so on; I didn't dream about random people hundreds of miles away.

So what was my connection with Jack Wilson?

Maybe I *did* dream about random strangers now. I had no reason to think my gift, or curse, or talent, or whatever it was, couldn't change.

Or maybe I was going to be accused of attacking Jack; after all, Mrs. Shotgun had seen me acting suspiciously.

But I wouldn't have been there at all if I hadn't dreamed about Jack. The dreams had never been self-fulfilling prophecies before; they were always about people I would have been involved with anyway. Had that changed?

I had come to Kentucky to head off whatever bad things might be coming my way. If I hadn't ignored the dreams I might have been able to prevent Mom's death, and I wasn't going to make the same mistake again.

Or maybe I couldn't have prevented it. Maybe I would have just died with her. I couldn't know. Or she might have died no matter what I did. But I didn't *try*, because back then I didn't know the dreams meant anything.

I was in Kentucky to try to prevent whatever new horror might be coming, but I didn't know what it was. I hadn't had a chance to save Jack's finger, but there might be worse coming.

Or there might not.

My thoughts were going in circles, and I decided I wasn't going to figure it out sitting in the parking lot; I started the car and headed for the Wilsons' neighborhood.

Their car was in the driveway, but I didn't see anyone out in the yard; presumably they were all indoors. It was a pretty hot, sticky day, so there wasn't anything unreasonable about staying inside with the air conditioning on. I cruised on past and down to the end of the street, hoping Mrs. Shotgun didn't notice me.

There was no sign of Jenny anywhere, but that was no surprise in bright sunlight. I was pretty sure at least some of the night-creatures were still out there, though weaker or even dormant, but I also knew I couldn't see them in daylight. Anything supernatural and inhuman that was visible in the daytime was very,

very bad news; I hadn't seen anything unnatural in full sun since Mrs. Reinholt died. I had *felt* things – if nothing else, Mel's curse was just as strong by day as by night – but I hadn't seen them.

I didn't feel anything now.

I didn't linger; I didn't want to attract attention. I turned the car around and headed back out.

I didn't know what to do with myself all day; I really did want to give the dreams another chance to make themselves useful, and I couldn't talk to Jenny until sunset. Eventually I decided I might as well enjoy my visit to the Heart of the Bluegrass, as the tourist brochures called it, and I headed downtown looking for local attractions.

I've got to say, Lexington seems as if it might be a nice place to live, but if you're a visiting tourist, you better like horses. There's a house where Henry Clay used to live, and if I'd remembered more of who Clay was I might have checked it out, but other than that pretty much everything I could find advertised was connected to horses and racing. If I'd wanted to drive a few hours out of town there were caves and distilleries and assorted scenery, but in Fayette County it was all horses.

The locals I talked to when I got lunch seemed more interested in the University of Kentucky sports program than in horses, but that didn't provide a lot to do in August.

I'm not horse-crazy, by any means, but I yielded to the inevitable and spent the afternoon at the Kentucky Horse Park. I'd probably have enjoyed it more if I hadn't been worrying about Jack, and if I gave a damn about horse-racing. Cooler weather might have helped, too; not only was it still humid, but it was sweltering hot in the sun. In the shade it was tolerable.

After supper I headed back toward Jack's neighborhood, hoping to talk to Jenny again, now that we'd had a day to calm down and consider things. I intended to ask her about her past, about her lost children and her last name. I still didn't know any way to harm a ghost, but I thought that if I knew her background I might do a better job arguing with her.

I noticed I was thinking of Jenny as "her," instead of "it," again. I couldn't really make up my mind about that. I don't suppose it really mattered.

I had the car windows open as I cruised down the street, taking in the sounds and smells.

The Wilsons' car was in their driveway, but I didn't see anyone in the yard, and I didn't look in the windows. A guy in his sixties was mowing his lawn, despite the heat, and the roar of the mower didn't quite drown out the hum of the air conditioners on every side.

That carnival smell was back. Was that real, or was it some psychic artifact? Did it have some connection with Jenny? I let the car drift to a stop in front of the guy with the mower. I threw the house at the end of the street a glance, but didn't see any sign of the shotgun-wielding hausfrau, so I thought I was safe.

The mower man noticed me; he let the mower's engine die, then pulled a big old handkerchief from his back pocket and wiped sweat from his forehead before coming over to the car.

"Can I help you with something?" he asked, leaning on the car.

"I'm sorry to bother you," I said, "but I was wondering if you know what that smell is."

"Smell?" He straightened up and sniffed. "You mean the peanut butter factory?"

"Is that what it is?" I suddenly felt like an idiot. Hot peanut oil – that's what I was smelling.

"Yeah, that's the Procter & Gamble plant over on Winchester Road. Usually the wind's wrong and you can't smell it here, but sometimes – well, there it is." He smiled. "Makes me feel like a kid again."

"I know what you mean," I said. Not everything odd in my life had to be supernatural, it seemed. "Thanks."

He was in no hurry to get back to his mowing. "You visiting someone around here?"

I couldn't get away with lying about that; he probably knew every family on the street. "No," I said. "I'm a botany student. I've been studying those trees at the end of the street."

"Those?" He waved his thumb at them. "Anything special about them?"

"Not really. I'm just looking at growth patterns, and those were a good sample." I hoped the old man wasn't a botanist himself, because I had no idea what I was talking about. "Why? Have *you* noticed anything strange about them?"

"Nope. Just trees. That big one drops a lot of twigs and stuff, though – maybe it's sick."

I shook my head. "No, tulip poplars just do that." There were enough of them around where I grew up that I knew that.

"Oh. So you're a student?"

"Yeah."

"U.K. or Transylvania?"

If someone had asked me that a day or two earlier I would have thought it was a joke I wasn't getting, but now I knew there really was a Transylvania University in Lexington. I didn't know much about it, though, so I said, "U.K."

He nodded. "And you're just looking at trees?"

"Yup."

He glanced at the Wilsons' house. "You aren't interested in any of the kids around here?"

There it was again, and I should have expected it – a stranger in the neighborhood right after a kid got attacked, of course I was going to attract suspicion. "Nope. Not big on kids, really. Why? Do they climb the trees?"

"Don't know. What if they do?"

"Well, that might affect growth patterns, having that weight on the big limbs."

"And I suppose you asked about the smell because you thought it came from the trees?"

"No, I knew it wasn't the trees. I wondered whether it might be an environmental factor I needed to check out, though."

"You didn't think it was candy?"

"Mister, I didn't know *what* it was. That's why I asked."

He didn't look entirely convinced.

"Thanks again," I said, and reached for the steering wheel.

"Hold up a minute," he said.

I waited as he walked around and looked at the back of the car; then I leaned out my window and asked, "Is something wrong back there?"

"Nothing wrong," he said. "I was just getting your license plate."

I blinked, trying to look puzzled. "It's a rental," I said. "Why'd you want the plate number?"

"We've had some trouble around here lately," he said.

"Really? Want me to keep an eye out for anything?"

He shook his head. "I'd suggest you not stay around after dark, though."

"I wasn't planning to," I lied. I put the car in drive. "Thanks again."

He stood and watched as I pulled away from the curb, but by the time I reached the end of the street the comfortable buzz of the mower was filling the air once again.

The sun was low in the west but still above the horizon as I stopped the car again and looking into the shadows beneath the big tree. I didn't see Jenny, but I wasn't sure whether that was because she wasn't there, or because there was still too much daylight. I scanned the area.

A curtain in the last house twitched.

I bit my lip, considering what to do. I'd told two different lies now, that I was an actor practicing lines and that I was a student studying trees; if the mower man and the shotgun woman ever compared notes I was screwed. They were both suspicious of me, and I couldn't really blame them; this was a dead-end street in the sort of neighborhood where anyone other than the people who lived here, and maybe the ice cream truck or the trash collectors or the postman, was out of place and going to be noticed. My cover stories were both pretty weak.

I thought of a better one, but I really didn't want to try it. I could claim to be some sort of official investigating the attack on Jack Wilson. The problem with *that* one, though, was that someone would want to check it out – they'd want to know whether I was a cop or what, and how to verify my story.

I could say I was a reporter, but that wasn't much better; they'd want to talk to my editor. Or they might just want me to leave; everyone here seemed to know about the attack, but none of them seemed to want to talk about it. My guess was that they really didn't want any publicity; it would be bad for the real estate values, bad for the neighborhood.

The sound of the mower cut off; the guy had finished his lawn. I looked back and saw him pushing the mower toward the garage. He looked at me, at my car, as he did.

The sun was well below the treetops now, brushing the horizon, but I still didn't see Jenny anywhere, and either Mr. Mower or Ms. Shotgun might be calling the cops to come check out the suspicious stranger. I decided staying around wasn't a great idea. I could come back again after everyone was in bed.

I started the car, turned it around, and drove away.

Sure enough, as I headed out Strader Drive I passed a cop car heading the other direction.

It might have been coincidence, of course. They might have been coming to cruise the neighborhood for whatever had attacked Jack anyway.

Or they might have gotten a call about me, and Mr. Mower had my car's license number, not to mention PT Cruisers are pretty recognizable. I half-expected them to U-turn and come after me, with lights and sirens.

They didn't. They drove on into the quiet little neighborhood, and I drove out, with no idea where I was going.

Chapter Six

I debated whether or not to take a nap. I worried that if I did, I'd sleep through until morning, since didn't have an alarm clock. I hadn't thought to bring one, and if my phone had an alarm as an option, I didn't know where.

The thing is, I didn't know what else to do. I wasn't sure I dared go back to talk to Jenny again – what if the cops were patrolling the area? I hadn't seen any before, but that was before Jack came home.

I had two days before my flight home, but I didn't know what to do with them. I didn't know what Jenny wanted, not really. I didn't know how to find her if she wasn't staying under the big tulip poplar. I didn't know what I really hoped to accomplish.

I pulled the car over on a quiet street and tried to think, and the question became moot – I dozed off without meaning to. After all, it wasn't as if I'd been getting lots of sleep.

I dreamed, of course. I saw Jack and his folks finishing their supper, and I saw his parents trying to be nice to him, and I saw his kid sister staring at the bandage on his hand where his finger used to be. I saw him say he wasn't feeling well and wanted to go to bed early, and of course his parents bought that. His mother even came to tuck him into bed, over his half-hearted protests. I saw her turn out the light and leave the room, closing the door behind her.

And I saw Jack wait a few minutes to be sure she was gone, then climb out of bed, throw on a bathrobe, and climb out his bedroom window, lowering himself until he was hanging by his fingers from the sill and then letting go, so that he dropped into the bushes around the air conditioner.

"Oh, crap," I said to myself – I don't know whether I said it aloud or not. I tried to wake up, so I could go to help, but I couldn't, not yet.

I saw Jack slip through the back yards, climbing hedges and fences, staying out of sight of the street as he made his way down to the end of the road, past the big tulip poplar, past the other trees, into a clump of bushes that might have been forsythia, but I couldn't be sure in the dark. He ducked down and pushed through the overhanging branches and crawled into a little hollow inside the thicket.

Jenny was sitting there waiting for him. *You came*, she said.

"Of course I did," he said. "I told you I would."

I knew you would.

"No more fingers," he said.

But I'm... no, I'm sorry. Did it hurt? I didn't want to hurt you.

"You didn't hurt me," he said, but I didn't believe him. I didn't think he would ever admit *anything* hurt.

I love you, Jack.

"I love you, Jenny."

And then he was in her arms, and she clutched him to her, and I could see her claws digging deep into the back of his bathrobe.

"No," I said, but I still couldn't wake up. "Get away!"

I'm so hungry, she said. *I love you so much, and I'm so very hungry.*

"I know," he said. "I know. And I'll feed you. Just give me a minute."

"No!" I shouted – and that did it; I woke up, soaked in sweat, sitting in the driver's seat of my rented Chrysler, staring out at an empty street.

"Oh, *crap*," I said, and I reached for the key.

Five minutes later I turned onto the Wilsons' block, and I had been so desperate to get to those bushes and stop whatever was happening there that I had forgotten all about my earlier worries.

I shouldn't have. There was the cop car, parked in front of the Wilson house. A reddish night-thing was crouched atop it, but I ignored that; I was more concerned with its human occupants than any supernatural manifestations that might have attached themselves to the vehicle.

I had a pretty good idea what would happen if I drove down to the dead end and got out of my car – within two minutes there would be a cop with a flashlight asking me what I was doing there, and the odds that he'd cut me enough slack to get to those bushes and drag Jack out weren't very good.

I tried to think of something I could tell the cops that wouldn't make me sound insane or dangerous, and even as I did I was wondering whether the neighbors had talked to them about the strange young man in the gray PT Cruiser.

I didn't have time to come up with anything before I was driving past the police cruiser. I glanced over and saw two cops sitting in their vehicle, both of them watching me intently, and the red thing on the roof, also watching me, and I lost my nerve.

The cops weren't going to believe a word I said. I couldn't think of a convincing lie, and the truth sure wasn't going to work. I flew out here from Maryland because I was having dreams about this kid feeding a ghost woman his own finger? Oh, they'd believe that, of course they would!

Right.

I turned at the next corner, the last corner; I didn't dare go on down the dead end. And once I'd done that, I couldn't circle back; that would *definitely* attract the cops' attention.

I looked at the GPS, flipped it to map mode and tried to figure out whether there was somewhere I could park to come at those bushes from the other side.

It looked as if there was, but it involved getting back out on Winchester Road, then turning into the next development over and making my way to the back, where there was another dead end that should connect up. Except, of course, there might be fences or ditches or other obstacles in there that didn't show up on the little diagram.

Still, I didn't have a *better* idea. I headed out of the development.

It took about ten minutes to get to the spot the GPS said was closest, which was directly in front of someone's house. I wasn't eager to cut through someone's yard, so I cruised slowly up the block, looking for an alternative.

I found one, a playing field that backed up to a bunch of trees, and if I cut through those trees I *should* come out at the end of the Wilsons' street. I parked the car, hoping it wouldn't be too conspicuous.

There was a fence around the field, of course. Wouldn't want stray balls sailing off into the woods. I went around the end and hurried, stumbling over tree roots and beer bottles in the dark, and uncomfortably aware of the things in and around the trees that were watching me. Something big and white was stalking up and down the field, and black or gray things crouched or fluttered on every side.

I was still trying to find my way in the dark when I heard the whimpering, and saw something moving ahead of me, something that wasn't just the usual sort of night-creature – though it didn't look exactly *right*, either. "Jack?" I called.

I didn't care about maintaining the dreams anymore. If he was out there, hurt, bleeding, whatever, I intended to find him and do whatever I could to keep that Jenny thing away from him.

The whimpering stopped for a moment, and then that not-a-voice said, *Help him!*

"I'm trying!" I shouted. "Jack, where are you?"

"Over here," a boy's voice said, weak and unsteady.

I followed the sound, and found him lying on the ground beside the bushes – not under them, he'd made it that far. He was face-down on the dirt, but I spotted him easily, even in the dark.

For one thing, he had that wrongness that meant he could see the supernatural; he didn't blend in with the background. I'd wondered about that, and now I knew. It hadn't shown in my dreams, but in real life it was obvious, even at night – he had it *strongly*.

More obviously, though, Jenny was standing over him, not touching him, her long, bony fingers clutching helplessly at the air above his back. I could feel her desperation – and that despite whatever she had done, she was still hungry. *I can't help him*, she said. *I can't lift him. My touch would draw blood.*

"Then get away from him," I said, as I knelt down and rolled him onto his back. I looked him up and down quickly.

That strange distortion made it hard to really look at him, but I forced myself.

His nine fingers were all still there, clenched into trembling fists, and his clothes were intact; his shoes were still on. I didn't know whether she could eat parts of him right through the shoes or the other clothes, though.

His eyes were squeezed tightly shut, his whole face contorted with pain, and I thought his face was wet with tears. Then Jenny shifted position, and a glint of light reflected off her white dress, and I realized that the "tears" were too dark. It wasn't just the psychic thing; those weren't tears at all.

"Oh, my God," I said, as I slid an arm under his neck and scooped him up.

He gave it freely, Jenny said, and I felt a wave of pride and love and guilt – and that insatiable appetite was still there, as well. *I didn't want to hurt him – but I was so hungry!*

"Shut up," I told her. "I'll talk to you later." I stood up with Jack in my arms, trying to orient myself, and I spotted the big tulip poplar. I hurried toward it.

Jack was whimpering again. I glanced back, and saw that Jenny was following us. The hair fell away from her face for a moment.

I refused to think about what I saw; I turned around and staggered out onto the street, where the police car still sat against the curb in the next block. "Hey!" I bellowed. "Help! Officer, help!"

A light came on in the house with the shotgun, but no one answered, and no doors or windows opened. I kept shouting.

I was halfway to the corner before the cops finally heard me and turned on their spotlight. The passenger-side door opened, and one of them got out, his hand on his gun.

"He's hurt!" I shouted. "Call for an ambulance!"

"Stop right there!" the cop shouted back.

I stopped; I wasn't stupid enough to disobey a cop in a situation like that. "This kid's hurt!" I called. "Come see for yourself!"

He came. The driver had his door open now, and was talking into his radio; I couldn't hear what he was saying.

I looked down at Jack's face. He still hadn't opened his eyes, not once since I first saw him there. Now that I was out on the open, with the police searchlight shining on us, I could see that the "tears" on his face were red; blood was trickling steadily from his left eye.

The right looked okay, except for being jammed shut with pain.

And the left eye – blood was oozing between lids that were sunken in, not rounded out.

There wasn't any eye there anymore. He didn't need to open it and show me the empty socket; I knew it was gone.

I'd seen Jenny's face, where her right eye was still just a dark patch of nothing, but her left was now a real eye, an eye that had been wide with dismay.

Then the cop was there, shining a flashlight in Jack's face. "What happened to his eyes?" the cop demanded.

"I don't know," I said. "I found him like this, back there in the bushes."

"You found him?" The cop moved the light up to my face. "What were you doing there? Do you live around here?"

"No, I was out for a walk, and I heard him whimpering."

He turned the light back to Jack. "Kid? Can you hear me?"

Jack made a noise. I'm pretty sure that if he'd opened his mouth to speak he wouldn't have been able to keep from crying, and he wasn't about to do that, so it was just a wordless noise, his lips tightly closed, and even that wasn't very steady.

"It's gonna be okay, kid; we've got you now. The ambulance is on its way."

Jack whimpered.

"Can you tell us what happened? This guy holding you, did he have anything to do with it?"

Jack bit his lip and shook his head.

"Hey, I just found him," I said. "I never laid eyes on the kid until then." I wasn't lying. Whatever I use to see in my dreams, it's not my eyes.

"Do you know who he is?" the cop asked.

I shook my head – and that was a lie, I suppose, but what was I supposed to say?

"Kid, can you talk?"

A sob escaped; then Jack closed his mouth tight again, and shook his head, just once.

"Bring him over here," the cop said, directing me toward the car.

That was fine with me. I walked slowly up the street.

The other cop had finished talking to the dispatcher, apparently; he called, "Is it the Wilson kid?"

"Looks like," the cop with the flashlight said. He turned the light on Jack's left hand. "He's missing the same finger."

"Jesus." He stepped away from the car, slammed the door, and headed for the Wilsons' front door. "What happened to him?"

"I dunno, but there's blood on his face."

Then the door opened and Jack's father stepped out. "What's going on?" he demanded.

"Sir, it appears your son has been injured," one of the cops said.

Wilson's face went pale – I could see it even in the gloom. He hurried down the steps and across the lawn. "What happened?" He glanced at me. "Who the hell is that?"

I didn't know what to say, and I was exhausted; I didn't say anything, I just handed Jack over. Then I stepped back as Wilson and one of the cops talked, the cop filling him in.

I took another step back, and was wondering whether I might possibly slip away, when the other cop grabbed my arm. "Sir, if you could come with me? I think we need to ask you some questions down at the station."

"Oh, my God," Wilson said, loudly. "What happened to his *eye*?"

Jack's mother was standing in the open door. "Is he all right?" she called.

"No," I called back. At the time I just wanted to tell the truth, but when I saw her reaction I realized that I'd been cruel.

And then the ambulance arrived, with lights and sirens, and woke up the whole neighborhood, and the cop who had my arm decided not to risk losing me in the confusion and shoved me into the back of the car.

I sat there watching as the paramedics strapped Jack to a stretcher and loaded him into the ambulance, and I saw his parents huddling together looking broken, and I saw his little sister standing in the open doorway staring out at the chaos in the street, and I saw a dozen neighbors standing in clumps on the sidewalks, watching everything from a safe distance. I heard them asking whether I was the maniac who'd attacked Jack, and the cops saying no, I was just a witness who might have seen something.

And I saw Jenny standing unnoticed in the darkness down the street, taking it all in, watching it all with her one empty hollow and her one bright young boy's eye.

Chapter Seven

I gave my real name and my real address and showed them my real ID. I told them where I'd parked the rental car. I answered all their questions about what I had seen and heard and done as truthfully as I could.

But what I couldn't tell them was why I had come to Kentucky in the first place, or why I was in that particular neighborhood. I wasn't going to tell them I was a psychic who'd had visions about Jack; they wouldn't believe me.

And when you get right down to it, I didn't *know* why I was there.

"It was a whim," I said. "I just wanted to get away for a few days, so I stuck a pin in a map and hit Lexington."

They didn't believe that; maybe I should have gone with the psychic story after all.

At least I could prove I had been home in Maryland when Jack's finger was gnawed off; I think that was all that kept them from settling on me as the psycho responsible for everything.

I don't know how long I sat in that grubby little interrogation room, answering questions, telling them that no, I never met Jack before I found him lying there in the bushes, and no, I'd never been in Lexington before, and no, I didn't know anyone in Lexington, and yes, I'd been sleeping in the rental car, and no, I wasn't really an actor or a botany student, I'd just made those up for fun. Finally, though, they took a break and let me make a call, and I called Mel.

I was so tired, so worn down from the questioning, that I didn't even brace myself; I didn't anticipate the curse at all. It wasn't until I heard her voice that the dread swept over me.

"Greg! Why are you calling at this hour? Why are you *awake* at this hour?"

I didn't point out that *she* was awake at this hour; what was the point? She'd always been a night-owl. Everything seemed to catch up with me at once, and I was suddenly so frightened and miserable I could barely hold the phone to my ear.

What was the point of anything? I was doomed. I was going to rot here until they could arrange a good frame, and then they'd scapegoat me for Jenny's snacking and send me to some prison hellhole, where some other inmate with a grudge against child molesters would cut my throat – if I was lucky, it would be my throat. I shuddered.

Even though I knew that it was at least partly her curse that was affecting me, I wasn't able to fight it off – after all, that *might* be what was going to happen to me.

"I'm in Lexington, Kentucky," I told her. "I'm in the police station. I haven't been arrested, but I think I would be if I tried to leave."

There was a moment of ominous silence, and my stomach knotted in fear.

The curse, I told myself. It's just the curse. She's not angry.

"Why?" she asked.

Officially, no one was listening in, but unofficially I would not be at all surprised if everything I said and did there was being recorded. "A kid got hurt," I said. "Lost an eye. Maybe he was attacked – the cops seem to think so. I found him and called for help, but you know how it is, I was a stranger and I didn't have a good explanation of why I was there in the middle of the night, so they're asking me a lot of questions."

I didn't say Jack's name, or mention any dreams, but Mel knew the situation. She would figure it out. That was why I had called her, rather than anybody else.

Not that I really *had* anybody else anymore, I thought hopelessly.

"What do you want me to do?" she said, and while I knew she meant it and wanted to help, it sounded to me as if she was telling me to leave her alone, keep her out of it, it wasn't her problem.

"I... I'm not sure," I said. "I wanted *someone* to know where I am, though."

"I bet."

I knew I was imagining the venom that seemed to drip from those two words, but I still felt sick at the sound of them, and almost dropped the phone.

The curse wasn't actually hitting me as hard as I had feared, or as hard as it had when I called her from my apartment; the hundreds of miles between us might have been helping a little. It wasn't easy to judge.

Still, I was feeling it. I was awash in despair and fear, struggling to keep myself behaving rationally and not collapsing into a sobbing mess.

"Listen, Mel," I said, "I'm not feeling well. I mean, I still have some of that kid's blood on my shirt, and I haven't eaten in hours. I'm going to hang up, but if you think of anything I should do, let me know, okay?"

"It's getting to you?" She knew I was talking about the curse.

"Some, yeah."

"You want me to find you a lawyer?"

I didn't really, but it was so very hard to disagree with Mel that I said, "Maybe. I don't know if I need one – I shouldn't, but maybe."

"Okay, I get that. Take care, Greg, and I'll see what I can do."

"Thanks, Mel. Take care." I thumbed the red button to break the connection.

Then I just sat there with my head down, trying to fight off the effects of her curse. That's how I was when the plainclothes detective came in.

He sat down across the table from me and said, "Hello there, Mr. Kraft. I'm Ben Skees." He had a warm, reassuring voice with one of those friendly accents that always sounds like he's about to offer you a beer, like the prosecuting attorney in "My Cousin Vinny." I'm generally not very fond of southern accents, but his was kind of nice.

"Hi." I didn't raise my head. I really wasn't up for more conversation at that point.

"I'm going to just go over a few things, and we can wrap this up for tonight."

"Uh-huh."

"Jack Wilson is missing the little finger on his left hand, and his left eye. He's maimed for life."

I blinked. I sat up and looked at him. I recognized his face from one of my dreams; he'd been one of the people investigating Jack's lost finger.

More importantly, he wasn't asking me questions. He was telling me things, instead. I wasn't sure what that meant.

"We want to catch the bastard that did that to him. We know it's not an animal because there's no way any animal could have popped his eyeball out like that, and we're assuming it's the same guy who did both, because getting mutilated by two sickos in a single week is too much of a coincidence for me to buy into."

"Okay," I said warily.

"If it's the same guy, then it looks like you aren't him – your alibi for the finger is pretty solid, though we're going to check with your boss – Armando Sanchez, is it?"

"Yes."

"We'll be checking with him and your co-workers in the morning, and maybe your neighbors, and maybe some of the people who were on the flight you say you took. That plane ticket's pretty convincing, but there are ways you could have faked it."

"Uh-huh."

"So right now, we don't think you're the guy we're after, which I'm sure is good news. The *bad* news is, your story doesn't make any sense."

"I know," I said unhappily.

"We've got a couple of people in the neighborhood who say they talked to a young man in a gray PT Cruiser. That was you?"

"Yes," I admitted.

"One of them says you claimed to be an actor."

"I told her I was practicing lines, yeah."

"The other says you claimed to be a science student at the University of Kentucky."

"I said that, yeah."

"So you lied to both of them?"

I nodded.

"Why?"

I shrugged. "I didn't want them thinking I was the guy who cut off Jack Wilson's finger."

"You knew about that?"

"The woman who chased me away the first time said a kid had been attacked."

"She said that *before* you told her you were practicing lines?"

For the first time, I'd been caught out. I blinked. "I guess," I said. "I don't remember for sure."

"You aren't an actor."

"No."

"And you aren't a student, at U.K. or anywhere else?"

"No, I'm not."

"So what *were* you doing out there?"

"I don't know," I said miserably.

He sat back and started tapping a pencil on the table.

"I told you that two guys mutilating the same kid was too much of a coincidence for me to swallow, right?"

"Yeah." I nodded.

"You turning up in that same neighborhood, poking around that empty lot, and finding that kid with his eye out, with no explanation of what the heck you're doing there – I can't buy *that* as a coincidence, either, Mr. Kraft."

I just stared at him. I was still a little disturbed from talking to Mel, and not at my best.

"Now, I told you, I don't think you did it, but I think you know *something* about who did. I think you came to Lexington because you thought he might strike again. I think you didn't find Jack Wilson by accident; I think you were out there *looking* for him. Parking the car where you did and cutting through the park – that *can't* have been an accident."

"I don't..." I stopped. I had no idea what to say to that.

"So is this guy a friend of yours? Are you trying to cover up for him until you can get him some help? Is that it?"

I shook my head. "Whoever did this is no friend of mine," I said.

"But you know something about him?"

"Her," I said.

I didn't intend to; the word slipped out. I'm not good at keeping my mouth shut. I could claim I was still shaken from talking to Mel, but I don't really know whether that's why I did it.

The pencil stopped tapping, and the detective stared at me silently for a moment.

"Her," he said finally.

I nodded. "Jack said... he called her Jenny. When I was carrying him."

"And you didn't think to mention this until now?"

"He asked me not to."

"I'd hate to have to call you a liar, Mr. Kraft."

"Ask him."

"We'll do that. So you didn't know who was responsible until tonight?"

I shook my head.

"Then why'd you come to Lexington? Why were you out there tonight?"

"I don't know," I said.

Ordinarily I think I'd have been pretty miserable at this point, but where I'd just been talking to Mel, Detective Skees was downright comforting by comparison, even when he was poking holes in my story. I wasn't all that bothered by his questions.

"You haven't been in communication with this Jenny?"

I hesitated. I debated admitting I'd been talking to Jenny when I was "practicing my lines," but that was before I'd met Jack, so that wouldn't work.

"I don't know who she is," I said at last.

"Mr. Kraft, would you mind if we checked your cellphone records? I can get a warrant if I have to, but it'd be much easier..."

"Go ahead," I said, interrupting him. "I'm not... there's nothing there. I've made a couple of calls to an old friend from high school, and that's about it for the last week or so." I handed over my phone.

He accepted it, then said, "This old friend from high school – she wouldn't happen to be named Jennifer, would she?"

"No, her name's Melisandra de Cheverley. She lives in Sandy Spring."

"Sandy Spring – is that in Kentucky?"

"Sandy Spring, Maryland. She's not involved in this."

"Are you sure?"

"Pretty sure."

He nodded.

"Mr. Kraft, we've got men out there searching the area, and we'll have the forensics boys out there once we have daylight to work with, but that didn't help much the first time, when the Wilson boy lost his finger. Do you think you could show us exactly where you found him?"

"I think so."

"So you don't mind staying around until daylight?"

I shrugged. "I don't have anything better to do."

"And maybe once you've had some sleep, you think you might tell us what you were really doing there?"

I looked at him.

He was probably twenty years older than me, with dark brown hair that could have used a trim, and a jaw a bit like Basil Rathbone's. He didn't look stupid.

"Detective – Skees, was it?"

He nodded. "Ben Skees."

"Let me ask you a purely hypothetical question."

"Be my guest."

"Suppose I said that I came here because I saw Jack Wilson's attacker in a dream? Suppose I had a dream where I saw the whole thing, and it seemed so intense, so real, that I bought a plane ticket and came out here to see whether it *was* real. If I told you that, would it make my situation better or worse?"

He leaned back and put a finger across his lips as he considered that. "You claiming to be psychic?"

I shook my head. "I'm not claiming anything. I'm asking a hypothetical question."

"Well, son, *if* you were claiming to be psychic, and solving crimes in your dreams, I'd think you'd been watching too much TV. I'm pretty sure most psychics are, to be blunt, full of crap, and aren't any more in tune with the spirit world than I am. But on the other hand, I'm a God-fearing man, and I've heard a few stories about the Lord working through signs and visions, so I won't say it can't happen."

I nodded. "I'll agree most psychics are full of crap. But just hypothetically, still, I suppose I'd be making my own position worse if I claimed that in my dreams the attacks were committed by the ghost of a woman who murdered her own kids."

"I can tell you it sure wouldn't help us find the son of a bitch." He leaned forward again. "You believe in ghosts? Enough that you'd have bought a plane ticket to come see one?"

I hesitated. I bit my lip. I'd already told a few lies, and telling another shouldn't have been a big deal, but all the same, what I finally said wasn't a lie. "Yeah, I think I do."

He considered that, then nodded. "I think we're done for now," he said. "How about you get some sleep in a holding cell, and in the morning you can show us where you found the kid? It ain't much of a bed, but it's better than that car."

"Fine," I said. "That'd be fine."

So that's what I did.

The holding cell had four or five phantoms lurking in it, but they were all pretty insubstantial, and even though the one that kept pulling its own guts out through its navel was seriously disturbing, I decided I could put up with them. After all, I didn't need to watch, and it always put the innards back, apparently unharmed. I curled up on the cot and went to sleep.

And for the first time in several days, I didn't dream.

Chapter Eight

I was roused by someone calling, "Gregory Kraft! Front and center!"

I rolled off the bunk and stood up, and wished I'd somehow managed to get my bag from the car, because my clothes were disgusting. Not only had I slept in them, but they had Jack's blood on them, not to mention plenty of dirt and sweat. I tried to brush them into some semblance of presentability as I looked around and spotted the cop holding the cell door open.

Detective Skees was standing in the hallway beyond. I was not happy to see that he looked annoyed; I had thought we were going to go out to the crime scene on friendly terms. "Good morning," I said to him as I stepped out.

"For you," he said. "Your alibi's been confirmed, among other things, and I'm supposed to release you. Not that I was actually holding you." He jerked his head, and I followed him.

I wasn't sure at first where we were going; I'd assumed we were heading for somewhere I could reclaim my cellphone and then we could drive out to the scene, but he led me back to the interrogation room.

There wasn't anyone else there, which I was pretty sure wasn't standard procedure; there'd always been two cops around when I was being questioned. The red light on the camera wasn't on, either. I had a momentary fear I was about to get the crap beaten out of me, though that didn't really seem like Skees' style and I didn't know any reason he would be any angrier with me than he was the night before. He was obviously not happy with me, but I didn't know why.

"Mr. Kraft," he said, "I can't hold you, or ask you to do anything you don't want to, but because of *why* I can't, I'd like to."

"You said my alibi was good," I said, trying to speak as calmly and mildly as I could. "Is there a problem?"

"Your alibi for the *first* attack is absolutely solid," he said. "Your boss and your co-workers all swear you were at work that day, there's no record of anyone flying here, and you didn't have time to drive. So you're off the hook for Jack Wilson's finger, but you *were* here when someone or something popped his eye out of its socket, and I could have held you for that if it weren't for your friends."

I blinked. I wasn't very awake yet. "What friends?" I asked.

"Two congressmen and a senator." The look on Skees' face as he said it made me rethink that whole thing about beating up suspects not being his style.

"Oh," I said. I didn't know any congressmen, but I could guess who did. "Um... did you talk to..." I caught myself before saying "Mel," and finished, "...to Melisandra de Cheverley?"

He shuddered. "I did. That is one scary friend you have there, Mr. Kraft, and she did not appreciate being woken up by my call. I would guess that was why I heard from those other folks not long after."

"I didn't ask her to call anyone, Detective, honest."

"I believe you, which is why I'm not going to make trouble for you about this."

"If you really thought I'd ripped out that kid's eye, I don't think you'd let me go no matter who Mel sicced on you."

"You're right."

He didn't say anything more, and for a moment we both just stood there, looking at each other. When the silence started to get uncomfortable, I said, "You wanted me to show you where I found the kid?"

"We probably already have the spot, but yeah, if you could come verify it, we'd appreciate it."

"I'll do whatever I can to help," I said.

He nodded, then pulled my phone out of his jacket pocket and handed it to me. I took it without saying anything and put it away.

We didn't talk as we made our way out of the police station and into his car, but when he put the car in gear and started backing out I said, "Detective, I'd like to clear the air here, if I can. I swear, I didn't ask Mel to do anything. I said she could find me a lawyer if she thought I needed one, but that's all. She... she's just used to getting her own way."

He didn't answer right away, but once we made the turn onto Midland Avenue he said, "I'll bet she is. How does she *do* that?"

I didn't need to ask what he meant. "I don't think she can help it," I said. "It's been like that since high school."

He hadn't expected that. "Are we talking about the same thing?" he asked.

"The fact that you can't talk to her without being frightened half to death?"

"Yeah, that."

"She can't help it. She can't turn it off. She's *always* like that. It's a curse."

I thought he would assume I was speaking figuratively, but I underestimated him. He thought about it for a moment, and then, as we turned off Winchester Road, he asked, "Do you know who cursed her?"

"Mrs. Reinholt," I said. "Our high school history teacher."

He glanced at me. "You're serious?"

I lost a little of my nerve. "Let's just say, I'm as sure of it as I'm sure that I came here because I dreamed about Jack Wilson talking to a woman's ghost."

He grimaced. "Your history teacher?"

"Eleventh grade," I said. "Mrs. Audrey Reinholt. The *late* Mrs. Audrey Reinholt."

"So Ms. de Cheverley wasn't born with it?"

I shook my head. "You think she'd have survived infancy if she was? Babies have enough problems when their parents *aren't* terrified to be near them."

He took that in silently, then nodded. He didn't say anything more until we pulled up to the side of the street, right behind a cop car that was parked just behind my rental car. "Mind if we search that?" he asked, pointing at the Chrysler as he put the car in Park. There were two uniformed cops standing beside it.

"As long as you don't damage it," I said. "It's a rental, and I waived the optional insurance." I fished the keys out of my pocket and handed them over.

He took them, and as we got out of the car he tossed them to one of the cops. "Search it. Don't break anything."

"We looking for anything in particular?" the cop asked, eyeing me.

I expected him to say something about blood or weapons, but his first words surprised me. "A phone," he said.

Then he got to the obvious. "Blood. Fibers. Hair. Photos. Notes. The usual."

"A phone?" I asked, as we walked past the car onto the field. "I gave you my phone."

"You're smart enough to give us one and hide another."

"I am?"

He didn't deign to answer that. "Show me where you found the kid," he said.

I led him past various people who were looking at the ground, or photographing the area, or otherwise inspecting the scene, to the spot where Jack had been lying. Skees beckoned to a couple of cops.

"Here," he said. "This is where the kid was." He bent over, looking at the ground; I couldn't tell whether Jack had left a mark, but maybe Skees could.

Then he looked at the bushes.

"So," he said, "where was the ghost?"

I blinked. "What?"

"The ghost."

I pointed at the forsythia. "In there," I said.

"Is it there now?"

This was not a line of questioning I was prepared for; up until now the only person who had ever taken my visions seriously was Mel. "I can't tell," I said. "I can't see ghosts in daylight."

He turned to stare at me. "But you can see them at night? When you're awake?"

I met his gaze. "Sometimes," I said. Which wasn't quite a lie; if it was very, very dark, or if I had my eyes closed, I didn't see the night creatures, and 95% of the time was technically "sometimes."

"You aren't still claiming it's all hypothetical?"

I shrugged. "I will if you'd prefer that. Last night you didn't seem to like the idea that I see things other people don't."

He turned away. "Last night I hadn't talked to the de Cheverley girl. She told me about your dreams."

"You believe her?"

"I sure believe that there's something unnatural about her. My hands were shaking, you know that? Just talking to her on the phone."

He didn't look at me while he spoke; he was studying the forsythia. Before I could reply, he called, "Jensen, I want these bushes checked out – I think our perp may have hidden in there."

"Yessir." One of the cops signaled to someone carrying a leather case.

"Show me where you went," Skees said.

I showed him, retracing my steps as best I could given the drastically different circumstances – walking in bright sunlight is not the same as carrying a bleeding kid in the middle of the night.

When we came out on the street I walked a little further, then stopped. "This is where your officers took over," I said.

Skees nodded, and looked around, taking in every detail. "Was Jenny still around?" he asked. "Or did she take off?"

"She followed us," I said. I pointed. "She stopped over there and watched. Once Jack was in the ambulance, I didn't see her anymore."

"She didn't want another bite?"

"I don't know what she wanted," I said. I hesitated, then asked, "How's Jack doing?"

Skees didn't look at me. "The doctors say he'll live."

That wasn't actually very helpful; I'd never thought his injuries might be fatal. "That's good," I said.

At that the detective turned to look at me. "You want to talk to him?"

I hadn't expected that. "I... I don't know," I said.

"His parents might want to talk to you."

"Anything I can do to help," I told him.

He looked at me for a moment, then nodded.

The hospital was on the University of Kentucky campus, halfway across town. We didn't actually get there for about another two hours, what with looking over the scene, and more questions, and paperwork, but eventually I was in a waiting room with the Wilsons, explaining that I'd been out for a late walk and heard Jack whimpering and found him, and I didn't see who attacked him, I didn't know anything about it.

Skees knew I was lying, but he didn't contradict me. We both knew I wasn't about to tell them the truth, after all. In fact, while he didn't actually confirm my story, he said, "We've been interviewing Mr. Kraft, and while we haven't finished our investigation, we don't believe he was a party to the attack."

That was good to hear.

We talked a little more, and then came the moment I'd been both dreading, and hoping for – Bill Wilson said, "You want to see Jack?"

"If I could," I said.

"You may have saved his life," Jack's mother said – I'd been introduced, so I knew her name was Emily.

"I didn't do anything special," I murmured.

Then they ushered me into the kid's room. It was a double room, but the other bed was empty. Jack had the one by the window.

He was lying on his back, the head of the bed raised slightly, with bandages and tape covering the empty socket while he stared at the ceiling with his remaining eye. He looked strained and tired, and he didn't move when we entered, didn't acknowledge us.

He almost shimmered, though. The kid definitely had psychic ability – either that, or for the past eight years I'd been misinterpreting that weird badly-photoshopped effect.

"Jack?" Emily called. "There's someone here to see you."

Jack still didn't move.

"He's sedated," Bill said.

That wasn't a surprise. I stepped up to the bedside. "Hi," I said. "My name's Gregory Kraft; I was the one who found you last night."

At that he finally turned his head a little and looked at me. Then he looked past me at his parents and Detective Skees.

"Make them go away," Jack said. His voice was weak.

"What?"

He pointed at his parents. "I want to talk to you without them in here."

"Jack, that's crap," Bill began, but Skees held up a hand. He leaned over and whispered to Wilson.

I couldn't make out all of it, but I heard the word "disturbed," and the phrase "further our investigation."

Emily tried to argue, and Skees more or less pushed the two of them out of the room, which gave me a few seconds to tell Jack, "The cop's okay."

Jack didn't care about the cop. "You can see her," he said. He was looking less sedated now that his parents weren't there – still groggy, but less so.

I didn't pretend. "Yeah, I can see her," I admitted.

"How can you see her? Nobody else can."

"How do you know?" I asked.

"She came to the house once," Jack explained. "And I've seen her in the street, and no one else ever seems to see her, but *you* did."

Then Skees was back, closing the door gently. Jack glanced at him. The kid was definitely not as out of it as he had first appeared.

"He's okay," I said again.

"Can *he* see her?"

I glanced at Skees. "I doubt it."

"Why can you?"

"I just can," I said. "Something happened to me eight years ago, and now I can see them all."

"All?"

"All the night things," I said. "The ghosts, and the other creatures."

"I wasn't... I can see others, but not as well as I see Jenny. She's more real."

I nodded. "I see all of them," I said. "Some are blurry and faint, some are pretty solid. Jenny's pretty solid, but she's not the only one."

"Can you hear them?" Jack asked.

"Some of them."

"You heard Jenny. You told her to shut up."

"Yeah, I heard her."

"Is she okay?"

I closed my eyes and let a breath out slowly.

I didn't want to answer that. I wanted to yell at the kid, ask why he cared, point out that the damned thing *stole his eyeball*, and was now using it herself.

But I didn't yell. Instead I said, "She's fine. Or at least, she was the last I saw."

"Can you take her a message?"

I glanced at Skees again, but he was just standing there listening, keeping his face still.

"I don't know," I said.

"Will you try?"

"What's the message?" I said, without actually agreeing.

"Tell her where I am," he said. "And tell her I still love her."

Chapter Nine

I heard Skees grunt at that. I ignored him and stayed focused on Jack.

"You still think you love her after what she did to you?" I said.

"I *do* love her!" he said. "And she loves me."

I closed my eyes, sighed, then opened them again. "Kid," I said, "you don't know that. You don't know what she is, what she wants, what she feels. She isn't human. She's something that *preys* on humans."

"She loves me," he insisted.

"The way I love chocolate," I said. "Jack, she *bit off your finger.*"

He screwed his face up into a pout. "I *asked* her to," he said.

"And your eye? You asked her to take that, too?"

"Yes, I did!"

That stopped me for a moment, but I regrouped. "*Think* about that a minute, Jack," I said. "Think about how crazy that is. She's gotten inside your head somehow, and she's making you feed her pieces of yourself. That's not love. That's... I don't know *what* that is, but it's not love."

"It is! I did it because I love her! She was so hungry, and she can't eat anything else."

"You love her, so you offered her parts of yourself?"

"Yes!"

I shook my head. "If *she* really loved *you*, Jack, she wouldn't take them."

"She does love me!"

"It's an *act*, Jack," I said. "She tells you lies so she can eat."

I didn't know whether that was true, really, but it seemed to make sense, and besides, I was perfectly willing to lie myself to keep this kid from losing any more fingers or other body parts.

"It's real! It hurts her that she needs to hurt me!"

"But it doesn't stop her, does it? What are you going to do, Jack, keep feeding her bits of you until there's nothing left? Or until you bleed to death? Maybe next time no one will find you in time, or the ambulance won't be quick enough. Do you love her enough to *die* for her?"

"I..." He stopped and blinked his one good eye at me. "I don't know," he said quietly. "Maybe."

"And what do you think is going to happen when you're dead?" I asked. "Do you think she'll just disappear? No, she'll find some other desperate kid she can convince to feed her. It's what she *does*, Jack. It's what she *is*."

"I..." He paused, and his mouth twisted into a frown. "How do you *know* that?" he demanded.

It was my turn to be caught without a good answer. I'd never had an argument like this before, and I wasn't doing a great job of it. "It's obvious!" I said.

"No, it's not," Jack retorted. "It's not what *she* says. She says that if she can just... well, that she'll get another chance! She'll be alive again!"

I stood there looking stupid. I'd never heard of such a thing happening; I'd never heard anything claim that it *could* happen.

But then, I'd never met anything quite like Jenny before. Most of the night things aren't anywhere near as human-like as her. Most of them can't talk at all, let alone carry on a coherent conversation. The ones I *had* talked to up until then had mostly been either too stupid or too sure of themselves to bother lying about what they were, what they wanted, what they could do. Mostly they do the same things over and over and over, no matter how pointless that is.

One of the ones that got Mrs. Reinholt, the big one, had lied to her, fooled her into thinking it was under her control and couldn't hurt her, but it didn't bother lying to me after it killed her. It hadn't pretended it was going to ever be anything but what it was. It had boasted about how it had tricked her, how it had promised her power.

Was Jenny something like that, but promising love instead of power? Maybe her whole grieving-mother thing was an act; maybe she wasn't a ghost at all, but just something that pretended to be one.

Once again, I wished that the supernatural world I saw matched what was described in a book somewhere. In the stories the monster hunters and vampire slayers could just look in a book and find descriptions of whatever they were facing; they could tell whether it was a ghost or a ghoul, a demon or demigod. Me, I never knew. Nothing I saw ever followed the rules. I'd tried exorcisms and wards and protective spells; none of them did anything at all. The night things didn't even bother to laugh at me; half of them didn't even *notice* me. I didn't know whether Jenny was a ghost or a demon or a vampire or a succubus or a lamia or a goddamn Chinese fox spirit, or something that had never been reported anywhere.

All I knew was that she was biting pieces off this kid.

"Is that what she told you, Jack?" I said quietly.

"Yes!"

"And you believe her?"

"Yes, I do!"

"Why?"

That threw him for a moment, but then he went back to, "Because she loves me, and I love her! We trust each other!"

"And you think you'd know if she was lying about all of it, if she were a monster trying to lure you into letting her kill you? It could all be lies, Jack; how would you know?"

"I just *know*, all right?"

"No, it's *not* all right! Think about it! She killed her children when she was alive, right? Starved them to death?"

Jack stared at me. "How did you know that?"

"She told me. Did she tell *you* that?"

"Yes. How... when did she tell you?"

"So you're telling me that if she kills *another* kid, she'll get a second chance at life? Jack, how does that make *any* sense?"

"Because... because this time she'll have *permission*. She can't hurt anyone who doesn't want to help her."

"But she'll still be *killing another kid*! How can that be right? It's ridiculous! And turning human again – have you *ever* heard of a ghost being given a new life?"

"Why not? What do *you* know about it?"

"I know I've never heard of it happening, and I've studied this stuff. It's just something she made up to get you to do what she wants."

"No, it isn't! It's the truth! Just because you never heard of it doesn't mean it isn't possible."

"And you're sure enough of that to *die* for it?"

He didn't answer at first; he just stared at me. Then he said, "Tell her I love her, okay? We'll figure the rest out later."

"I'm not making any promises," I said. "I don't know whether I'll see her again."

"*I* will," he said. He glanced at Skees. "Someday." Then he rolled over to face away from me.

I looked at Skees, and he shrugged. I looked at Jack, and saw his shoulders hunched defensively.

"Let's go," I said to Skees.

We went.

Bill and Emily were waiting for us outside the door. "What was *that* about?" Bill demanded.

"He wanted to know whether I'd seen who did this to him," I said. "He... he wanted to say he forgave them."

"*Forgave* them!" Bill said. "The people who ripped out his eye? He forgave them?"

I shrugged.

"*I* sure as hell am not forgiving anyone!"

"I wouldn't ask you to," I said.

"Why didn't he want us...?" Emily asked.

I glanced at Bill and didn't answer.

There was an awkward moment of silence, and then Detective Skees said, "I want to have a few more words with Mr. Kraft, and see that he gets back where he belongs. I'll be back to talk to you later, if that's all right."

"Sure," Bill said. He stood and watched as the detective escorted me down the corridor.

We took the elevator down, and walked back to the garage across the street where he'd left his car. We got in, but Skees didn't start the engine immediately.

I didn't rush him; I sat there and waited.

"That kid's pretty screwed up," he said at last.

"Yeah," I said.

"Do I have it right, that he *let* that thing bite off his finger and pull out his eye?"

"I think so. He says he did."

He shook his head, staring out the windshield rather than looking at me. "That's bad." Then he did look at me. "You think he's under some kind of spell or hex or something?"

"I don't know, sir. Honestly."

"Is a spell like that *possible*?"

"I don't know. I wish I did."

"So there wasn't anything in your dreams about that?"

"Not really." I hesitated, then said, "Look, I don't know how any of this really works, but I don't think it's really a *spell*. I think here's this miserable kid who's constantly fighting with his dad and neglected by his mom, and he meets this ghost-woman who showers him with attention and tells him everything he wants to hear – she doesn't *need* a spell to get him devoted to her."

"I can see that," Skees said. "You think he'll really go back to her?"

"I don't know," I said. "He might. Or maybe when the drugs wear off and he realizes what she's done to him, he'll realize how stupid he was, that she's just a monster trying to feed on him."

"That might screw him up worse, when he realizes he gave up a finger and an eye for nothing."

"Yeah," I said. "It'll be rough."

For a moment neither of us said anything. I was about to suggest starting the car when Skees said, "I can't believe I'm sitting here talking about flesh-eating ghosts as if they're real."

I grimaced at that. "I wish *I* didn't have to believe in them."

He looked at me. "Maybe you don't. Maybe this is all some goddamn hoax you and your girlfriend put together. Maybe that whole thing on the phone was some kind of hypnosis."

"I don't think you can hypnotize someone over the phone," I said.

"Then it's drugs, or subliminals, or something – isn't there supposed to be some kind of sonic vibration that scares the crap out of people?"

"Subsonics," I said. "I think I heard something about that."

"Well, maybe that's what your Madame Melisandra uses."

In all the eight years since Mrs. Reinholt cursed Mel, that had never occurred to me. I'd seen it all happen, so I just accepted it as... well, magic. Now that Skees mentioned it, though, I wondered. Oh, I don't mean I suddenly didn't believe in the curse, or witchcraft, or any of the rest of it, but maybe that was *how* the curse worked. Maybe that was why it was so much worse when she spoke than when I just looked at her. Maybe earplugs would help. It was something to try, anyway.

I shrugged. "She doesn't do it on purpose."

"So you say. People say a lot of things that aren't so, Mr. Kraft."

I sighed. "I can't prove anything, Detective. I haven't even made any claims, really, I just gave you some hypotheticals."

"That's bullshit, kid, and you know it."

I got angry at that. I was short of sleep, I hadn't had a real shower, I'd just talked to a kid who thought the monster trying to eat him loved him, and here I was with this cop calling me a liar. "You believe whatever you want, then," I said. "You think I'm lying to you, and there isn't any Jenny? Fine, you believe that if you want, but you still don't have anything on *me*. I don't have any reason to hurt that kid, and I wasn't even in this *state* when something gnawed his finger off. If you think *I'm* the one who ate it, then let's go back inside and find a doctor who'll pump my stomach, so you can see I'm not a cannibal."

"Wouldn't prove anything," he said calmly. "No reason to think you swallowed; if it *was* you, I figure you'd have spit it out."

I didn't have an answer for that, and the image was just so grotesque I almost laughed. I didn't, though; I didn't say anything at first. When I had a better handle on myself I asked, "So what are you going to do?"

"I've got no reason to hold you," he said. "You may be telling God's own truth and you may be right about everything, that it really is this ghost monster that's responsible. The kid's story matches yours well enough. Or maybe you believe what you're telling me, but have it wrong somehow – the kid thinks you do. Maybe you and the kid are both crazy as a two-dick dog and believe it all, but it's got nothing to do with what's really happening. I don't *know* what's going on. If you and your girlfriend *are* running a scam of some kind, I'm damned if I can figure out what the point of it is. And if I tried to hold you, tried to get a warrant as a material witness or whatever, I'd need to show the judge some reason to think you're involved, and the only reason I've got is that you've got no business in Lexington, but here you are, and somehow I don't think being a tourist is gonna play as evidence against you. So what I'm gonna do, Mr. Kraft, is take you back to your car and let you go about your business, but I want to know how to get hold of you if I think of any more questions – your cell number, any other phones you've got, e-mail, whatever."

"Sure, that's no problem, Detective." I tried not to sound as relieved as I felt. I'd been thinking that at the very least he was going to tell me not to leave Fayette County, and that would've meant paying a penalty to change my flight home, or maybe needing a whole new ticket, and probably losing my job, on top of it.

"And if any of your ghosts or dreams or witches tell you anything more about what's going on, you tell me, no matter how stupid it sounds."

"You've got it, sir."

"Good."

And with that, he finally started the car.

Chapter Ten

I didn't get a chance to talk to Jack again. Detective Skees didn't tell me anything more, or ask me any new questions. But I did go looking for Jenny again that evening, right after sunset, and I found her, back under the tulip poplar.

There were two cops sitting in a car in front of the Wilsons' house, and I knew they could probably see me if they bothered to look the right direction, but I didn't worry about it; I wasn't doing anything illegal, and if they arrested me I'd just go back to Ben Skees.

Jenny was sitting cross-legged under the tree, leaning forward, staring at her hand – staring at Jack's stolen finger, staring at it with Jack's stolen eye. She was rocking gently back and forth in utter silence, radiating woe and hunger.

"Jenny," I said.

She didn't look up.

"Jenny!" I repeated, more loudly. She stopped rocking.

"You need to leave Jack alone," I told her.

I love him, she said.

"So you want to kill him?"

I don't want to. I need to.

I hadn't expected that; I'd expected denials and evasions. "You intend to kill him?"

I need to.

"You're going to eat him away, little by little, until there's nothing left? Is that the idea?"

She finally looked up at me, with the one dark, empty eye and the one bright one. *I have to. I love him.*

For a moment I thought I might throw up, but I didn't. "And then what?" I asked. "You go on to the next kid?"

She didn't answer; she just stared at me. I don't know whether she didn't want to say, or whether she really didn't know herself, or what.

"He thinks you'll turn human and live happily ever after," I said. "Did you tell him that?"

She still didn't reply.

I decided to try a different tack. "You don't really love him, do you?" I demanded. "If you did, you wouldn't want to kill him."

I love him. I must devour him. I love him so much I want to eat him right up.

That sounded supremely creepy, but I didn't let that deter me. "The way you loved your own kids? The way you killed little Susie and Bobby?"

She blinked her stolen eye. *Susie? Bobby?*

I gestured wildly. "Whatever their names were. *I* don't know – do you? Do you even remember?"

Ashley. Sarah. Jason. My babies. I killed them. I loved them, so I killed them, and now they're dead, all dead dead dead.

Okay, that was interesting. I had names for her children now. Maybe I could track down Jenny's past; maybe that would give me some way to stop her.

"What were their full names, Jenny? Ashley Ghost? Ashley Smith?"

Ashley Derdiarian. My poor lost Ashley.

Derdiarian? That was a stroke of luck, I thought – that wasn't a common name. I wasn't sure I'd ever heard it before. There couldn't be that many people out there named Ashley Derdiarian.

"Derdiarian? D E R D A..."

She didn't actually say anything, but I knew she had somehow corrected my spelling, that there was a silent I I'd missed.

"Ashley, Sarah, and Jason? You starved them to death?"

I did, yes, I did, I locked them in their room and listened as they cried and begged and screamed, and I would not let them out, and they died, and I went in and saw their poor dead bodies lying there, and I cried and wailed...

With that, she fell forward onto her elbows, her long black hair falling down to hide her face, and she shook with inaudible sobbing. I could feel her grief. It wasn't unusual for spooks to have a sort of emotional aura, and hers was pretty strong.

It wasn't even close to Mel's, though. I had no trouble dealing with it, not after eight years with the Queen of Despair. "Where was their father?" I asked, trying to make sense of this. "Didn't anyone else hear them screaming?"

No father, no others, just Jenny, just me and my babies.
Something about this didn't make sense.

Well, really, *nothing* about it made sense. I was listening to a ghost explain how she had murdered her children, and how that meant she had to eat Jack Wilson alive – how could it make sense?

But I had to try to understand it, if I wanted to stop it. I couldn't physically stop Jenny, and I hadn't been able to talk Jack out of seeing her – though I thought he might balk at dying for her. At the hospital he had seemed unwilling to go that far.

That assumed, though, that her hold on him wouldn't be as strong as ever when they were together again; being away from her for a day might have made him more rational. When he actually saw her again, he might agree to anything.

But maybe if I could convince her to leave him alone, I could save him.

Of course, she might just go looking for a new victim, but surely there couldn't be very many kids with a home-life as miserable as Jack's, miserable enough to make a ghost's carnivorous love more precious than life itself.

Or maybe there could. I didn't know much about abused kids. Maybe there were thousands of them, and Jack was just the first one who could see her and hear her...

If he *was* the first. Maybe she didn't always start with eyes and fingers as appetizers; certainly plenty of kids went missing.

"So have you killed anyone else?" I asked. "Your own three kids, and now you're working on Jack – were there any others?"

Go away. Let Jenny mourn. I could *feel* her desire to have me leave, as well as sensing her words, but I ignored it.

"Tell me, first," I said. "Have you loved any other children, besides your own and Jack?"

Go away. The psychic push increased.

"Were there others?"

Go away. She seemed to have reached her limit, and it was still scarcely an echo of Mel's curse. I had no trouble resisting it and staying there.

I argued for awhile longer; I offered to give Jack a message for her if she told me the truth, I begged and I shouted, but she didn't answer, she just told me to go away. I had apparently gotten everything out of her that I was going to get – and I was tired and hungry and I wanted a shower, and fighting her rejection eventually took a toll, so I gave up. I turned and walked back to my rental car, leaving her curled up under the tulip poplar, her white dress a bright patch in the darkness, while darker, less human night-things moved silently through the surrounding brush and climbed on the branches above.

It wasn't over, I knew that – Jenny was still there, and Jack still loved her, and he had another eye and lots of fingers left, and I didn't really believe he would stay away from her, or that she wouldn't find him.

Besides, I'd dreamed about him, and always before that had meant there was going to be something important between us, something that would change my life; I didn't think carrying him out to the street and calling the cops, or promising to give Jenny a message and then not being able to find her, was really enough to account for it. I thought that not only would Jack and Jenny probably see one another again, but so would Jack and I.

But I didn't know of anything more I could do, and my plane ticket was ready, so I waited around that night, but when Thursday came I went home.

The whole way on the plane I was thinking about it, trying to decide what I should do, what I *could* do, but I kept coming up blank. Jenny had no material presence – at least, I didn't think she did, though maybe her new eye and finger did. It occurred to me, a little too late to be useful, that maybe I should have taken someone else to meet her, to find out whether that eye and that finger were visible to ordinary people, and not just to freaks like me and Jack.

But aside from those added body parts, I knew she was invisible and intangible to anyone who didn't have my special abilities. She could probably pass right through physical barriers; certainly other phantoms I'd seen could do that. She couldn't be arrested or imprisoned, and I didn't know of any way she could be hurt. This was why I hated the spooks and apparitions so much – they couldn't be stopped. Most of them were harmless and didn't *need* to be stopped, but the bad ones, the strong ones, the dangerous ones, could go about their business unmolested, because except for talking to them, there wasn't any way I knew for a human being to interfere with them.

Maybe there were things I didn't know; after all, Mrs. Reinholt seemed to be able to control them, up to a point – but only up to a point, as her death demonstrated.

I landed in Baltimore and got the B30 bus to the Greenbelt Metro, then walked home from the Takoma station rather than wait for another bus. It gave me a chance to stretch my legs and think some more.

I couldn't be sure whether Jack was still in danger, but if he was, and if I was going to do anything to save him, I had to talk either Jack or Jenny out of resuming their nasty little pact. Neither of them was rational, but if I could find a strong enough argument, maybe I could get through to one or the other.

That was why, when I got home to my apartment, I made a sandwich and then settled down at the computer to eat it while looking for background on Jenny Derdiarian, the mother who had murdered her three children.

I didn't find any.

You'd think that a gruesome triple child murder by starvation would be easy to research, wouldn't you? There should have been tabloid accounts all over the web; it should have been archived on a hundred news sites, and mentioned on dozens of true-crime compilations, but I couldn't find a damned thing.

And that was when I began to wonder whether the entire story was a lie, whether Jenny wasn't really a woman's ghost at all, but just a ghoul with a convincing cover story.

But why? Why make up names and specifics? Why not just say she couldn't remember the details? Instead she genuinely seemed to be... well, *haunted* by it.

Maybe she was really a ghost, but her kids had survived. Maybe they had been rescued in time, and she had somehow blanked that out. I started searching obituaries for a Jenny or Jennifer or Genevieve Derdiarian, and I didn't find one.

But I *did* eventually find a Jenny Derdiarian. She was still alive, and living in Winchester, Kentucky, which was only about twenty miles east of Lexington, in the next county over – presumably, that was the town Winchester Road ran to. That was close enough that it didn't seem likely to be mere coincidence.

I didn't have anything about her except a name and phone number, and that she was on her church's Bible School committee – that's where I found her name and number, on the church website. It was her only online presence.

Somehow, I didn't think a Baptist church would put a triple murderess on the school committee; that was carrying forgiveness a lot farther than most Christians could manage. And the webpage said it had been updated just a few days ago, getting ready for the new school year, so she had presumably been alive then, and probably still was.

Which meant she couldn't be my ghost, who had been seeing Jack for weeks, but there *had* to be a connection. Maybe a relative?

I sat and stared at that phone number for about ten minutes, but then I looked at the clock, and saw how late it had gotten, and I knew I wasn't about to call her that night, in any case. I didn't know whether I was *ever* going to call her – I mean, really, what would I say? But I wrote down the phone number – two copies, in fact. I stuck one in my pocket and left one next to the computer.

Then I picked up my phone to call Mel, who didn't mind late-night calls, and I scrolled to her number, but I didn't hit SEND; I was tired, I'd had a long day, and the thought of talking to the Queen of Despair was too much. I knew I would want to tell her about it all sooner or later; I owed her a thank you for trying to get Skees to lay off me, even if it hadn't been necessary. She would want to hear the whole story, but I just wasn't up to it. She could wait until tomorrow.

I put the phone down, shut down the computer, and went to bed, and if I had any dreams I didn't remember them.

In the morning I went to the store and gave Mr. Sanchez some half-assed story about where I'd been, which he pretended to believe. I still had a job, which was a pleasant surprise, and I didn't want him to regret it, so I put in a full day, no slacking, doing my best to get stock on the shelves and help every customer I saw.

That gave me time to think, to plan a little. It doesn't take a lot of brains to pull things out of boxes and stack them on shelves, so while my hands were earning my pay, my brain was mulling over what to say to Jenny Derdiarian.

There wasn't really any doubt that I was going to call her; I had to know what her connection was to that thing that bit off Jack's finger, and I couldn't see any better way to find out than to call her and ask.

But I couldn't jump right in with the whole story. If I accused her of murdering three kids she'd probably hang up on me, and I'd guess it was a fifty-fifty shot as to whether she'd call the cops. I needed to approach it carefully.

And if I just said I was some random stranger, she probably wouldn't talk to me at all. She'd probably think I was a telemarketer trying to sell her something. I needed an explanation for my questions.

And in the end, I decided to go with the truth – not all of it, but some.

Chapter Eleven

I got some supper on the way home, got settled at the computer, then called the number from the church website. She answered on the third ring.

"Hello?"

I felt a chill at that – not the same kind of chill I would get talking to Mel, not terror or despair, but a little tremble of excitement. I recognized her voice.

Now, that may seem crazy, since I'd never actually *heard* the ghost at all, I had only sensed its words in my head, but the words had had a tone, all the same, and this woman's voice had that exact tone.

"Hello, Ms. Derdiarian? Jenny Derdiarian?"

"Yes?"

"You don't know me, but my name is Gregory Kraft, and I'm... well, I guess you'd say I'm a psychic."

I know it's stereotyping, and it might not have worked, but I thought a church-going woman from Kentucky would be willing to listen to a psychic; I held my breath as I waited to hear whether I was right.

"Oh?" she said.

That wasn't exactly enthusiastic, but she hadn't cut me off.

"Yes," I said quickly. "I had... well, a sort of a vision the other day, and I'm trying to figure out what it means. I was hoping you might be able to help me."

"Well, *I'm* not a psychic, Mr. Kraft. I'm sure I don't know what your vision was about. Are you positive you have the right number?"

"I believe I do, Ms. Derdiarian, but no, I'm not positive. Your name is Jenny Derdiarian, yes? That was the name in my vision. But to be honest, I'm not sure you're the right one. Do you know of anyone else named Jenny Derdiarian? A relative, maybe?"

"No, I can't say I do. The only people I ever even heard of named Derdiarian are my first husband's folks, and I don't think a one of them is named Jenny."

"Then I think you must be the right one. Tell me, do you have any children?"

"Not that it's any business of yours, but yes, I do have children. Three of them."

I spoke quickly again, before she could tell me anything more. "Two girls and a boy?"

"That's right." She sounded wary.

"Ashley, Sarah, and Jason?"

"Now, how did you know *that*?" For the first time she sounded interested, rather than impatient.

"Those were the names in my vision, Ms. Derdiarian. May I ask how old they are?"

She hesitated for a moment, then said, "Well, Ashley's just turned twenty-four, and Sarah's in college, and Jason graduated high school this past June. What is this *about*, Mr. Kraft?"

I swallowed, surprised. Those kids were older than I'd expected, much older.

"And they're all okay, so far as you know? They're well?"

"They're fine. Jason's right here with me, and it looks as if he wants to know why we're talking about him. If you're trying to scare me, Mr. Kraft..."

"No, no! Nothing like that. I'm just concerned. In my vision they were younger than that, so perhaps this is related to something that happened some time ago."

"*What* is? What is this vision you keep talking about?"

"Well, that's why I'm calling. I don't understand it myself, and I was hoping you could help me make sense of it. In the vision you were very upset, so upset that you had locked all three of your children in their rooms, and they were saying they were hungry, and you were refusing to let them out or let them have anything to eat."

For a long moment she didn't say anything; then she said, "Where did you say you are, Mr. Kraft?"

"I'm in Maryland, Ms. Derdiarian. Just outside Washington, D.C. I live here, in a place called Takoma Park."

Her next sentence wasn't addressed to me, and she wasn't speaking directly into the phone, but I heard it clearly enough. "Jason, honey, would you go check on the car? I think I left the keys in the ignition again."

I couldn't make out the words, but I thought I could hear Jason arguing.

"Just go, sweetie, and make sure, okay?" she said.

I thought I could hear some further protest, but apparently Jason went.

Then she was speaking into the phone again. "All right, now, Mr. Kraft, or whoever you are," she said, quietly and intently, "how did you get this number? Was *that* in this vision?"

"No, I found it on the web," I said. "On your church's website."

"That doesn't have my kids' names."

"No, it doesn't. Those were in my vision, along with *your* name. I did a search for it – listen, I know how creepy this must sound, but my dream, my vision, was really disturbing, and I wanted to make sure it wasn't... well, that everything there was all right."

"Well, it *was*, until you called me just now." She sounded genuinely distressed, and I felt a stab of guilt.

"I'm really sorry if I've upset you," I said, and I meant it.

"Well, bless you, I'll be fine. You know, I was never too sure whether there were any real psychics, because I know a lot of them are fakes, but I think you must be a real one, Mr. Kraft, because I can't think how else you would know about... about that. You got my number from the internet, and you could probably find my name and my kids' names, but what you're talking about, *that* isn't on the web anywhere."

"What I'm talking about? Ms. Derdiarian, I don't *know* what I'm talking about. I was hoping you could help me understand it."

"You really saw it in a vision?" Now she sounded more curious than upset. "Me locking the kids in their rooms and starving them?"

"Well, more... more heard it than saw it, really," I explained. "That's why I didn't know how old the kids were, I never saw them. And I don't know whether the Jenny Derdiarian I saw looked anything like the real one; she was thin, with a pale complexion and long, straight black hair..."

"It's been a long time since I'd say I was thin, Mr. Kraft, and I cut my hair a few years back, but at least you've got the color right."

"Then... then was it you that I saw?"

"You tell me, Mr. Kraft. Just what *was* in this vision of yours?"

"I told you – you had locked up your children and were denying them food. You were pale and thin, with long black hair, wearing a plain white dress, and... well, you seemed a little hysterical. Does that make any sense to you?"

She didn't reply immediately, and I began to wonder whether she'd put the phone down, but at last she said, "I'm going to tell you something I've never told anybody else, Mr. Kraft, and it's *because* I've never told anybody else that I'm taking you seriously, and why I think you really are psychic. When my children were little, when Ashley was about seven and Jason was just a baby, I got feeling more than a little overwhelmed. My first husband, their father, had left me, gone off somewhere to drink himself to death, and I hadn't met Chester yet, so there was just me and the kids, and not enough money, and I felt more than a little trapped, and I used to have these fantasies of just locking the kids in their rooms until they starved to death, and then I'd have my life back. I never *did* anything like that, thank heavens, I never even seriously considered it, but I *thought* about it, and I thought about it *all the time*, it got to be a real obsession, you know? It started out just a harmless little fantasy, but I couldn't stop thinking about it, and it got more and more real. Whenever I had a spare moment I would sit and play it all out in my head, like I was watching some horrible movie. Half the time I couldn't think about anything else. I started worrying that maybe someday I might actually do something about it, and hurt my kids. I was thinking of maybe talking to someone about it, but the preacher at the church I went to back then, he wasn't all he could have been, and I couldn't afford a psychiatrist, and I didn't really have the time to talk to anyone anyway. It was pretty troubling; I prayed a lot, but I couldn't make myself quit."

I made a noise to indicate I was still listening, that I understood.

"And then one day, it stopped. It was just gone. I didn't think about it anymore. Oh, things were still rough, money was tight, and I won't deny I had some hard thoughts about the kids and maybe yelled at them a little more than I oughten, but that whole idea of locking them up to starve, it was just gone. I thought God must have just plucked it out of me, as a burden I didn't need anymore, and I'd hardly ever thought about it since then, until tonight. And here you are, and it sounds like you dreamed that whole thing just the way I used to. That thin woman in a white dress, I don't know if I ever *really* looked like that, but that was how I saw myself when I dreamed about... about doing that."

"In... in your daydreams, if that's what they were," I asked, "did the kids actually die?"

"Oh, yes," she said, and her voice had gone strangely calm, the distress that had been there a moment before gone, as suddenly as she said her obsessive fantasy had gone. "I'd listen to them crying and screaming and begging for food, right up until they stopped. And I opened the door and went into the room to be sure they were dead, and I cried over the bodies, and then sometimes I'd die, too, or I'd just fly away by magic, or – well, it didn't matter, once they were gone."

"Oh."

"But you know, Mr. Kraft, if I'd ever *really* locked them up until they died, they'd have died of thirst, not hunger, wouldn't they? Or of something else, anyway. Or they'd have smashed a window and climbed out, at least Ashley would have. She's always had a mind of her own, that one."

"I guess you're right," I said. "It *couldn't* have been real." I felt a bit stupid for not realizing that myself.

"But you *saw* that?" she asked. "You really had a vision?"

"Yes," I lied.

"That's surely strange. I guess God does work in mysterious ways."

"I guess so," I said.

This was all beginning to make a sort of sense. I didn't really understand it entirely, but it fit together. The ghost-Jenny had somehow gotten hold of this woman's obsessive fantasy, taken it out of her head and believed it was real.

That was strange, but it made more sense than the ghost of a murderess wanting to eat kids.

"Thank you, Ms. Derdiarian," I said. "You've put my mind at ease, knowing it was just a daydream you used to have. I don't know how it came to me, but I'm glad to know it wasn't any more than that."

"It was pretty intense for a daydream, Mr. Kraft; I don't know that's the word I'd use.

"Well, it wasn't real, anyway."

"No, it never was. I used to think I was a monster for even *thinking* about it; I can't imagine how it could be real."

"No," I said. "Is there anything more you can tell me about it? Because it seems to me there must be some reason for me to see it now."

"Well, I don't know what it could be. Hold on a moment, Mr. Kraft." I heard her do something to muffle the phone, and then say something to Jason – I couldn't make it out exactly, but I'm fairly sure he had returned and she was sending him on another pointless errand, out of earshot.

"Are you still there?" she asked, when Jason was presumably gone.

"I'm still here, Ms. Derdiarian," I said.

"You know, I do believe things happen for a reason, so if you had this vision, maybe it's important, though I can't imagine how." She sounded thoughtful.

"I don't know myself, but I have a feeling that someone may be in danger, and there's something in your story that might help save him."

She caught her breath. "Oh, my – really?"

"I don't *know*, but I think there might be."

For a second she didn't respond, and when she did she seemed almost wistful. "It must be very strange, being psychic. You just *see* these things, out of the blue?"

"Sometimes, yes." I didn't want to get distracted by any details of how my talents worked. "Now, about your... your daydreams. Was there just the one?"

There was a pause before she said, "No, there was one other."

"What was it?"

"You didn't see it in your vision? Or hear it?"

"I'm not sure," I said cautiously. "If I did, it wasn't clear."

"The other one came first. Do you have any children, Mr. Kraft?"

I resisted the temptation to say, "Not that I know of," and just said, "No."

"But you've seen people play with babies?"

"Some," I said, wondering if maybe I should have spent more time with my stepmother and my half-sisters.

"Well, you know how someone will say, Oh, you're so cute, I could eat you right up! You've heard that, haven't you?"

"Sure," I said, suddenly afraid I knew where this was going.

"Well, when Ashley was a baby, I used to say that – I would hold her in my arms and look down at her and smell her and I would say I could eat her right up, and at first it was just one of those things you say because it's what you've always heard, and she was so adorable, but then I began to wonder what it would be like to actually eat her. Isn't that awful?"

"It's... I don't know, Ms. Derdiarian."

Suddenly I wasn't sure I wanted to hear any more of this. I wondered how psychologists could stand listening to some of their patients' secrets.

"I would hold her tiny little hand and kiss her fingers, and everyone would smile at me," the voice on the phone said, "but while I was doing that I was wondering what it would taste like to bite those fingers right off. I loved her so much I wanted to get her back inside me – isn't that crazy?"

"I don't know, Ms. Derdiarian," I said, a little desperately, while the image of Jack's left hand filled my thoughts.

"They say that new mothers are a little crazy sometimes, from all the hormones and sleep deprivation, so at first I thought it was that, but the idea kept coming back. Every time I held Ashley, and then again after Sarah was born, and again with Jason, I'd think about eating them alive. Those cute little fingers and big bright eyes – I never *did* anything, of course, but I *thought* about it, every time I picked one of them up. I've never said a word about it to anyone before right now, but you asked."

"Yes, I did," I agreed, though now I almost wished I hadn't. "Thank you." It sounded as if Jenny's appetite had nothing to do with becoming human; it was just another nasty involuntary fantasy this woman had once had.

"That went away, too. I'm not sure whether it was at the same time that the one about locking them away to starve went away, or whether it might have been maybe just a little earlier. I mean, Ashley and Sarah weren't babies anymore, and even Jason was running around on his own, I wasn't carrying him all the time, so I hadn't been thinking about eating him so much, I was dreaming about locking him in his room so he would be *still*, so I wouldn't need to worry about him anymore."

"I understand," I said, though I didn't really.

"I'm sure you think I'm really horrible," she said. "*I certainly used to think so!* I remember how awful I used to feel about these things just as much as I remember the... the urges themselves."

"You *used* to think so?"

"That's right. When the... when the obsession went away, so did the guilt. It was *all* gone – it was like it wasn't even me who'd had all those terrible thoughts, like that was just something I'd seen on TV, or read in the newspaper, not anything that had been in my own head."

"Really?"

"Really. It just stopped. The good Lord took it away."

I didn't think it had been God who took it away. "And that was when?"

"Oh, goodness, I don't know. At least fifteen years ago."

Did that mean that ghost-Jenny had been lurking there for *fifteen years*, waiting for some kid like Jack to come along? Was it because Jack had that psychic talent so strongly?

Or had she victimized other kids, and for some reason no one heard about it? Maybe I should check into any missing children in that neighborhood.

But that wasn't Ms. Derdiarian's business. There was no reason to upset her, when she was being so open and cooperative.

The mere fact that she hadn't hung up on me immediately was more than I'd had a right to expect.

"You haven't had any nasty feelings like that since?" I asked.

"Not a one, Mr. Kraft. At least, not one that ever repeated. Nothing that kept *going*. I admit I've had the occasional wish that something bad would happen to someone, that someone with her nose in the air would trip over her own feet, or that sort of thing, but we're none of us perfect, are we? And I never once, since that day, dreamed of hurting anyone myself; at worst I wished that the bad things would just *happen*, never that I would *do* them."

"I see the difference," I said.

"I told you, it was as if God had just pulled that darkness out of my soul, cast out the devils that troubled me."

"And that was fifteen years ago?"

"Thereabouts."

That fit, except that I was still wondering whether it had really taken ghost-Jenny that long to harm anyone. I also wondered why a spook would have latched onto this woman's guilty obsession, in particular. If it had needed a victim who could see it, like Jack, maybe it had needed a source with the same talent. I hesitated, then said, "I do have one more question, Ms. Derdiarian."

"What's that, Mr. Kraft?"

"Have you ever seen a ghost?" I thought that even if she didn't always have the ability, perhaps she had seen the thing when it stole her obsessions, or perhaps it had hung around her for awhile.

She didn't answer right away. Then she asked, "What do *you* think?"

That almost answered the question right there. "I think you have," I said. Then I added, "But maybe not recently." After all, she hadn't been bothered in years.

"Mr. Kraft, you are truly beginning to scare me. I don't know whether I've seen a ghost, but I used to see *something*. Or several things, really; they were pretty common. Only I haven't seen a one since the day I stopped imagining what you saw in your vision. I saw them many a night, prowling out there in the dark. I didn't think they were ghosts, I thought they were devils come to torment me, and that maybe they put those bad thoughts in my head. Sometimes I even thought I was going crazy, what with seeing those things and getting obsessed with those horrible ideas about killing my darlings. But then that whole nasty fantasy went away, and the ghosts or demons or whatever they were went with it, and I haven't seen any since, and I'll tell you, Mr. Kraft, I'm much the happier for it, and I really hope this vision of yours doesn't mean they'll be coming back."

She had seen *several* ghosts? She *had* been able to see them all, not just the one that took her fantasy?

But she *stopped*. There was a way to make it *stop*. How had that happened? Was it something *I* could do?

Had the phantom taken more from her than her obsession?

"I don't think it means they'll be back, Ms. Derdiarian," I said. "I think they've moved on. But I want to say thank you for talking to me – I don't really know what it all means, but you've been very helpful, and I really appreciate it."

"So you're all done, then? No more questions?"

"Nothing important, no. I admit I'm still curious about a few things, but it's none of my business and you've been more than kind."

"What sort of things?"

"Well, I was wondering – you said Derdiarian was your first husband's name, and if I understood correctly you've remarried, but you're still using it?"

"Yes sir, I am. I tell people it's so as to have the same name as the kids, but the truth is – well, Chester's last name is Craig, and my name's Jenny."

I was so focused on supernatural weirdness that it took a second for me to see the problem, but then I got it. "Oh," I said. "Lucky for me, then – I don't know if I'd ever have found you if he'd been named Jo... I mean, Smith."

"I don't suppose you would. Was there anything else?"

"Did you ever live in Lexington?"

"Well, sure. For about thirteen years, when the kids were little."

"Near Winchester Road?"

"Now, there you go again, being psychic. If you're faking, Mr. Kraft, you're awful good at it. Does this have something to do with your vision?"

"Yes, it does." I hesitated. "I think there's something there in Lexington that remembers your... your daydreams, and that was communicating with me."

"One of those devil-ghosts?"

"I think so."

After that neither of us had anything more to say, until finally she said, "The Lord works in mysterious ways, but I'm sure it's all for the best. It's been interesting talking to you, Mr. Kraft."

"Thank you for your help, Ms. Derdiarian. I really appreciate it." Then I ended the call.

And of course, I immediately thought of something else I should have asked her – had she ever known the Wilsons? But it wasn't worth calling back, and I didn't think it really mattered.

What mattered was that Jenny the ghost wasn't really a ghost at all. No one had starved three children to death. A thing had somehow latched onto this woman's guilty fantasy, that was all. How and why it had done so, I didn't know, but it had.

In fact, it had apparently stolen the whole evil fantasy right out of the real Jenny's head, probably about fifteen years ago, going by the kids' ages.

So had it been preying on the local kids for fifteen years? Even if it had never actually harmed one before, it seemed to me that someone should have mentioned that the local kids talked about a hungry ghost, if they did.

Maybe Jack really was the first. Maybe Jack was the first one who could see and hear the specter – or maybe he was the first one desperate enough to listen to it.

Or maybe it was growing stronger.

I didn't know; all I could do was guess.

I picked up the phone again and called Mel.

I told her about the trip to Kentucky, but I didn't mention my call to Jenny Derdiarian at first. Just telling her what had happened in Lexington was hard enough. Talking to Mel at all, about anything, was difficult, and I intended to take it in stages.

When I had given her the basics she had questions, and I tried my best to answer them without screaming or slamming down the phone.

Mel thought I should have talked to Jack more while I had the chance, asked him more questions about Jenny, spoken to him back on his own street, but the problem there, I pointed out, was that I was a strange man from out of state, and he was a vulnerable twelve-year-old, and if I went anywhere near him once he was out of the hospital, anywhere we could talk privately, everyone was going to take it for granted that I was a pedophile grooming my next victim.

"You could have had Detective Skees play chaperone," Mel said.

That image filled me with dread, but I knew that was at least partly the curse; Ben Skees meant me no harm. "I think he's got better things to do with his time," I said. "Not to mention, Jack's parents would want an explanation."

That didn't really satisfy her, but she didn't argue the point, and besides, it was too late; I was back home in Takoma Park, in my apartment on Maple Avenue, not in Kentucky.

Then I told her about my phone conversation with the original Jenny Derdiarian.

Mel was very quiet for a moment.

"That's really interesting, Greg," she said at last, and I struggled not to read any mockery into that.

"Yeah," I said.

"No, really," she said. "I mean, we've been trying to make some sense out of this supernatural stuff since high school, and this is... well, this is something new. It might be important."

What I intended to say was, "Or it might be random," but I was talking to Mel, so all that came out was, "Or... or not."

"Or not, yeah, but it's still interesting. Do you think this ghoul got its kid-starving, kid-eating obsessions from Jenny Derdiarian, or did it give her the obsessions in the first place?"

"I don't know," I said. I hadn't thought of that, that maybe the monster had inflicted this on her and then relented. It didn't seem to fit, not really; it felt over-complicated.

"But it never was human, so would eating a kid really turn it human?"

"I don't... I doubt it."

"You think it's lying."

"Yes." I swallowed. "Or maybe it believes it, but it's still wrong."

"I guess it might be. I mean, from what you've said, it seems to think it's really Jenny Derdiarian."

"Or it's all an act."

"But why would it bother? Why tell Jack it killed those three kids, when they're alive and well? Why not make up some nicer story? Besides, if it was acting, why choose a real person, and one who's still alive? I think it really *does* think it's Jenny."

I couldn't argue with that; it did make sense. "Maybe," I said.

"And she used to see supernatural things, but that stopped when the ghoul took away her fantasizing. How does *that* fit in?"

"It thinks it's her, right?" I said. "So it can't have any contact with the real Jenny; that would be like being in two places at once."

"We don't know whether that's a problem for it," Mel replied. "And that doesn't explain why she can't see the others that are out there."

"Maybe it took that along with her fantasy."

"Is that possible? I didn't think it could work like that."

"*I* don't know. I don't know anything." I felt utterly helpless; this was all so overwhelming and mysterious.

"See if you still think so when you aren't talking to me," Mel said, and I realized she might have a point, but even so, at that moment it seemed impossible that I could do anything to help Jack, that I could ever figure out what was really going on.

"I can't save the kid," I said.

"He may save himself. Hey, do you think you should call Detective Skees and tell him that you found where the ghost's story came from?"

"I don't see how it could help."

"Could it hurt?"

"I don't know. I can't think, Mel." I tried desperately not to sound as if I was blaming her for that, but we both knew that the curse was responsible. That I even mentioned it showed how much it was wearing on me.

"I suppose not. Maybe we should call it a night, Greg. Get some sleep, take your time, think it over, and then you can call Skees or not, whichever you like. Maybe you could see if the two of you can come up with a good explanation for all this."

"Maybe." I knew she could hear my doubts in the tone of my voice, but I didn't care. It had been a long talk with Mel, and my nerves were shot.

When I was a kid, I used to hate calling strangers on the phone. Now, though, talking to my best friend was so miserable that calling strangers was nothing. Talking to Jenny Derdiarian was easy compared to talking to Mel.

That was just so *wrong*.

"Good night, Greg," she said.

"Good night, Mel."

And that was the end of the call.

I took her advice and went to bed, and slept heavily; I was more tired than I'd realized.

That was Friday. By Monday I'd decided there wasn't any point in calling Ben Skees; what difference would it make to know a partial history of a creature he couldn't see or hear? He would just have to keep an eye on Jack; Jenny was not part of the detective's world.

All any of us could do was try to keep Jack away from Jenny, and Skees already knew to do that – though he didn't know how, and neither did I. We would just have to hope that Jack had come to his senses and wouldn't go near Jenny again.

That should have been the end of it.

But it didn't *feel* like the end of it, to either me or Mel.

And of course, it wasn't.

Chapter Twelve

My little trip to the Bluegrass State had been in August; it was a Tuesday in late September, and I was on my lunch break, when I got a call.

It wasn't Mel's number, or Dad's; it wasn't any number I recognized. It didn't give a name. The area code was 859, and I didn't know where that was. "Hello?" I said.

"Mr. Kraft?"

I recognized the voice, even if I hadn't recognized the number. "Detective Skees," I said. I dreaded what he was going to say. I felt almost as strong a sense of impending doom as if I were talking to Mel, and I knew it wasn't because of any curse.

I hadn't dreamed about Jack since I carried him out to the street the night he lost his eye, but I had thought about him. Those dreams – I knew I wasn't done with Jack. He hadn't yet had enough of an impact on my life to justify the dreams.

I had tried to tell myself that this just meant I'd had the rules wrong, and it didn't *always* have to be some great life-changing event that triggered the dreams, but I hadn't really believed it.

And sure enough, here was a phone call that pretty much had to be about Jack, and it wasn't coming from Jack himself, or a family member, or a teacher or counselor; it was coming from a police detective.

Not a good sign.

"I was wondering whether you might have heard anything from Jack Wilson recently," Skees said. "Or from Jenny."

"No," I said. "Not a word. What's happened?"

"It seems our boy Jack didn't come home from school yesterday," Skees said. "Didn't come home at all last night. His classmates swear he got on the bus same as always, and got off at his own stop, but no one's seen him since. I'd hoped, since you two seemed to hit it off so well this summer, that he might have contacted you."

I felt slightly ill. It had taken a month, but I was pretty sure what must have happened. He'd gone back to Jenny, and this time she might not settle for just a little piece.

"No," I said. "I haven't seen or heard a thing from Jack since that day at the hospital."

"I was afraid of that. Mr. Kraft, I realize this isn't really your problem, but if you have any suggestions I'd sure like to hear them."

I was completely at a loss. "He was out all night? Then he's probably already dead," I said.

"I sure hope not."

"Well, if he isn't, then maybe he can take care of himself. He's twelve years old, Detective, he's not a baby."

"Yeah, but he's not alone this time."

"What, you mean Jenny? I don't follow you."

"I mean Katie. Jack's little sister. She's gone missing, too."

Suddenly I felt ill, remembering the frightened little girl in my dreams, the girl no one seemed to pay much attention to. "Katie?"

"She's seven, Mr. Kraft. We've got men out looking for the two of them, but so far we haven't found a thing, so I figured I'd give you a call and see if you had any ideas."

I had an idea, all right, but it wasn't a helpful one; my idea was that Jack had found another child to feed to the monster he thought he loved.

If I understood it right, and if Jenny hadn't lied about this, Jenny couldn't eat Katie unless Katie offered herself, but Katie was *seven*, and her big brother was probably there trying to convince her to help the nice lady...

"I'll get the earliest flight I can," I said. "I don't know what I can do, and it may be too late, but I'm coming to help you look."

For a moment he didn't respond; then he said, "You don't have to do that."

"I want to help. Maybe I can see something you can't."

"What might that be?"

"I don't *know*. Maybe something."

"Well, maybe you can. If you really think it's worth the trip, I can't stop you, but I'm not advising you to come."

"I'll see you soon, then." I ended the call, shoved the rest of my lunch in the trash, and headed out. I told Mr. Sanchez I was leaving, family emergency, but didn't stop to give him a chance to argue, just ran past and out the door.

I barely made a 3:40 flight out of Reagan. It stopped in Charlotte, so it was about eight and I'd missed dinner by the time I reached the rental car desk at Blue Grass Airport, and close to nine by the time I got to the Wilsons' street. The sun was long gone, the streetlights were lit, and there were a couple of police cars pulled up at the curb. Four policemen were standing on the sidewalk, three of them in uniform; the fourth was Detective Ben Skees. That thing that looked like a bent old woman in a brown robe was crouched a few yards away, watching the cops, and a few other phantoms were in sight, but there was no sign of Jenny, and none of them looked threatening.

It didn't look as if much was happening, which puzzled me – shouldn't everyone be out looking for the missing kids, rather than just standing there calmly?

I had a little Chevy this time, not a Cruiser, not that it made much difference, but it meant Skees didn't recognize me until I leaned out the window and called his name.

He was talking casually to a couple of the other cops; the Wilsons were nowhere in sight. At the sound of my voice the detective turned and spotted me.

"Kraft," he said. "You came all the way from Maryland?"

"Of course. I got here as quickly as I could," I said.

He gestured to the other cops, then walked over to my car. "You've wasted your time," he said. "We found the kids hours ago."

I felt like an idiot. It had never occurred to me that they might turn up before I got there. "Oh," I said. "Are they okay?"

"They're both fine, physically – I mean, other than what Jack was already missing. Katie was pretty upset, and Jack's mad as hell but won't say why."

"How'd you find them? Where were they?"

He grinned at me. "McDonald's," he said. "Katie got hungry, so Jack went to get her a Happy Meal, and the clerk got suspicious at the sight of kids with no adults, and called the cops. We found them sitting there eating french fries."

"You could have called and saved me the trip."

"I was kinda busy at first, and by the time I had a moment, my call went straight to voice mail. You must have already been on the plane with your phone turned off."

"Oh." In fact, I realized when he said it that not only had I not checked my voice mail, I hadn't even turned the phone back on. It had slipped my mind. I fished it out and remedied that little oversight.

As I put the phone back in my pocket I asked, "If it was all over hours ago, why are you still here?" I gestured at the cop cars.

"Just keeping an eye on things."

"Making sure Jack doesn't take off again?"

He shrugged.

"Slow night, huh?" I asked.

"I like slow nights," he said, smiling.

"I do when I'm home."

"I *did* tell you that you didn't need to come here."

"Yeah, you did," I admitted. "But I'm here now, so can you tell me anything more about what happened?"

Skees glanced at the other cops, then leaned down into the window. "I did not call you," he said, as he set his crossed arms on the bottom of the car's open window. "You understand that?"

"Sure," I said, startled.

"I do not believe in ghosts or ghouls or things that go bump in the night. The Lexington-Fayette police department does not consult psychics or pay attention to visions."

"Of course not."

"This whole thing is the Wilsons' business, and not yours."

"Got it."

He glanced back at the others again, then turned back to me. "So long as we understand that, and that I'm not talking to you – it looks like they spent the night out under the trees somewhere. Jack's not talking, but Katie says they went to see the hungry lady, the one in the white dress who's hard to see, and Jack said they had to feed her, but Katie wouldn't, because the hungry lady was scary. She and Jack argued all night, she says, and when the sun came up the hungry lady went away, and they went to sleep for awhile, and then when they woke up Katie was hungry, almost as hungry as the hungry lady, so they went to Mickey D's for lunch, and then the policemen came and got them. So that's her story."

"Jack tried to feed his sister to the ghost," I said.

"That's what it sounds like to me, all right."

"Can I talk to the kids?"

Skees hesitated. "I don't see as how I can explain that," he said. "Mr. And Mrs. Wilson are pretty upset, as you can imagine."

"I'm sure they are," I said. I looked out through the windshield, peering into the gloom at the end of the street; I wasn't sure whether I saw something white down there under the tulip poplar, or not.

The imitation Jenny was probably pretty upset, too – she didn't get her meal.

"Could you ask?" I said. "Because I don't think Jack and Jenny are going to give up. If Katie won't cooperate, maybe they'll find someone who will."

The detective considered that for a moment, looking back over his shoulder at the Wilson house, then he turned back to me and said, "We can do that. We can ask."

Then he turned and headed for the house.

He didn't say whether I should follow or wait where I was, so I followed, about three steps behind him, as he marched up to the door and rang the bell.

Bill Wilson answered the bell; he spoke quietly, and I was still hanging back, on the path below the stoop, so I didn't catch his words.

"Mr. Wilson, we're about done here. I'm going to leave one car here, with Officers Fahey and de Witt, but the rest of us are heading out soon."

"Thank you, Detective," Wilson said.

"There's one thing – do you remember Mr. Kraft, who found Jack after he lost his eye last month?" He gestured in my direction. Wilson looked at me, but didn't answer. Skees continued, "He heard about what happened and wanted to lend a hand, but we'd found the kids before he got here. Since he came all this way, he was hoping he could talk to them, just to see how Jack's doing. He's been worried. Of course, it's entirely up to you, but if they aren't in bed yet it'd be a nice gesture."

"Katie's asleep," Wilson said, staring at me. He hesitated, then said, "Let me see what Emily thinks."

That didn't sound like the household tyrant I remembered from my dreams. I guessed that Jack's adventures had gotten to him. He went back inside, but left the door cracked.

"You do understand you can't talk to Jack *alone*, right?" Skees said over his shoulder. "I'll be there."

"That's fine." I hadn't expected anything else.

Then the door opened again, and Jack stepped out. He was wearing a black eye-patch and looked tired and angry, and had that eerie, out-of-step look. I wasn't sure whether it was a little more intense than it had been in August, or whether I'd just forgotten how strong the effect was in him.

Skees backed down the steps to make room; the boy stood on the top step and closed the door behind him.

He wasn't looking at Skees; he was looking at me. He obviously intended to talk to me whether his parents liked the idea or not.

"You didn't give her my message," he said. "You told her to leave me alone."

"That's right, I did," I said.

"What gives you the right to do that?" he demanded. "What business is it of yours?"

"The same right any responsible adult has, to keep a kid from getting himself killed," I answered.

"Did you tell Katie about her?"

"I've never met Katie. I've never spoken to her at all."

"So it wasn't you that convinced her not to help Jenny?"

"*Convinced* her? Jack, don't be stupid. No one needs to be *convinced* not to be eaten."

"But someone needs to help her!"

"Jack, she's a *monster*. She wants to *kill* you."

"She's not a monster!"

"Oh, sure, every nice lady tries to eat children."

"She *has* to, so she can be human again!"

"She never *was* human, Jack. I did some research. The *real* Jenny Derdiarian is alive and well; your friend is just pretending to be her."

That clearly caught him off-guard, but he recovered quickly. "You're lying!" he said.

"No, I'm not."

"It's a different person!"

"I don't think so. Same name, three kids with the same names – how many people named Derdiarian do you think there *are*?"

"Then you're wrong!" He looked like he wanted to hit me, or to burst into tears, or both, but he didn't do either one.

"She's lying to you, Jack," I said, trying to sound reassuring. "She doesn't love you. She just wants someone to eat."

"She *does* love me!"

"Did she tell you to bring Katie to her?"

For the first time he hesitated.

"She asked if I knew any other kids who could feed her," he admitted. "When I wouldn't let her eat any more of me."

"So you brought her your own kid sister." I didn't try to sound contemptuous, but I didn't need to.

"Nobody cares about Katie!" Jack retorted furiously. "Even Katie says that. She said she didn't care what happens to her, but then when she saw Jenny she changed her mind."

I glanced at Skees, who had eased back onto the lawn, out from between the two of us. I couldn't read anything on his face, but I knew he'd heard what Jack said. He could guess what a great family life these kids had, that they'd say things like that.

"Of course she did," I said. "She's not crazy. She never meant what she said about not caring what happens to her; that's just something people say when they're upset. No matter how miserable she is, I'm sure she wants to grow up and make a life for herself; why should she give up her whole *life* just so you can make your cannibal friend happy?"

"She's not..." he began. Then he stopped, because if Jenny really was human, then she really was a cannibal. He couldn't very well deny that after she ate his finger.

"Jack, Jenny's a monster," I said, trying to be gentle. "Maybe she doesn't want to be. Maybe she doesn't know she is. But just stop and think about it – she eats human flesh. She wants to kill a child. That makes her a monster. You shouldn't be helping her. If it's a choice between killing someone who's got her entire life ahead of her, or letting a monster go hungry, I'm sure you know which is the right thing to do. Just stop, okay? Stay away from her. Don't help her."

"But I *love* her!"

I shook my head. "She's fooled you, Jack. Really, truly, she's tricked you. It's not real. It's not love."

He glared at me. "What do *you* know about it?"

"I'm the only adult who can see her, remember? I know about these things. I've been watching them for the past eight years. She's not what she says she is; they never are. They're monsters. They're not people, they just pretend to be."

"You're wrong! She's different!"

I didn't bother to answer that; I just looked at him.

"I'll find a way," he said. "I know there's a way for her to be well again."

"She never was, Jack."

"Then I'll find a way to *make* her well!"

Before I could answer he turned and threw the door open, then stamped inside and slammed it behind him.

For a moment Skees and I just stood there, looking at the closed door. Then Skees said, "I don't think you convinced him."

"You noticed that, Detective?"

"But on the other hand, Katie's alive and well. That thing didn't eat her."

"Yeah. *I* noticed *that*."

"Why is that?"

I shrugged. "Jack and Jenny both say she can't eat pieces of anyone without their permission. Katie won't give permission. End of story."

"So she's really pretty harmless?"

"Unless she finds someone suicidal, yeah, I guess she is."

"You think she'll ever convince Jack to pick suicide?"

I sighed as I stared at the door. "I don't know," I said. "I just don't know."

Chapter Thirteen

There wasn't much to say after that. Skees hung around while I walked down the block to the big tulip poplar looking for Jenny, but I didn't find her, and after about fifteen minutes I gave up.

As I was walking back to my car he asked me, "What was that you said about a real Jenny?"

"Oh," I said. "The ghoul says her name is Jenny Derdiarian, and that she murdered her three kids, Ashley, Sarah, and Jason. Except I found a Jenny Derdiarian who used to live in this neighborhood, with three kids named Ashley, Sarah, and Jason, and the four of them are all alive and well. I talked to her, and she said she had a bad stretch when the kids were little when she used to fantasize about killing them and starting a new life, but she never did it. I figure this ghost, or whatever it is, somehow stole her fantasy and pretended it was real."

Skees cocked his head. "How could it do that?" he asked. "*Why* would it do that?"

"I have no idea," I said. "I can *see* these things, but I don't *understand* them. I don't know how they work, what they can and can't do."

"That's not what you told Jack."

I shrugged. "So? I wasn't under oath; I was trying to talk a kid out of being stupid. It's all in how you look at it."

"Uh huh. So what are you going to do now?"

"Find a room," I said. "It's too late to get a flight home tonight, and I don't want to sleep in the car." The Chevy was even more cramped than the Cruiser had been. "Got any recommendations?"

He didn't, but it wasn't hard to find a motel – a decent one, one that called itself a hotel and had a lobby and a coffee shop, but it was still a motel, out the north end of town.

I felt like a fool tucking myself into that fifty-dollar bed. Why had I come here again? What had I thought I could do? If I had the timing right, the kids had been found before I even got to the airport; why hadn't I thought to call and check before boarding?

What could *I* do to help? Sure, I could see the phantom Jenny and talk to her; so what? It hadn't done anyone any good yet, so far as I could see. Neither she nor Jack would listen to reason.

At least Katie had resisted. She was apparently a bit smarter than her big brother, or maybe she just had more of a sense of self-preservation. Or maybe she was less sensitive to Jenny's emotional radiation; I could certainly feel the ghost's hunger and misery, but maybe that went with being psychic. There hadn't been any sign that anyone else felt it, any more than they could see or hear her.

That might be why Jack was more susceptible than Katie, especially if Jenny could transmit love as well as she did hunger – Jack could feel it, and Katie couldn't.

Jack hadn't mentioned that, but it would help explain why Jack was so certain Jenny loved him; if I was right, he could actually *feel* it.

But normal kids couldn't, and most kids weren't psychic. And even Jack, who looked like the most powerful psychic I'd seen since Mrs. Reinholt died, hadn't let Jenny kill him.

Skees had a point when he said Jenny was pretty harmless. Apparently she really *couldn't* hurt anyone who didn't volunteer. She hadn't touched Katie, not so much as a finger, so either she really did need willing victims, or there was some reason Katie didn't suit her. Maybe she preferred boys? Maybe her prey had to be hitting puberty? But the real Jenny Derdiarian had said her fantasy was about eating babies, so I'd think the younger, the better, and it had started with her daughter, so girls should do just fine.

So something else was holding the ghoul back, and presumably would keep most kids safe.

On the other hand, ghost-Jenny wasn't *entirely* harmless – she'd bitten off a kid's finger and eaten one of his eyes. What if, once Jack got back within range of those emotion transmissions, he decided it *was* worth his own life to help her? Or what if he found some other kid stupid enough to fall for her line and volunteer? Just because Katie didn't buy it didn't mean no one would.

But there wasn't anything I could do about it.

For eight years I'd been able to see the night-things and apparitions, and I could spot my fellow psychics, and I had my prophetic dreams, and what good had it *ever* done me? I knew who killed my mother, and what happened to Mrs. Reinholt, but I hadn't done anything to save either of them. I hadn't been able to do anything for Mel other than be a shoulder for her to cry on. I'd warned a few people about supernatural dangers, and about half of them had listened to me, but I didn't know whether any harm would have come to them if I'd kept my mouth shut.

What was I doing here?

I was still trying to figure it out when I fell asleep.

There wasn't any rush the next morning; there were plenty of flights, through various cities, and I wasn't in a big hurry to spend hours either wedged into what the airlines considered a seat, or running through some unfamiliar airport to make my connection. I took my time about getting breakfast. I was sitting in the motel coffee shop eating pancakes when Ben Skees came in and stood by my table.

"This seat taken?" he asked, pointing to the bench opposite mine.

"Suit yourself," I said.

He slid into the booth. "I wanted to chat a bit. Unofficially."

"Chat away," I said, pouring syrup.

"I'm trying to get a picture of just what's happening with this Jenny that Jack Wilson's been talking to."

I shrugged. "I told you what she looks like."

"You said there's a real Jenny still alive? Then this one isn't really a ghost?"

"That's right." I put a fork-full of pancake in my mouth.

"So are *any* of the things you see really ghosts?"

I chewed and swallowed, then said, "I don't know. I don't know *what* they are. Some of them look more or less like people, and some don't. Some are just blurs. Most of them act like automatons, doing the same pointless things over and over."

"Have you ever met the ghost of someone you knew? A dead relative, maybe, like one of your grandparents?"

"No," I said. "For one thing, half my grandparents are still alive."

"But the other two are dead?"

"So is my mother. I've never seen their ghosts. Is this going anywhere, or are you just curious?"

"Mostly just curious. Trying to get a handle on just how much danger our boy Jack is actually in."

I shrugged. "I don't really know."

"And you don't know whether there are any real ghosts?"

"No. I don't know whether the things I see at night are all the same, or a thousand different species. They don't all look alike, but that doesn't mean much. I know they aren't *all* ghosts, but some of them might be."

"This particular one, though, isn't a ghost."

"Not in the sense of being the spirit of a dead person, no. It may be some kind of ghost image of the real Jenny."

"Does it look like her?"

I shook my head. "I didn't see the real one, I just spoke to her on the phone, but she says no, she's not that thin and her hair's not like my description, though maybe it used to be. But she says she used to imagine herself looking like that."

"So did she somehow imagine her doppelganger into existence?"

I stopped with another fork-full of pancake halfway to my mouth, and lowered it back to the plate.

"Maybe she did," I said. "Not intentionally, but maybe she did."

Skees' question had reminded me of something Mrs. Reinholt had said, back in school. She had been warning us to behave in class, and she said, "Any punishment I can imagine, I can make it happen." I remember it exactly because at the time I thought it was odd that she said "*I* can imagine," instead of "*you* can imagine."

I'd thought it was an exaggeration, an empty threat, but maybe not. Mrs. Reinholt was a witch, or something like one – the only real one I ever found. I never had any idea how she did the things she did – how she cursed Mel, how she gave me my dreams and the ability to see the night-things and other psychics. After she died, Mel and I broke into her office – yeah, I know, but we were looking for a way to break the curse. Anyway, we broke into her office, and into her house, looking for a book of spells or a magic scroll or a cauldron or a broomstick or a voodoo doll or *something*, some sort of tool or recipe for her magic, anything that would give us a hint of how she did it.

We came up empty. There wasn't a thing. We thought maybe she'd had a hidden stash we didn't find, or maybe everything vanished when she died, or maybe she did it all through some sort of demon familiar, like the one that killed her. If there *had* been a book of spells, we thought maybe the demon took it with him.

And then things got busy and we didn't have time to think about it for awhile, and eventually there just didn't seem to be any point anymore.

But now a lot of things I'd seen over the past eight years were beginning to fit together, and I was wondering whether maybe she really *did* just imagine those things into existence. Maybe what she did on purpose, Jenny Derdiarian did once by accident.

Maybe that was where a *lot* of the night-things came from.

Maybe that was where *all* of them came from. Maybe that's what they were, pieces of people's imagination that got loose and became... well, *sort* of real.

But not just anyone's imagination, and maybe not just any *kind* of imagination. Jenny said she used to see ghosts, but that she never did after her obsession went away; maybe whatever let her see them was all used up in creating ghost-Jenny. And the obsession itself shaped the night-thing.

I didn't know whether the thing had existed at all before it got Jenny's fantasy, or whether it *was* Jenny's fantasy. Or maybe it was Jenny's psychic ability, all tangled up with the fantasy and cut loose. Maybe dumping it, turning it into ghost-Jenny, had been some sort of subconscious defense mechanism, a way to get rid of her fantasy before she got so obsessed she actually hurt her kids.

I had lots of theories, or anyway lots of variations on my basic theory, but then I realized that it didn't matter very much which one, if any, was right, because none of them told me anything about how to *stop* ghost-Jenny. Mrs. Reinholt had originally been able to pull her spells, or demons, or whatever you want to call them, back into herself, but I couldn't imagine Jenny Derdiarian doing that – and after all, Mrs. Reinholt had lost control eventually. If she hadn't, my dreams might be gone, Mel's curse might be gone, and Mrs. Reinholt might still be alive.

Maybe she overreached herself, trying to keep up the spells on both Mel and me while still doing other stuff. The thing that killed her had said she only *thought* she was in control, that it had been growing stronger...

Was ghost-Jenny growing stronger? After all, real Jenny got over her fantasy something like fifteen years ago, but ghost-Jenny was only now giving Jack trouble.

If it was growing stronger, maybe it wouldn't always need permission.

"You think this person has any idea what she did?" Detective Skees asked.

I'd been so caught up in my thoughts that I didn't know what he was talking about until I mentally replayed the conversation. Then I understood.

"Jenny Derdiarian? No. I don't think she knows anything about it at all."

"So you don't think she can *un*-imagine it?"

I shook my head. "I don't think so. But I could be wrong. I told you, I don't understand what's going on here."

Except I was beginning to think maybe I *did* understand it a little. If the night-things were independent chunks of imagination, then that would explain ghosts, and why they did weird things over and over instead of acting like people – they were left-over bits of dead people's imaginations, doing things that those people had obsessed about doing.

And werewolves – people would have fantasies of turning into monsters and killing their enemies, and those fantasies got loose.

Vampires? Maybe people fantasized about drinking blood. I didn't *get* that, but people do lots of things I don't get. Biting pretty women on the neck wasn't any stranger than putting on a rubber suit and being tied up, was it? And any browse on the internet could find people who were turned on by *that*.

But that didn't tell us anything about making them go away.

"So this ghost – what does it really *want*?"

"It wants to kill children," I said. "To either starve them to death, or eat them alive."

"*Starve* them?"

"Yeah, that's the main fantasy Jenny had – starving her kids to death. Eating them was an earlier, less upsetting fantasy she had."

"*Less* upsetting?"

"Because it was less real."

He nodded. "So it's all about food, somehow?"

"It's about food and love and death and guilt and possession, all tangled together."

"Possession? Like devils?"

"Like ownership. It's about control."

Skees looked down at the table, then at the pancakes I wasn't eating anymore, then at me. "You know anything about Jack's home life?"

"In my dreams his father yelled at him a lot," I said.

"About what?"

"About everything. Belittling him, telling him he was a worthless little loser, stuff like that."

"And his mother?"

"She stayed out of it. She sat there and let her husband yell."

"Katie?"

"Hid in the corner and hoped her father wouldn't notice her."

"Did the father ever hit the kids?"

I shook my head. "Not that I saw."

"You think Jack's looking for love from the ghost because he doesn't get it at home?"

"Well, yeah. That's pretty obvious, isn't it?"

"Maybe to you. Not all of us have psychic visions."

"You heard him at the hospital."

"Yeah, I did. That's why I'm asking." He glanced at the pancakes again, then looked me in the eye. "We talked to the neighbors, when Jack was missing, and before, when he got hurt. It's routine, you know? Just trying to figure out whether the kid ran away or was abducted, or maybe whether his parents might know more than they're saying. It's never happened in a case I handled, thank God, but you hear about parents who kill their own kids and then report them missing. So we ask a lot of questions."

"I figured."

"There's no evidence of physical abuse – no bruises, no broken bones, nothing like that. No limps or shiners or bloody noses. But there were a lot of neighbors who weren't surprised by the idea that Jack and Katie might run off, and the psychologists who interviewed them say both kids have lousy self-esteem. Emotionally they're pretty broken, both of them. We don't have enough to take them away, get them declared wards of the state or anything, but we could make some recommendations, ask for observation, that kind of thing. There's a social worker, Angie Ballard, keeping a case file on them. You think getting them away from their parents might help?"

I shrugged, and picked up my fork. "How would I know? I'm just a retail clerk from Maryland."

"Come on, Kraft. You're a retail clerk from Maryland who talks to ghosts and has prophetic dreams."

"Yeah, okay, but I'm not a social worker. I don't know what those kids need. Ask this Angie Ballard."

"I will, but you know more about Jack's dealings with Jenny than any of us. You think maybe if we could give the kids some support system, a counselor they could trust checking in on them regularly, they'd stay the hell away from this ghost?"

"Katie would," I said. "She doesn't want anything to do with Jenny, does she?"

"No, she doesn't. But what about the boy?"

"He's stubborn. And he really thinks he loves her and she loves him." I hesitated, because I really didn't want to get into this, but I said, "She can radiate emotions a little – sort of like Melisandra de Cheverley, but nowhere near that strongly, and I don't know whether it's under her control or not. And it doesn't seem to affect everyone, but *I* can feel it, and I'm pretty sure Jack can. He can feel her hunger, and I think she can make him feel that she really loves him. So she's got that hold on him, and I don't think he's going to give it up. It might be the closest thing to actual love that he's ever experienced."

Skees frowned thoughtfully. Then he said, "So you don't think counseling would work."

"Probably not. But it couldn't hurt to try, could it?"

"Oh, we'll try. We'll set something up through his school to start. He's had truancy issues, but we've already told the family that any more unexcused absences will mean we call in the child welfare folks."

"You haven't already? I thought you said this Ballard person was in charge."

"Of course we called them, and yes, Angie has an open file, but we're keeping it quiet, so far. There's no direct intervention. Besides, the youth services people are understaffed and there's no extra in the budget, so Angie's trying to avoid turning this into an active, hands-on case."

"Right." I stuffed some pancake in my mouth.

"So, let's say we do keep Jack away from Jenny, one way or another – what happens then?"

I chewed, swallowed, and said, "She doesn't eat him."

Skees looked annoyed. "Yeah, but what *does* she do? Does she go after some other kid?"

"If I answer that, I'm just guessing." I lifted the fork again.

"You've talked to her. Go ahead and guess."

I considered it for a moment as I ate, and then I said, "I think she does, yeah, as soon as she can find another one who can see her."

"So how does that work?"

I shrugged for what seemed like the hundredth time. "I don't know," I said. "I can see her, but I can see all the ghosts and monsters. Jack can see her, but I don't know why, or whether he can see other things. Katie could see her a little, but said she was hard to see, right? You told me that."

"That's what she said," Skees agreed.

"Some people can see these things. It's a talent. I can tell who's got it and who hasn't, but I don't know why some people have it and others don't. I don't know whether it runs in families, whether it's something you're born with, how you could get it, whether you can lose it once you've got it. If it does run in families, maybe that's why Katie saw something – or maybe Jack was able to *make* her see it somehow; the talent's really strong in him. Or maybe this particular monster is something special, and *lots* of kids could see Jenny. I don't know. I've always heard that little kids can see ghosts better than grown-ups can, but I don't know whether that's true; I haven't really done a count. I'm not around kids much."

"Think Jack might know what the story is?"

"He might. Doesn't mean he'd tell us."

"He sees her better than Katie."

"Oh, yeah, Jack's got it really strong," I said. "I don't know whether it's because Jenny's been working on him, or whether he was born like that, but there's something special going on there."

"So she might not be able to find another kid who can see her."

"Maybe not right away," I acknowledged. "As far as we know, it took her fifteen years to find Jack."

I didn't mention my own suspicion, since all it was at that point was an unfounded suspicion. I thought that maybe Katie could see Jenny now not because she was a kid, or because she was Jack's sister, but because Jenny was getting stronger. She might be feeding off Jack's psychic ability somehow. I thought maybe *any* kid Jenny wanted might be able to get a glimpse of her now.

But I didn't have any way to test it. I didn't have any evidence at all. It was just a feeling.

I hoped I was wrong.

Chapter Fourteen

The rest of the conversation went in circles. I finished my breakfast and paid the bill, but we kept talking until finally I said I had to get my stuff together and head for the airport. I started to get up.

That was when the detective's cell phone rang. I slid out of the booth and straightened up, and started toward the door while Skees answered the call.

I was just past the hostess station when Skees called, "Hey, Kraft! Hold on!"

I stopped and turned, thinking that he had some parting remark to make, or maybe he wanted to make sure I had his number. He was out of the booth, the phone still open.

"Jack's gone missing again," he said.

My mouth literally fell open. For a second I had no idea what to say.

"He was on the bus this morning, but when the school psychologist went to talk to him just now the teacher said he'd never shown up for class."

"Are you *serious*?" I said.

"Yeah." He looked disgusted – and angry.

"That is one stubborn kid," I said.

"And a screwed-up one," Skees agreed.

"Any idea where he went?"

"I was hoping *you* might have a suggestion."

I shook my head. "I don't know," I said. "I don't know whether he can see Jenny in daylight. I'm pretty sure *I* can't, I've never seen a ghost in daylight before, including her, but maybe his connection with her gets around that somehow."

"Katie said the hungry lady disappeared at sunrise."

"Yeah."

"So you don't think he can go to her until it gets dark?"

"That's my theory, yeah. But I don't know for sure."

"So what would he do instead?"

"I don't have a clue," I said. "But Katie might."

Skees frowned at me. "The kid sister? Why?"

"Because this may be something Jack and Jenny planned yesterday morning, before he took Katie to McDonald's, and Katie might have heard them talking about it." I remembered my chat with Jack on his front stoop, and his insistence that he would find a way to make Jenny well. He might have already known exactly what he was going to do.

If so, he'd done a pretty good job of hiding it, for a kid.

But then, with *his* parents, he was probably used to keeping secrets.

"That's a good idea," Skees said. He raised one hand to indicate I should wait where I was, then talked into his phone, telling whoever was on the other end to get some men to look around those trees at the end of the Wilsons' street, and to find someone non-threatening to question the sister at school, see if she'd heard her brother make any plans.

"If she did, don't try to make sense of what she says," Skees told whoever it was. "Just write it down and get it to me. There's a whole big fantasy thing going on here, role-playing stuff."

He listened, then said, "No, *not* like Dungeons and Dragons. Not a game. Just... role-playing."

There was a pause, and then he said, "No, don't take her home. Talk to her at the school. It's okay if there are teachers present, but I don't want her parents in the room if we can help it."

He listened for another moment, then said, "Right. Get on it." He closed the phone, and looked at me.

"You think he's got a plan?" he asked.

"Probably," I said. "I mean, he's screwed up, but he's not stupid. He wouldn't just take off without *some* idea what he was going to do."

"Kids do just take off sometimes."

"I'm sure they do, but Jack – I don't think Jack would."

"Neither do I. And I'm pretty sure this has something to do with Jenny, even if he can't see her in daylight. The kid's obsessed with her."

"Oh, yeah, it never even occurred to me that it might not."

He hesitated, then asked, "So you can't see her in the daytime?"

"Nope."

"Does she even *exist* in daytime?"

I thought that was a pretty good question. "I think so, but I couldn't swear to it."

"Could she hear you, if you talked to her? I mean, if you were in the right place?"

"I don't know," I said. "Sorry, I just don't."

"Think you might want to take a walk under that big tree and talk to yourself a little?"

"I won't hear her answer."

"I figured that, but you could maybe let her know that we aren't going to leave her alone there."

I nodded. "I can do that," I said.

"I take it you aren't leaving town quite yet after all?"

"I guess not," I agreed.

"Thanks." He handed me a card. "Give me a call if you think of anything."

I took the card and stuck it in my pocket, then turned and headed to the front desk, to let them know I might be staying another day or two.

I considered calling Mel to bring her up to date, but it was still early, by her standards, so I decided to hold off. Instead I went out to the car and headed for the Wilsons' street.

There was a cop car in front of the house, but I drove past it and parked at the end of the street. I sat in the car for a moment, looking at the trees.

By daylight, I couldn't see anything remotely strange or supernatural about the big tulip poplar; it was just a tree. There were a lot of twigs scattered around, a few leaves, and that black dust that tulip poplars drop, but that was all.

Still, I got out of the car and walked over to the tree. I stood there and said, "Jenny, if you hear me, I've got a message for you. We aren't going to let you have Jack, or anyone else. We're going to watch this place, and if he comes here we'll find him. We won't let you be alone with him again – not tonight, and not ever. Give it up. Go away."

When I was done I stood and listened, but I didn't hear anything except wind in the leaves overhead, and the distant hum of traffic on Winchester Road. I could smell mown grass and the peanut butter factory.

I repeated my message.

Still nothing – but then, what did I expect? I'd told Skees I couldn't see or hear anything supernatural by daylight, and that was the truth, plain and simple. I didn't know whether Jenny was there; she could have been standing right in front of me and I wouldn't know it. I'd thought maybe her stolen finger and eye would show up somehow, but there was no sign of them. Which didn't mean she wasn't there, but it didn't mean she *was*, either. I didn't know *where* she was.

I didn't know where Jack was, either, but I knew it wasn't here, because I *would* have seen *him*.

But Jenny wasn't a real person; she was a twisted fantasy that had taken on an independent existence, and so far as I knew, I could only see her at night.

And apparently Jack, like me, could only see her at night, so there wasn't any reason for him to come here by daylight. He would need to wait until dark to talk to her again.

So why had he taken off first thing in the morning this time, instead of after school? What was he planning to do all day? Was there somewhere he needed to go, something he needed to do?

I was standing there, staring at the tree, when a thought struck me – what had he and Katie been doing yesterday morning after sunrise? They had spent the night out here somewhere, talking to Jenny, but once the sun came up and Jenny wasn't visible, why hadn't they gone straight home? Why had they waited until lunchtime to go to McDonald's – and a late lunch, at that? What were they doing for all those hours?

Had Jack been trying to talk Katie into letting Jenny eat her?

Was he going to meet Katie somewhere later, to feed her to the monster? That didn't seem right; how could he hope to get at Katie again? She was going to have cops and counselors around her all day, and Jack must know that.

Was he going to try to feed some *other* kid to the ghost?

I got my phone out of my pocket, then went digging for Detective Skees' card.

He answered on the third ring. "Skees," he said.

"Detective Skees, this is Gregory Kraft," I said. "You may have already thought of this, but I was wondering whether there were any other kids missing from Jack's school. He may have taken someone with him, same as he took his sister last time."

"Yeah, we checked that," Skees said. "No one's missing. While we were at it we asked about friends, and it seems he doesn't really have any, so we're not too concerned about anyone skipping out later to join him."

"Oh," I said.

That was a disappointment. I'd been hoping I'd come up with something useful that the cops might have missed, but they'd been all over it.

I wished I'd been surprised that Jack didn't have any friends, but I wasn't.

"Did Katie say anything useful?" I asked.

"We're just now getting to her. Checking attendance and asking teachers about a kid's friends takes five minutes; setting up to interrogate a seven-year-old calls for jumping through a few more hoops than that."

"Oh."

"Anything else?"

"No," I said, and ended the call. I looked up the street; that cop car was still parked in front of the Wilsons' house, but otherwise the neighborhood was quiet and calm.

I'd really thought I had something there, but if all the other kids were still in school, then Jack wasn't dragging one of them off to be ghost food.

It was sad that the teachers said he had no friends, but I really wasn't surprised. That was one screwed-up kid. If he'd had human friends, he might not have bonded with Jenny so strongly.

What else could he need the day for, other than talking some other kid into feeding the ghost? Had he just run away? The cops would presumably check the bus stations, and he was awfully young to hitchhike; most drivers wouldn't pick up a lone rider that young.

I still liked the idea that he was looking for a victim, but where would he look, other than his school? Where else would he find kids? Did he maybe have home-schooled friends?

What *had* he and Katie done all yesterday morning? I doubted anyone had really asked, or had paid any attention to the answer; the only ones who really had any idea what was going on here were me, Jack, and Ben Skees.

I walked slowly back to my car, trying to think what I should do next.

I didn't have any special abilities that were useful in daylight. I wasn't going to dream about Jack again, and I couldn't see Jenny in sunlight. The only thing I had going for me that the cops or Jack's parents didn't was that I knew more about Jenny than they did, and more about what Jack wanted.

Jack wanted Jenny to love him, and to be a real woman, someone who would be there all day, not just at night. He thought he could get that by feeding her a child. He had wanted it so much he almost fed himself to her – no, not almost; he *did* feed her one of his fingers and his left eye.

Anything that intense wasn't something that was just going to go away. Wherever he was, and whatever he was doing, it almost certainly had something to do with finding prey for Jenny.

That made finding him more urgent; I wasn't just trying to save Jack this time, I was trying to save some innocent sucker *from* Jack. If we didn't find him, some poor kid might die tonight.

But how did Jack plan to do it? How did he expect to get his victim to her? He must know that someone would be watching the tree. He couldn't come here, let alone bring another kid with him, without being seen.

So obviously, they weren't going to meet here. He must have arranged to meet Jenny somewhere else, somewhere he could bring another kid, or where he could meet Jenny and lead her to the kid.

Katie must have heard them making plans; Jack wouldn't have let her get far enough away that she wouldn't.

I got into the Chevy, but once I was there I got out my phone and called Ben Skees again.

"Listen," I told him, "I'm sure that Jack's going to rendezvous with Jenny somewhere different tonight, but Katie must have heard them discussing it."

"Yeah, we thought of that," Skees said. "It's on the list of questions we'll be asking her. Near the top."

"Oh," I said, a little deflated.

"Any idea where it might be?"

"I think it'll be somewhere near other kids," I said.

"So – a park or playground, maybe? Or a school?"

"I don't know," I admitted.

"Kids he knows?"

"Probably."

"The teachers were pretty definite that he doesn't have friends at school."

"From church, maybe? Someone he knows from summer activities?"

"We'll check that out. Thanks."

I wasn't sure just how sarcastic he was being; surely, those suggestions would already be on their list. Probably he was being polite, to encourage me so that I might come up with something that *wasn't* on the usual list.

But I didn't know anything about Jack that they didn't, not really.

I did know things about *Jenny* that they didn't, though. I knew what she looked like, and that she had probably come from a real person's imagination...

And that person lived in Clark County, only about twenty miles east of Lexington.

"Hey," I said. "I think I might drive over to Winchester after lunch, and talk to the original Jenny Derdiarian."

"She's in Winchester?"

"Yeah."

"That's outside my jurisdiction. I work for Fayette County."

"But that doesn't affect *me*."

"True enough. And if I had some real evidence that she's connected with this, I might want to go with you, but as it is, Mr. Kraft, you're on your own."

"Sure, I figured I would be."

"Don't do anything actionable, okay?"

"I won't," I said, annoyed. "Talk to you later."

I ended the call and put the phone back in my pocket, and as I did I realized that Skees wasn't treating me like an idiot; he was giving me good advice. I wasn't a cop; I had no right to go around questioning anyone. If I did anything to upset Ms. Derdiarian I might wind up in the Clark County jail on some sort of stalking charge.

I got lunch at a Wendy's just off Winchester Road, near I-75, and called Jenny Derdiarian when I'd finished eating.

She was sufficiently intrigued by the idea of meeting a real psychic face to face that she agreed to meet me, and gave me her address. I didn't ask for directions, since I had the GPS.

I'd have figured Winchester Road had to be the best route to Winchester, but the GPS put me on I-75 north for one exit, then east on I-64. I guess the higher speed limit made the difference. I got there quickly enough.

Winchester turned out to be a fairly pleasant town with some factories along the interstate north of town, some old brick storefronts and a classic county courthouse on Main Street, and a lot of ordinary houses on quiet little streets on the hillsides east of Main Street. One of those ordinary houses was where Chester Craig and Jenny and Jason Derdiarian lived.

Jenny Derdiarian was waiting on the porch for me, and offered me a glass of lemonade before I'd even gotten up the steps.

She wasn't bony-thin, but solid. Not fat by any means. Her black hair was cut off at her shoulders and permed, and she had two ordinary brown eyes. She was wearing a floral print sun-dress and not a white slip, and her skin, while still fairly pale, had clearly been exposed to some sun that summer, but all the same, I saw the resemblance instantly. The ghost could have been her goth daughter, or her younger sister – or her younger self.

I looked for that oddness I saw around Jack and other ghost-watchers, and I didn't find it. I didn't see anything like the darkness around Mel, either. Jenny Derdiarian looked completely normal, and fully part of her surroundings.

I didn't know what that meant. I'd assumed that anyone with any sort of psychic power, or magic, or whatever it was, had that unnatural look, and I thought Jenny must have some of the talent if her imagination had shaped her ghostly doppelganger, but there was no trace of it, so far as I could see, even when she was well out of the sunlight, in the shadows of the open front door.

I remembered that she said she hadn't seen any ghosts for fifteen years, not since the obsessive fantasies about killing her children went away. Could whatever took the fantasies taken *all* her psychic power?

I took the porch chair she offered, and accepted the glass of lemonade.

"You're younger than I expected," she said, as she poured herself a glass and settled in the other chair.

I didn't have anything intelligent to say to that, so I just said, "Hmm," as I sipped the lemonade.

"You live in Maryland, don't you?" she asked. "That's what I think you said on the phone last month."

"That's right," I agreed. "In Takoma Park."

"Near Baltimore?"

"Washington."

"Oh, yes. Well, then, what brings you to Kentucky?"

I hesitated. I'd given this some thought during the drive here, but I wasn't entirely happy with the approach I'd settled on. Still, I didn't see a better choice.

"I came to help the Lexington police with a missing child," I said.

"Oh, you work with the police? I've heard about psychics doing that."

I hesitated again, and then decided to tell the truth.

"I've never worked with the police before," I said, "and it's not official this time. I came on my own, they didn't invite me."

She frowned. "Oh?"

"I had dreams about this kid. His name is Jack Wilson. He's twelve."

She looked concerned. "Have they found him? Is he all right?"

I shook my head. "They haven't found him yet. That's why I'm here, talking to you."

"I don't understand," she said. "What does this have to do with me? Since it's you who came here, and not the police, I guess you've seen some connection – you had a vision of some sort?"

"Something like that." I sighed. "Jack wasn't abducted or anything," I explained. "He ran off. He doesn't get along with his parents, and he met a woman who's become a sort of mother figure to him, so we're pretty sure he's run away to be with her."

"And you think I know something about her?"

"I hope so."

"Who is she?"

I grimaced.

"She calls herself Jenny Derdiarian," I said.

Chapter Fifteen

She sat and stared at me silently for a moment before saying, "Go on."

"I know it isn't you," I said hastily. "In fact, even calling her a woman isn't accurate. She's a... a night creature, a sort of ghost."

"Like the ones I used to see."

"I think so, yes. In fact, I'm pretty sure she's the one that took your old fantasies about hurting your children. Those were so strong that they've taken her over completely – she thinks she's you, or your ghost, and that you really did murder your three kids."

Actually, I had a strong suspicion that it wasn't so much some wandering ghost or devil taking those fantasies as that the fantasies themselves had taken on a life of their own, but I didn't want to get sidetracked by arguing about it. I didn't think it mattered.

"How do you know that?" she asked. "How do you know what she thinks?"

"I've met her," I said. "I've talked to her."

"This wasn't just a dream?"

"No. I met her, in Lexington, in your old neighborhood there. She seems to live under a big tulip poplar at the end of the street."

"A tulip tree?"

"Yes. Do you know the one I mean?"

"I might. Tell me about this ghost – how did you meet her?"

I explained. I didn't go into all the details of my dreams, I just said that I'd dreamed Jack was in trouble, and I had come to Lexington to check on him, and that was how I had met ghost-Jenny.

But I *did* go into detail talking about the ghost. This was the part that concerned her, and I wanted to get everything out in the open. I told her almost everything I could remember that the apparition had said and done, as close to word-for-word as I could make it. She listened intently.

I told her *almost* everything. I did not mention Jack's missing finger or eye, not yet. I didn't want to risk upsetting her if she felt responsible for any of it. I did say that the ghost had talked about eating him.

When I was done, she asked, "So Jack Wilson can see this ghost?"

"Yes."

"And you can?"

"Yes."

"But no one else?"

"No adults that I know of, but I can't really be entirely sure. I've met other people who see ghosts, but not here in Kentucky. Jack's little sister Katie said she could sort of see the ghost, but that might have just been suggestion from her brother."

She nodded. "You think Jack's run away to be with this ghost?"

"I do," I said. "That's why I'm here – I'm hoping you can tell me where they might have arranged to meet."

She shook her head, startled. "Bless your heart, how would *I* know?"

"Because this ghost thinks it's *you*," I said. "It's acting out those horrible old fantasies of yours. Where would *you* have arranged to meet Jack?"

"He can't go back to the big tree?"

"He knows the police will be watching it."

"Of course they will; how silly of me. Well, let me think – though I don't see how you think I'll know anything more than *you* do. After all, you're the psychic."

"I'm not that kind of psychic. Ms. Derdiarian, after I spoke to you on the phone I did some reading, and from what I read, when people have the sort of obsessive fantasy you said you had, the fantasies usually get very elaborate. The more people think about them, the more details they add – sounds, and smells, and exactly what everything would look like." I didn't mention that most of my reading on the subject had been in books and articles about criminal psychology, particularly about serial killers. "Was it like that for you?"

She was taken aback. "I... I hardly remember," she said. "It's been fifteen years, and as I told you on the phone, when they went away, they went away *completely*. Wasn't a thing left. I hadn't given them a moment's thought for that entire fifteen years until you called last month."

"This ghost hasn't thought about anything *else* for fifteen years, though, so anything you could remember would be helpful in getting a handle on how it thinks."

"Mr. Kraft, whatever this thing is, don't forget, it isn't me. My own belief is that it's a demon that possessed me, all those years ago, and made me obsess on all those horrible things, and that in His own good time God cast it out of me. I wouldn't know the first thing about how a demon thinks."

"But this demon lived in your head for years, and it *thinks* it's you!" I insisted. "It's doing its best to *be* you, to do whatever you would if you had really killed your children."

"And I can't imagine ever doing that. Yes, I know I *did* imagine it, over and over, for years, but I *stopped*. That all went away. I can't get it back, and I don't want to."

I sat back, disappointed. "Of course you don't." I sighed. "I guess I understand, Ms. Derdiarian, but this boy Jack could be in real danger, so I'd appreciate it if you could tell me everything you *do* remember about your fantasies. There may be some little detail that could be useful."

She sighed. "This is... this is very embarrassing, Mr. Kraft. These were things I never told anyone, and never intended to tell anyone. It's a little like letting a stranger read my diary."

"I can see how it would be, but please, if you could try..."

She sighed, and she started talking.

I didn't say much for the next hour or so; I nodded occasionally, and once or twice I asked questions, but mostly I just sat and listened.

Some of it was scarily relevant. Her baby-eating fantasies had included biting the fingers off one by one, then popping the eyes out and eating them like candy. She had imagined them tasting as sweet as candy, too – it had been a *fantasy*, with no attempt at realism. No blood, no pain, no guilt. The baby in her fantasy had laughed and giggled and enjoyed the entire experience.

That was probably why ghost-Jenny had needed her victim's cooperation; it was part of the original fantasy. She had probably been shocked by how Jack suffered; that hadn't been how it was supposed to go. In Jenny's long-ago daydreams eating the baby was supposed to be fun for everyone involved.

One of the strangest details, to me, was *why* Jenny said she had fantasized about eating the baby – that had been a way to put it back inside her, which would somehow make her a *real* mother more than anything external could.

I'm sure a psychologist would have a field day with that.

But at any rate, that whole thing had really been a harmless daydream.

Starving the kids to death had been very different; that had definitely included plenty of pain and guilt, though still no blood. I'm not going to go into the details, but listening to her calmly describe the whole thing was utterly horrifying – and part of the horror was because it clearly didn't bother *her* anymore. Oh, she was a little embarrassed to be telling me about these ghastly scenes that belonged in a horror novel, but the heavy emotional content that had obviously been there once really was gone, completely gone. She felt no guilt, no shame, no pain about any of it; it might as well have been a party game for all the impact it had on her.

As for how it had all ended, one day she had been so angry with the kids and with her desperate situation that she had walked out the front door, afraid that if she stayed in the house a minute longer she might really hurt someone – maybe one of the kids, maybe all of the kids, maybe herself, but *someone*. She had walked down to the end of the street and sat down under the tulip poplar and put her face in her hands and cried.

And then, she said, she had felt something change, as if a weight had been lifted off her, and the idea of hurting her kids was just *gone*. She was still worried, still concerned about money and debt and keeping the family fed, but all the lurid, complicated fantasies about starving the kids, or eating them, were gone. She had stood up, dried her tears, and gone back to the house, and from that moment on her life had started to improve. She didn't know whether there was any connection, or whether it was merely coincidence, but nothing else important went wrong for months – no one got sick, no appliances broke down, nothing went wrong at work or at Ashley's school. She met a nice man who convinced her that she wasn't completely unlovable despite what the children's father had said, and then not long after that she met Chester Craig, who showed her that she could still love someone else besides her kids. That afternoon under the tulip poplar had been a turning point in her life; no wonder she thought God had intervened for her then.

It must be nice sometimes to believe in God; I haven't been able to manage it since I was a kid, especially not after Mrs. Reinholt and my mother died.

Anyway, her story explained a lot about why ghost-Jenny was what she was and did what she did, and it gave me a new and unpleasant awareness of how horrible even the nicest, most ordinary people could be under the surface, but I didn't see anything in it that helped me figure out where Jack might be, or where he planned to meet his Jenny.

I wondered what would happen if ghost Jenny met real Jenny; would the phantom realize that it wasn't a ghost at all?

Would it *recognize* the real Jenny? *I* could see that they were the same woman, but would a ghoul, ghost, devil, or demon see it?

One of the things that worried me the most was that even if I found Jack, even if I kept him away from Jenny, I didn't know of anything I could do to stop Jenny from eventually finding some other kid to eat. I really did think she was getting stronger somehow, and if she wasn't stopped I thought that in time, she would be strong enough to coerce a child into being eaten.

Or maybe she would eat a baby, as in the original fantasy – one too young to object...

When that idea struck me I almost said something aloud, almost interrupted Ms. Derdiarian's narrative, but I caught myself at the last moment. I let her finish – after nagging her into this, I couldn't very well tell her to stop, and besides, there might be something else.

But if there was, I missed it.

When she had finished I thanked her, promised I'd let her know what happened to Jack, finished my lemonade, then went back down the steps to the street, where my rental car was waiting.

I hesitated for a second, debating whether to call Mel or Detective Skees first, and settled on Skees. I raised my phone and found his number.

"Skees," the familiar voice said.

"This is Greg Kraft," I said. "Did Katie say anything useful?"

"I'm afraid not," Skees said. "She claims that Jack and the hard-to-see lady sent her away while they talked and wouldn't let her hear anything."

"What about later, after Jenny was gone?"

"Funny you should ask. It seems our boy Jack asked his little sister about all her friends. Were any of them sick? Did any of them have new brothers or sisters? But she says she didn't tell him anything. So did you hear anything interesting?"

"I'm in Winchester," I said. "I just talked to the original Jenny Derdiarian, and she says that it should really be a baby that gets eaten, not a kid Jack's age. I think Jack's looking for a baby, someone too young to object when Jenny gets hungry."

Skees didn't reply immediately, but eventually he said, "Okay, I can see that. So where does that put us?"

"Well, I'm kind of hoping it puts a cop in every maternity ward in Lexington, especially whichever one is closest to Jack's school," I said.

"You think he'd just pick a baby at random?"

"He's twelve, Detective. What else is he going to do?"

"You may have a point. I'll see what we can do. And I'll ask the Wilsons if there are any babies in the neighborhood."

"I don't think he'll dare go near his house," I said.

"Neither do I, but we need to cover all the bases here." He paused, then said, "You know, I don't think there's a hospital anywhere near Crawford Middle School."

I wasn't happy to hear that. "He's had all day to get to one," I said.

"You don't think he's more likely to just find a playground?"

"I don't know," I admitted.

"Well, we'll keep it in mind, Mr. Kraft." He cut the connection.

I didn't like it. A playground didn't feel right, somehow; it didn't fit the way I thought Jack and Jenny thought. A hospital where they could find a newborn baby seemed like a better match to me. At a playground there would be mothers watching, and other kids, and everyone would be moving and active; in a maternity ward there would be a bunch of babies sleeping in those little plastic cribs with a bored nurse watching over them. Jack wouldn't need to catch anyone, or talk to anyone, or steal a baby out of a stroller; he could just let Jenny in and turn her loose.

Besides, it would need to be done after dark – Jack couldn't see or hear Jenny in daylight. Parks and playgrounds didn't have many babies around after dark, but hospital nurseries did.

I considered calling Skees back and explaining this to him, but so far he'd always figured things out for himself, so I thought he'd get this one soon enough, too. I glanced up at the sun, which was far to the west, but still well above the horizon. I had time; I didn't think Jenny could hurt anyone by daylight.

I called Mel instead, looking for advice.

She listened to my explanations without saying a word. With anyone else I might have thought that silence was rude, or that it meant they weren't listening, but with Mel I knew it was simple consideration – she knew what her voice did to me. Even when she didn't speak, just knowing she was there, on the other end of the connection, was enough to make me absurdly nervous. My hand got sweaty, so I tried to switch the phone from my right hand to my left, and dropped it down the side of the seat. I fished it out, started to ask whether she was still there, then decided I didn't want her to answer; I would just assume she was. The display didn't say I'd lost the signal.

I told her about meeting the real Jenny Derdiarian, and about her fantasies, including the baby eating. I didn't go into a lot of detail, though; it wasn't my story to tell, and repeating some of it felt like a violation of trust.

I said enough to convey everything I thought was important, though, and then explained my theory that Jack would be looking for a baby, the younger the better, to feed to the ghost. I told her about my call to Ben Skees, and my fear that he wasn't taking me seriously.

"He probably doesn't have the manpower to put guards on every newborn in Fayette County," Mel said. "After all, dear boy, this isn't a serial killer he's after, it's just a runaway kid. He can't send the entire police force out on some psychic's theory."

I instantly saw the truth in that, and my heart sank – but then, *anything* Mel said would provoke fear or despair; that was the nature of her curse.

"I'll bet he's phoning the hospitals, though, and asking the staff to check for an unattended boy fitting Jack's description."

That didn't raise my mood. Intellectually I knew she was right, and that it was a good thing, but because it was Mel I couldn't believe anything good would come of it.

"You think Jack will go to a hospital, then?"

"I can't think of a better idea."

"Which one? There must be dozens in Fayette County!"

"One with a maternity ward. One he's heard of, or seen. One that isn't out in the middle of nowhere."

"There still must be several of them."

"Maybe. Maybe not. Do you have your computer with you?"

"There's no wifi here."

She must have heard something in my voice that told her the curse was getting to me. "I'll call you back, Greg," she said, and broke the connection.

It was as if a weight had been lifted off my shoulders. The sun was suddenly brighter, and the situation seemed far less hopeless.

I *hated* that I felt relieved that Mel had cut me off. She was my best friend, and I owed her big-time for everything she had done for me, and I just hated the fact that talking to her was such a nightmare.

But my hands were trembling, and I had to wipe the sweat off my palms three or four times before I felt confident I could grip the wheel properly.

I put the phone away and started the car, heading back down to Main Street, where I turned right and drove toward the interstate.

Chapter Sixteen

I was most of the way to Lexington when my phone rang – or rather, when it started playing Dire Straits, which is what I had as my ringtone. I answered it.

"Greg," Mel's voice said, and I had to fight to not slam on the brakes – what had seemed like a reasonable highway speed a second before was suddenly a terrifying headlong rush that could only end in disaster.

"Yeah," I said.

"I'm not as good at this as I'd like to be, or even as I thought I was, but I've been searching the web and I think your best bet is the University of Kentucky's birth center on Rose Street. 800 Rose Street."

"Oh," I said, resisting the temptation to jerk the wheel over and slam the car into a railing.

"It's four or five miles from his school, but he's had all day to walk it, or to hitch a ride."

"Yeah," I said again.

"You're driving?"

"Yes, I am."

"Drive safely," she said, and ended the call.

I put the phone down and took a few seconds to calm myself. I almost missed the turn onto I-75, and I *did* miss the exit for Winchester Road. I took the next one instead, and let the GPS guide me down Man O' War Boulevard to Liberty Road.

I felt like an idiot. Trying to guess which hospital had been stupid. Not realizing the obvious until Mel called me back made me a moron.

The U.K. hospital was where they'd taken Jack when he lost his finger, and again when he lost his eye. He *knew* that hospital. Of *course* that's where he'd go. I hadn't realized it had a maternity ward, but why wouldn't it? It was obvious.

I hadn't said as much to Mel because there wasn't any point in making *her* feel stupid, and besides, saying *anything* to her was difficult. Maybe I'd been slow to make the connection before because I was rattled by talking to her, in fact – but that was no excuse. I should be used to it by now.

I thought about calling Skees, but I didn't do it. I'd given him that heads-up earlier, and if he didn't follow up on it, it wasn't my fault. He knew where Jack had gone before, and where the maternity ward was. The U.K. hospital would be the first one he'd try.

I glanced at the sky, and decided it wouldn't be dark for some time yet and I'd do better on a full stomach. I turned north off Liberty onto New Circle Road, which was lined with fast food and urban sprawl, and stopped at a place called the Parkette Drive-In that was a relic of the era of tailfins and rockabilly. I got a surprisingly tasty chicken sandwich that I ate in the car, then headed on toward the hospital on Rose Street.

Except I knew that it wasn't really on Rose Street, it was on South Limestone, or at least the parking garage across the street was. I'd been a passenger when I'd been there before, not driving, but I found it easily enough – the hospital complex was huge, impossible to miss.

The sun was low and the shadows were long when I got out of the car in the hospital garage. As Mel had said, the place was on the University of Kentucky campus, and everyone who'd mentioned it in my hearing called it the U.K. health center, but the sign on the main building said it was the Albert B. Chandler Hospital. It looked brand-new – at least, the part nearest Limestone, which was about a dozen stories of glass and red brick.

I didn't ask directions; I just walked across the pedestrian bridge from the garage and marched on in as if I knew where I was going, then followed the signs to the maternity ward – the birthing center, they called it – on the third floor.

It was pretty spiffy, lots of gentle lighting and soft colors, not much like the standard rows of machines and clear plastic cribs you see on TV, but the basics were unchanged – there were babies, mothers, and nurses, and fathers and siblings were visiting.

I didn't see Jack. I didn't see any sign of Jenny. Everything was calm and happy. I looked everywhere, opening doors I shouldn't have and apologizing when I intruded, getting more and more frantic that I hadn't found Jack.

I'd been there almost half an hour when I finally concluded that he wasn't there and wasn't coming. I thought I might have the wrong hospital after all – maybe Jack had deliberately picked a different hospital *because* this one was so obvious. I glanced out a window at the sun's glow fading behind the parking garage.

Had we picked the wrong hospital, or had my entire theory been wrong? For all I really knew, Jack was back under that damned tulip poplar – but I didn't think so. I thought I had the wrong hospital. I debated calling Mel and asking her to choose again, or calling Skees to find out whether there had been any new developments, but decided not to take the time to do either one; the car's GPS could probably find me other hospitals faster than Mel could, and if Skees had anything to tell me, he had my number. I headed for the elevator.

I'd been wandering around, though, and wound up in a different elevator than the one I'd ridden before. Also, I went down to street level, rather than heading for the bridge to the garage, so that when I came out on the ground floor I had no idea where I was. It was a big hospital, as I said, with multiple wings and various outbuildings, and I hadn't been in this part of it before. I headed toward what appeared to be an exit, and came out on a pedestrian plaza somewhere in the middle of the medical complex. I looked around, trying to get my bearings.

And I saw Jack, about fifty yards away.

It was unquestionably him, even at that distance; quite aside from that weird psychic sharpness, or whatever it was, the eye-patch and injured hand were pretty unmistakable.

I ducked back, making myself a little harder to see, and watched.

He had just emerged from another part of the hospital by yet another door, and was walking across the plaza, looking in all directions as he moved.

All I had to do was keep him in sight, and call Ben Skees to come get him. I reached in my pocket.

My phone wasn't there.

I froze, trying to think what could have happened to it, and I remembered – I had been driving on I-64 and talking to Mel, and when the call ended I had focused on my driving, on getting the right exit and finding my way to the U.K. campus. I had put the phone down – just *down*, not away in my pocket. It hadn't been there in my pocket when I ate my supper, or when I got to the hospital. I'd left it on the front seat of my rental, on the passenger side. It was probably still there, in the hospital garage.

If I went to get it, I'd lose sight of Jack and might never find him again.

That wasn't going to happen. I intended to keep him in sight. Sooner or later I'd have a chance to make a run back to the car, or to borrow a phone from someone.

Or maybe I could just grab him, and drag him to the car with me.

I wasn't about to just dash out there after him, though; if I tried that, and he put up a fight, strangers might misunderstand the situation and intervene. I would follow him, get closer, try to find out what was going on. He was here at the hospital, but he hadn't been in the birthing center; where *had* he been?

He was standing in the plaza now, looking around as if waiting for someone, and I was pretty sure I knew who the someone was. This was where he had arranged to meet Jenny.

And at that moment I caught sight of Jenny herself, black hair and white dress.

I couldn't really see her properly yet; it wasn't dark enough, the sky was still blue and gold. I had just caught a glimpse, a sort of flicker, like when you see something from the corner of your eye, and when you turn to look it's moved on.

I didn't try to watch Jenny; I watched Jack, trying to decide whether he had seen her yet. I didn't think he had.

But then he *did* spot her, and waved to her, and the next thing I knew they were both heading for a door into the hospital – not the big front entrance, just a smallish side-door into another part of the complex that opened off the plaza. I wasn't sure it was even the same building as the main hospital. I hurried after them, hoping they wouldn't spot me.

They didn't. They embraced, which looked very strange, since Jenny was still a barely-visible flicker rather than anything that looked like a real woman, and then they spoke – I couldn't hear what was said. I was able to gain some ground on them, but before I got close they walked back into that other part of the hospital.

I didn't think there were any babies over there; it certainly wasn't anywhere near the birthing center. I hurried after them.

I was so focused on not losing sight of Jack that I had walked right past the sign before I realized what it said.

Pediatric oncology. We were in the cancer wing.

Suddenly it all made sense. I'd guessed wrong, and it was sheer dumb luck I'd found them. Maybe *Jenny* knew she wanted to eat a baby, but *Jack* didn't. Jack hadn't gone looking for a baby; he had gone looking for kids who were dying anyway, and who might not mind dying a little sooner to help someone else. I didn't know whether any of them actually *were* willing to die for Jenny, but I could understand Jack's thinking. For a kid his age it probably made perfect sense – logically, a kid with late-stage terminal cancer didn't have much of anything to lose. It wasn't like Katie, with her entire life ahead of her.

I was old enough to know that people aren't logical, but it was possible Jack might find a willing victim all the same. Not many kids Jack's age or younger were suicidal, not when they still had their entire lives ahead of them, but some desperate cancer patient might decide that throwing away a few months of pain was worth doing.

I didn't think the patient's family would agree, and I didn't think feeding Jenny was a good idea in the first place. I picked up my pace, intending to catch Jack before he could introduce Jenny to anyone.

And I lost them. They went around a corner ahead of me, and when I turned that corner they were gone. There was only an empty corridor. There were stairs on one side, and a dozen doors opening off the passage beyond, but I didn't see Jack anywhere. Had he made it to the next corner, or gone up the stairs, or into one of the rooms? Had Jenny hidden him, somehow?

I stopped, stunned.

I hesitated; should I go back to my car to get my phone, and call Skees to let him know where I'd seen Jack? But that would take several minutes, and that might cost some poor sick kid a few fingers or worse. Or I could call a nurse – we'd passed a nurses' station – but then I'd have to explain the situation, and nobody was going to believe a story like that without some pretty serious evidence. I had convinced Ben Skees and Jenny Derdiarian that I was a psychic because I knew things they couldn't explain any other way, but what could I say to prove to a nurse that I wasn't a pedophile, or a raving lunatic?

No, I had to find Jack and Jenny and stop her myself.

Not that I knew how I could stop her.

I hurried to the stairwell and looked up, but I didn't see any sign of them. I started trying doors.

The first one was locked; the next two opened on empty rooms, with bare beds and unused tables.

As I tried the fourth door it was beginning to register, despite my near panic, that I might not need to explain anything to a nurse beyond, "I saw a missing kid in here just now; can you call Detective Ben Skees and let him know?" I didn't need to say anything about psychics or cannibal ghosts. Except I wasn't sure I had Skees' phone number on me; that might be back in the car with my phone.

This room wasn't empty, but the little girl in the bed, and her haggard mother in the chair beside her, clearly weren't expecting company. "Sorry," I said. "Wrong room." I started to close the door, then asked, "You haven't by any chance seen a boy in an eyepatch, have you?"

"No," the mother said.

"Very sorry to bother you, then." I closed the door and took a deep breath.

And that was when I heard the first scream.

It was a shrill, high-pitched scream, a child's scream, and it was followed an instant later by another scream, a little lower, an older boy's scream.

Jack. I didn't know who the first screamer was, but the older boy was Jack.

I was too late. I'd failed again. I'd let the monster get at its prey.

I followed the sound, up the corridor and around the next corner, and almost collided with a young man in scrubs. There were nurses, as well, all of us converging on the room the screams came from.

One of the nurses got there first, and added a brief scream of her own to the racket.

I couldn't see what was happening; the door was jammed with hospital personnel, blocking the entrance and blocking my view.

I could *feel* something, though; I could feel Jenny's presence. I could feel hunger and fear and guilt – and a horrible satisfaction, a warm, comfortable pleasure in what she was doing.

Jack was still screaming, but the nurse had stopped after a single brief outburst, and the original childish shriek had trailed off to nothing. Someone was barking orders, and I was shoved aside as one of the other nurses pushed past me, heading for somewhere else.

I staggered slightly, then leaned against the corridor wall. Jenny's emotions were still reaching me in a dark, hideous cascade of feelings that I couldn't name.

Even though there was definitely pleasure in there, Jenny was definitely enjoying it, I don't ever want to feel anything like that again.

I decided to stay out of the way; there wasn't anything I could do. Hospital staff was rushing in and out, carrying various kits, calling instructions to each other.

One instruction was, "Get him out of here!"

"But don't let him leave!"

A moment later the young man in scrubs emerged from the room, dragging a sobbing Jack by one arm. Jack's face, arm, and shirt were wet with blood, but I didn't think it was his – I saw no sign of any new injuries. He looked as if he was on the verge of hysteria.

I felt sick myself. The wave of emotion had faded, and I knew I hadn't been in time. Jenny had attacked some other kid, and by the look of that blood, she hadn't settled for a finger this time.

"Jack!" I called.

He turned at the sound of his name and saw me, and the orderly or male nurse or whoever he was – I didn't think he was a doctor, but I could have been wrong – noticed me, as well.

"You know him?" he demanded.

"His name's Jack Wilson," I said. "He's a runaway; I've been helping the police look for him."

"Helping? Who are you?" The guy eyed me warily.

"I'm a friend of the family. Look, you need to call Detective Ben Skees at the Lexington-Fayette police – he's the man in charge of finding this kid."

The man looked at me, then down at Jack, then said, "Come on, both of you."

I followed as he hauled Jack along the corridor and into a small lounge of some kind. There he set Jack on one chair, and indicated another one to me. I sat, while he got out a cellphone and called someone.

I didn't listen in; I just sat and looked at Jack. I looked at all that blood, and suppressed a shudder.

One thing about being the Dark Lady's best friend was that I'd gotten pretty good at suppressing shudders, and other signs of fear. Jack probably had no idea I was almost as upset as he was. So very much blood, and the depth and strength of that loathsome enjoyment – what had Jenny *done*?

"Are you okay?" I asked.

He looked at me with his one good eye wide and bleak. "She ate him," he said.

I swallowed. He didn't say she'd eaten *part* of him.

This was bad. This was very, very bad. Phantoms shouldn't be able to hurt living people. And this Jenny monster, in particular – this was *really* bad. The thing that got Mrs. Reinholt had apparently never gone after anyone else after it was done with her, but it had never *wanted* to hurt anyone else – just her.

Jenny wasn't so specific. She wanted to eat children – *any* children.

I tried not to think about it. I had to stay calm so I could talk to Jack, so I could learn more without sending anyone into screaming fits, or catatonia. I hadn't been able to stop Jenny this time, but maybe I could find some way to keep her from doing it again.

"Well, yeah," I said. "But you sound surprised. She *said* she was going to, didn't she?"

"Yeah, but... She said it, yeah, and I... but not like *that*."

I wasn't sure I really wanted to know, but I asked anyway. "Like what?"

Jack closed his one eye. "She... she bit his entire hand off," he whispered. "Not just a finger. She didn't... she was *fast*. She ate the whole thing, she bit it off at the wrist and swallowed it whole. I don't even know how she *fit* it in her mouth. And then when Andrew started screaming, she just leaned over and tore his throat out with her teeth. And she was *enjoying* it. I could *feel* how much she enjoyed it."

His voice had gotten gradually louder as he spoke. The man in scrubs had stopped in mid-sentence to listen. "Who did?" he demanded.

Jack looked up at him. "Jenny," he said.

The young man looked at me, saw no help there, then looked back at Jack. "Who's Jenny? Is she still in the building?"

"She's... she was my friend," Jack said. "She was still in the room with Andrew last I saw."

I noticed the use of the past tense. It didn't sound as if Jack was still enamored of his flesh-eating friend.

I thought I understood that. As I said before, people aren't logical. Jack had known all along that Jenny wanted to kill someone, and he had helped her find a victim. He had watched her bite off his own finger and pluck out his own eye, too. He had known what she was planning to do.

But knowing it, and actually *seeing* her attack someone else, was different.

It was a cliché that dying wasn't as hard as watching a loved one die, that it was worse to see a friend or family member suffer than to be ill oneself, and it looked as if that had caught Jack unawares. Feeding bits of himself to a ghoul was painful and scary, but it was his own choice, almost under his control; watching the ghoul try to kill someone else was completely different.

And he must have felt what she was radiating, that dark joy and cruel guilt. There had been something horribly sexual about it; what would a twelve-year-old boy make of that?

"Still in the *room*?" the man in scrubs asked. "I didn't see anyone."

Jack gave him a look and then shut his mouth tight. He had clearly decided that he had said too much.

The young man stared at him for a moment, then turned his attention back to his phone.

I waited a few seconds, and then I asked Jack quietly, "Who was he?"

Jack looked up at me with a troubled eye. "His name was Andrew," he said. "He had cancer – leukemia. I met him in the cafeteria after I lost my finger. I thought since he was going to die anyway..."

"...you thought he might as well help your ghost friend," I said, completing his sentence.

"I didn't know it would be like *that*," Jack said. He glanced back toward Andrew's room. "Do you think he's dead?"

I looked at the blood on Jack's face and shirt, and the blood on the young man's scrubs, and I remembered what Jack had said about the monster tearing Andrew's throat out. I felt sick. "Yes," I said.

"I'm sorry," Jack said softly.

"I did tell you she was a monster."

Another voice interrupted us before Jack could reply. "Yeah, there's a man with him," the guy in scrubs said into the phone, a little louder than he'd been talking up to that point. "On the tall side, brown hair, jeans and a polo shirt. If he gave a name, I didn't hear it."

"Gregory Kraft," I called. "Kraft with a K, like the cheese."

"Gregory Kraft," he repeated.

"Is that Detective Skees?" I asked.

He ignored my question.

I sort of tried to hear what he was saying, but I was distracted. There hadn't been any more screams coming from the room up the hall since we followed this guy to the lounge, but there had still been a lot of talking and shouting going on back there.

Now it had stopped. I didn't hear anything from the corridor but silence, and somehow that was even more distracting than the shouting had been.

Whatever had been going on, whatever the doctors had been trying to do, it seemed to be done.

I assumed that meant Andrew was dead, and they'd given up any hope of reviving him. I felt sick to my stomach. Once again, despite my dreams, I'd failed to save someone. This time it was a kid I'd never met, not my mother or my teacher, but still, it hurt.

The guy on the phone was quiet, too – he was listening, but whether he was listening to someone on the phone, or to the silence outside, I didn't know. Whichever it was, he wasn't looking at me or Jack; he was staring at the lounge's open door.

Jenny had gotten a big taste of human flesh there. I didn't think it would turn her human, the way Jack hoped, but I didn't know what it *would* do – if anything. I didn't know whether it would satisfy her hunger, or whether she would want more. I didn't know whether it would make her stronger.

I didn't know what Skees was going to think about this, either officially or actually. I didn't know how Jack's parents would deal with it, or Andrew's parents.

I didn't know how Jack was going to react – but then he spoke.

"But she said what she was going to do," Jack said into the silence, more to himself than to me. "I mean, it was horrible, but did it work? Is she human again?"

I turned to stare at him.

He stared back. His expression had changed completely. He had regained his composure, and shaken off what he had seen. I couldn't believe he had really gotten over his shock and horror so quickly, but he looked calm.

"You can't be serious," I said. I was beginning to wonder whether Jenny was the only monster involved here. Had *Jack* enjoyed it, on some level? Had the rush of Jenny's emotions overwhelmed his natural revulsion?

I had seen someone change that quickly before, I realized. A guy I knew a few years ago had come into a party badly shaken; he had been driving drunk and had barely missed running down a little girl. He had walked in swearing that he'd never drink again, that he'd had it, he was giving up booze – and five minutes later he took a shot of tequila to steady his nerves.

He'd wound up in rehab. He was an alcoholic, an addict.

Was *Jack* an addict? Was he hooked on Jenny's imitation of love?

"I still love her," he replied. He stood up. "I need to see her. I need to know if it worked."

Chapter Seventeen

A twelve-year-old kid can move pretty fast when he wants to; Jack was out the door before I could grab him. I followed him while the guy in scrubs was still fumbling with his phone, trying to decide whether to drop it, put it away, or keep holding it.

Jack was headed back up the corridor, to Andrew's room. There were people in the corridor, people in white coats and in scrubs, but Jack was ignoring them, and none of them seemed to be reacting quickly enough to stop him.

I couldn't believe what was happening. Jack had deliberately helped the phantom kill a kid. He had watched her take bites out of a boy he had known, a boy he had befriended. He had been soaked in gore, and practically in shock.

But the instant he was over that initial shock, he was back to thinking he loved her. I wondered how a kid his age could be that messed up.

Then Jenny stepped out of the room, into the corridor.

She was smiling, her human eye bright, her white teeth gleaming, and she was drenched in blood. Her white dress was wet red, and her black hair was streaked with dark dampness where it reached past her shoulders. At the sight of Jack she raised a childlike hand, a warm brown hand, the fingers streaked with blood, in greeting. She was radiating satisfaction and contentment.

Jack and I saw her clearly. No one else saw her at all.

Jack stopped dead in his tracks, and half a dozen hands reached to grab for his shoulders.

Delicious! Jenny said. *So sweet!*

My mouth fell open in shock; then I forced it closed to keep from vomiting.

"Hold it, kid," someone said, as a couple of people got hold of Jack.

The guy in scrubs had emerged from the lounge right behind me; he called, "The police are on the way."

Jenny stepped forward, moving through the crowded corridor as if it were empty, and came right toward us.

Jack was frozen, staring at her, completely ignoring everyone else – and *that* didn't surprise me at all. She was an absolutely horrific apparition, that big splash of bright red in the cool earth-toned corridor, amid white coats and blue scrubs, and the waves of happy calm coming from her made it all the worse.

Jenny stopped and stooped down, and gave Jack a big hug. The various hands holding him didn't seem to interfere with her at all. I couldn't see whether anything actually passed through her, or whether she went through anyone else, but certainly nothing stopped her.

Thank you so much!

I couldn't see his face from where I stood, but from what I could see, he seemed stunned.

It was so kind of you to introduce us, and to convince Andrew to love me!

"He... I didn't," Jack said.

"Didn't what?" someone asked.

Then the guy in scrubs put a hand on my arm, and pulled me back into the lounge.

I didn't resist, and neither did Jack, when his captors brought him back, as well. I did call softly, "Jenny, come talk to us."

I hoped no one else heard that.

Then we were back in our seats, with the guy in scrubs and a security guard watching over us while we waited for the cops to arrive. They kept their attention focused on me and Jack, and this time they shut the door.

Jack and I kept our attention on Jenny. She had followed us into the lounge – I'm not sure whether she slipped in before the door closed, or simply walked through it. She settled cross-legged on the tile floor in front of us, smiling up at Jack.

"It didn't work," Jack said, staring at her.

The guard and the man in scrubs exchanged quick glances.

She smiled beatifically. *It worked beautifully! Bless you, Jack, I feel so much better now!*

"But it *didn't work*," Jack insisted. "They still can't see you."

"What's he talking about?" the guard asked me.

"He has an invisible friend," I said.

"Isn't he a little old for that?"

I shrugged.

But I'm not hungry, Jenny said. *And I feel like a real mother again, with so much of Andrew inside me.*

"But they can't *see* you," Jack insisted. He glanced at the guard, then turned back to Jenny. "You still aren't a live person."

It doesn't matter.

"It matters to me!" His shout caught the attention of the guard and the guy in scrubs, but they just stared, they didn't move any closer. I resisted the urge to shush the kid; after all, at this point, what difference could it make?

The monster's happiness was tinged ever so faintly with pity now. *Poor Jack. I'm sorry you couldn't really love me as I am.*

"I *do* love you!"

She shook her head, and I noticed that the blood seemed to be fading from her hair – not drying, but vanishing. *If you really loved me, you would have fed me yourself. Andrew loved me, and I loved Andrew.*

"You killed him!"

I loved him.

"She's insane," I murmured. "She's a monster."

"I'm not sure you two should be talking," the guard said.

"Sorry," I said.

"Will you be back at the tree when they let me go?" Jack asked, finally managing to speak quietly again, rather than shouting.

Oh, no, sweetie, Jenny said, grinning broadly and displaying what seemed like far too many teeth. The pity, never strong, had vanished. *I don't need to go back there, now that you've shown me where there are so many other children to love.*

Jack's face froze. I think mine might have, too.

That was when the door swung open and Ben Skees stepped in.

"You two," he said, gesturing at us. "Come with me."

"Excuse me, but..." the guard began, but then Skees held up his badge.

"You're welcome to accompany us, sir, but the boy's parents are on their way, and I'd like a chance to talk to him before they get here." He glanced at Jack. "And to get him cleaned up; we don't want his mother to see him like that."

"Come on," I said, getting to my feet.

"But..." Jack gestured toward Jenny.

"Come on," I repeated.

Goodbye, Jenny said. *Thank you, Jack. Goodbye.*

I looked at her, and I saw a spot of white fabric reappear at her shoulder. The blood was fading away.

I think Jack saw it, too. He stood up, and he and I followed Detective Skees out of the lounge, and then out of the hospital.

From her spot on the floor, Jenny watched us leave. She waved a farewell, but made no move to follow us.

I'd assumed Jack would be interviewed by a cop or two, maybe a social worker, and then returned to his parents. There was a little more to it than that. This wasn't just a missing child anymore. This was now a possible homicide. Andrew had died, and it didn't look like natural causes.

That meant Skees wasn't in charge; he worked missing persons, domestic disturbances, and the like, not homicide. An older man named McDonough was in charge. Skees was still involved, though, since Jack had been his case. Skees took us to the police station, looked us over, made sure that none of the blood on Jack was his own, got him into a clean T-shirt, and then turned us over to the homicide boys.

Jack and I were questioned separately, and at length. I assume they let Jack's parents see him at some point, but he wasn't going home, not that night.

Neither was I.

I thought I was going to have trouble answering their questions; I thought I would have to dodge a lot, maybe lie outright, to avoid being labeled a nutcase. Didn't happen. The homicide cops didn't really care about me; they were focused on what had happened to Andrew.

I'd never met Andrew. I could say that honestly. I'd never met him, never seen him, never spoken with him. I was at the hospital looking for Jack, and found him coming out of Andrew's room with blood all over him – that was my story. I'd never heard of Andrew before tonight, never heard Jack mention him. All the simple truth.

They never asked why I was in Lexington, or why I was looking for Jack; that wasn't their department.

They did ask if I knew anything about this Jenny that Jack talked about, and I said that Jack hadn't really told me much about her – which was true; I'd seen and heard her for myself, Jack didn't need to say anything – but that my impression was that Jack believed he could see and hear a ghost named Jenny, who served as a sort of mother figure for him. Jack and I had talked about her a little when I visited him in the hospital after he lost his eye.

They never asked if *I* could see her, so I didn't have to lie. They stayed focused on Andrew. Had Jack really never mentioned him? Had I ever seen Jack in the company of any dangerous strangers? Had I gone in Andrew's room? Had I looked in the door? Had Jack ever said what happened to his eye? Had he blamed Andrew for ruining it? Had he blamed Andrew for his lost finger?

I kept telling them that I had never heard of Andrew, that I was at the hospital because I thought Jack might have wanted to find a baby for Jenny to cuddle, and that it was pure dumb luck that I spotted him on the plaza and followed him into the cancer center.

I had a dozen witnesses who could affirm that I wasn't in Andrew's room – nurses, doctors, and other staff. I had no blood on my clothes. I wasn't a suspect, just a guy who had been in the area.

So after maybe an hour and a half, they were done with me.

They didn't release me immediately, though; they left me waiting on a hard chair in a small room. That's where Ben Skees found me.

"Okay," he said, as he sat down opposite me. "What happened?"

"Hypothetically?" I asked wearily.

"If you want to tell it that way, sure."

"Jack found another kid for Jenny. I was wrong – he didn't want a baby for her, he wanted someone who was dying anyway, someone he could convince to cooperate because he didn't have anything to lose. He found one, I guess – a kid with leukemia he'd met in the cafeteria last month."

"And how did *you* happen to be there?"

"I was checking out the birthing center, and wound up leaving by the wrong door and came out in that side-street instead of on Limestone, I guess it's Rose Street, and I saw Jack there. I wanted to call you, but I'd left my phone in the car – it's probably still there, on the front seat where I dropped it. I didn't want to lose sight of Jack, so I followed him, and he met Jenny in the plaza and led her inside, to Andrew's room. I got turned around and lost them, but when Andrew started screaming I followed the sound. I didn't get there in time to do anything except keep Jack out of the way of the doctors." I shrugged. "That's it."

"So Jack led the ghost to the McPhee kid?"

"I don't know Andrew's last name; I only know his name was Andrew because that's what Jack called him. I never saw him."

"Andrew McPhee, age eleven, leukemia not responding to treatment. We got the same story from Jack that you did, that he'd met Andrew last month and they hit it off."

"Is Andrew dead? No one's actually told me." I had a brief moment of mad, totally unrealistic hope – Skees was here talking to me, and he wasn't in homicide.

"Oh, yeah." Skees grimaced. "Several pieces missing, including his heart. He's dead, all right."

That irrational hope vanished. "I'm sorry."

"So's his mother. Father's out of the picture, apparently."

I didn't know what else to say, so I repeated, "I'm sorry."

"So your story is that this ghost tried to eat him?"

"She *did* eat him, or at least all she could." I shuddered. "She was covered in blood from her shoulders to her knees."

"You *saw* her?"

"Afterwards, yeah. She came to that room we were in, to talk to Jack."

Skees looked at me for a moment, then down at the floor, then back at me.

"Just how common is it," he asked, "for a ghost to kill someone? I thought they were mostly harmless, couldn't hurt the living."

I shrugged again. "I have no idea how common it is. Not very, I'd guess. This is the second confirmed case I've heard of in the eight years I've been involved with this stuff."

"That's more than I'd ever heard of," Skees replied. "Look, I'm a cop; we share stories about the weird stuff we see on the job, and we do get weird ones, but except for horror movies I have *never* heard about ghosts killing people before. This isn't even friend of a friend, I heard this but don't know if it's true stuff; this just *doesn't happen*, except in horror movies and campfire stories. People see ghosts, yeah, but the ghosts don't hurt people. So how come it happened here?"

I shook my head. "I don't know. There are a lot of malicious things out there – ghosts, if you want to call them that, and other things, too. I've seen them creeping around, stalking women, trying to hit people, things like that, but they can't hurt you; they aren't solid enough to harm *anything*. Jenny's an exception. I don't know why. I have a theory that maybe they get stronger if people interact with them, so maybe she got dangerous because Jack spent so much time with her. I don't *know*, I don't know anything for sure, but that seems to be how it works."

"How can people interact with them, though? They're fucking invisible!"

"Some people can see them. I can. Jack can. Mrs. Reinholt, my high school teacher, could, until one of them killed her. The original Jenny Derdiarian used to be able to, but lost the ability fifteen years ago when her ghost split off – I guess it took the talent with it. Over the years I've found a few other people who could see them, too. No one around here, though."

"One of them killed your teacher?"

It figured that he'd focus on that. "Yeah. That was the other case I know of. She'd learned to use them to do... well, magic, more or less. Witchcraft. Curses. Except the more she used them, the stronger they got, and eventually one of them got tired of being bossed around and tore her head off."

"You mean that literally?"

I looked him in the eye. "Yeah, I do."

He considered that for a moment, then asked, "Was the head still there when they found the body?"

I really didn't like to think about that. I closed my eyes. "Yeah," I said. "The head was there. You said some pieces of Andrew aren't?"

"That's right. And I'd like to know why the two are different."

"The one that killed Mrs. Reinholt wasn't interested in eating anyone – it was just pissed at her. Jenny isn't angry, but she's got food and love and guilt all tangled together. She's obsessed with killing children and eating them."

"Eating kids."

"That's right."

"So she ate Andrew."

"Apparently. I didn't see it." I didn't mention that I had felt how much she'd enjoyed it – or that Jack had, as well.

Skees contemplated me for a moment, then said, "Two doctors and three nurses did see it. They didn't all want to talk about it at first because they thought we'd think they were nuts, but once we got them started it all came out. When they got there, Andrew was still alive – his hand was gone, and his throat and shoulder were badly torn up, but he was still breathing.

"Except then more of him disappeared. The doctor who first told us about it said he'd never seen anything like it, and it didn't make any sense, but pieces of the boy's chest were tearing loose and vanishing. Nothing they did could stop it or even slow it down."

I made a noise.

"Eventually his heart disappeared, right out of his chest. That was when they gave up and pronounced him dead."

"I'm sorry," I said. "If I knew how to stop Jenny, I would have."

"We searched the room for... well, we didn't know what for. Something that might explain some of this. We didn't find much. But we did find a finger, the little finger from a child's left hand.

"Except it wasn't fresh enough, or the right color, to be Andrew McPhee's. I think it was Jack's."

Chapter Eighteen

I considered that finger silently for a moment before I said, "I suppose it's far too late to reattach it."

"After a *month*? Of course it is." Skees waved that aside. "I have a couple of concerns here, and that finger isn't on the list. I need to know what really happened, and I need to know what we can *say* happened, and I'm pretty sure they don't have much in common."

"I'm with you on that," I said.

"I guess you've told me the first part, and I think we can work something up for the second one. Last I heard, McDonough and Carrera had more or less decided to say it wasn't a homicide after all, or any kind of police matter, just some weird medical mystery, so that shouldn't be a big issue for us – the doctors get to make it up, we don't have to. What I also need to know, though, is maybe the most important thing – is it going to happen again?"

I considered that. I looked at Skees, and I wished I could give him some good news, that I could tell him yes, it was all over, Jenny had done her thing and that was it.

But that wouldn't be doing either of us any favors.

"I don't know," I said. "I really don't. But I'm assuming you want my best guess."

"If that's all you got, yeah, I'll take it."

"Okay, look, Detective, I don't know what I'm doing. Remember that. I've never had any other real psychics I could talk to, and I've never found any books or websites that match what I see and hear for myself. I talked to the thing that killed Mrs. Reinholt, and I've talked to Jenny, and to a couple of others. These ghosts or spirits or demons or whatever they are, they're all limited. They don't have real personalities, they just have obsessions. They don't get distracted, or change their minds – they stay focused on whatever they're about. Mrs. Reinholt's killer was all about who was in charge, who had the power, it was all anger and resentment, and once it was free of her control it was done; it went away and never came back, and so far as I know it never hurt anyone else. I'd like to say that's what's going to happen, but I don't think it is, because Jenny's not about power, she's about hunger and guilt and mother-love, and she's obsessed with devouring children. I think she's going to get hungry again, and now she knows that dying kids can be convinced to 'help' her, so I think she's going to eat more of them. I don't know how long it'll take her to get her appetite back, it could be a couple of days or a hundred years, but eventually I think she'll eat more."

"How do we keep that from happening?" He stared directly at me.

I met his gaze squarely. "I don't *know*," I said. "I swear I don't."

"Is she going to eat Jack Wilson?"

"No, I don't think she is," I said. "I think she's going after easier prey." I told him everything I could remember of Jack and Jenny's conversation in that little lounge.

When I was done Skees tipped his head back for a few seconds, then looked at me again.

"She jilted him," he said.

"You could look at it that way," I agreed.

"That would explain a lot about how he's been acting."

That caught my attention. "How has he been acting?"

"Pissed. Seriously pissed."

"That would make sense," I acknowledged.

Skees dropped that, and returned to what he considered important. "So you don't know who she'll eat next, or when?"

I shook my head. "I really don't. Some scared dying kid who thinks he can help her, would be my guess."

"And you don't know how we can stop her?"

"No. I wish I did."

"How did you stop the one that killed your teacher?"

"I didn't. No one did. It's still out there somewhere."

Skees considered that for a moment, then asked, "But it hasn't hurt anyone else?"

"Not that I know of."

"So why is our Jenny different? I know how you said she is; I want to know *why*."

"I don't *know*."

"You think it's something about the real Jenny? Maybe there's some connection between them?"

I shook my head. "I don't think that's it. The one that killed Mrs. Reinholt wanted to kill anyone who tried to control it. Jenny wants to eat children who love her. Nobody else is trying to control that one, but there are lots of kids out there who can love Jenny."

"Are there? Can they even *see* her?"

"I don't know. Jack can see her just fine, Katie could see her a little, I don't know about Andrew, but I'm not sure they need to see her to love her. If someone else *tells* them about her, that might be enough."

"Well, who's going to tell them? I don't think Jack's in any mood to talk about her anymore."

"Maybe," I said. I hesitated, then said, "Detective Skees, may I be blunt? I think you're trying to convince yourself that Jenny's not going to kill any more kids. I think you're doing that because there isn't any way you can catch her or make her stop. I don't think you really have any evidence."

He grimaced. "You don't have any real evidence, either."

"No, I don't. You're right. But I saw her, and I saw the one that killed Mrs. Reinholt, and they were really, really different. That one eight years ago didn't look remotely human, it didn't – " I stopped; I didn't want to explain that Jenny radiated her emotions, and Reinholt's bane didn't. It would just lead to a lot more useless questions. And it wasn't something unique to Jenny; lots of night-creatures radiated like that, maybe one out of every dozen, though not usually so strongly. "It was different," I finished.

"So then you don't really know anything about it, right? You keep saying that. So what makes you think it'll go after other kids?"

"Jenny said she was going to stay at the hospital where there are other children to love," I replied. "I think that sounds like a threat."

Skees didn't answer at first; he leaned back in his chair, folded his arms across his chest, and stared at me.

I stared back.

"You say there's nothing we can do," he said.

"I said I don't *know* of anything. Physical means won't work – you can't hold them, or hurt them. I drove a car through one once, and I've tried cutting them; it doesn't work."

"You've tried it?"

"Yes."

I didn't explain further, and after a moment's thought, Skees didn't ask. Instead he began, "This teacher of yours, Mrs. Reinhart..."

"Reinholt," I corrected him.

"Whatever. *She* could control these ghosts, right? Why can't you?"

"Because I'm not a witch, or whatever she was. I have some weird psychic abilities that she gave me, that's all. We had this strange relationship, where I was sort of a teacher's pet, but we kind of hated each other at the same time, and one day she said that I didn't know as much as I thought I did, and maybe if I saw what was really out there I'd be a little less of a pain in the ass, and that night I started seeing things. But I just *saw* them, I couldn't touch them, or make them obey me, the way she did. After that I watched her sometimes, and it seemed like she just summoned them up out of nowhere whenever she needed them, and I can't do anything like that."

I didn't mention that she had teased me with that, told me I would never be able to do what she did.

"But they *can* be controlled," Skees said. "*You* just can't do it."

"Well, yeah, I guess so. I'm not sure *anyone* can do it; for all I know, Mrs. Reinholt was the last of her kind."

"Doesn't seem real likely."

"I guess not. But Detective, I've been looking for real psychics or witches off and on for eight years now, and I haven't found any."

"Where were you looking?"

I grimaced. "Well, I started with the Yellow Pages. I tried the web, and the classified ads, and anywhere else I could think of that a psychic would advertise. I talked to a couple of professors at the University of Maryland."

"Did your teacher advertise any of those places? Would your professors have known about her?"

"No," I acknowledged. "She didn't work as a psychic; it was a hobby. She didn't advertise; she taught high school, and I don't think the school board would have been happy with her if she was moonlighting as a witch."

"So why would *any* real psychic advertise? *You're* a real psychic; can you do anything people would pay you for? Anything you could advertise?"

"No," I admitted.

I'd thought about that, of course, but my talents, if you want to call them that, weren't particularly useful. I could see night creatures, but I couldn't *do* much of anything about them. I could spot other psychics, and what good was that? And while I did have my dreams, I never dreamed about anyone I'd met, and I couldn't *choose* who to dream about. I couldn't see anyone's future, or talk to dead relatives, or find lost valuables. I was really something of a bust when it came to useful psychic abilities.

"If someone was looking for a real psychic, would they find *you*?"

"No," I repeated.

"So there are probably others like her out there; you just don't have any way of finding them."

I wasn't totally convinced, but I had to admit he had a case. "Maybe," I said. "But the thing is, I really *don't* have any way of finding them, so what good does it do us if they're out there?"

"Ah," he said. "Yeah. So you don't know anyone else with paranormal abilities – except your friend de Cheverley. Could *she* do anything?"

It wasn't literally true that I didn't know anyone else; I knew Jack, and a guy named Leonard who lived in Gaithersburg, and an old lady in Arlington, and a couple of others I'd lost track of.

But they couldn't do anything useful, any more than I could.

But Mel – maybe she could. I hadn't thought of that.

"I don't know," I said. "She can't see or hear these creatures, the ghosts or whatever they are; we've tested that. But I don't know whether she can affect them."

"Do you think she might be able to scare Jenny off?"

"I have no idea, Detective."

"Mr. Kraft, I really, *really* don't want any more dead kids. I think it's worth a shot. Think you could give her a call and ask her to come out here?"

I noticed he didn't suggest *he* should call her. "Even if she came, Detective," I said, "and did scare the ghost off, wouldn't Jenny just go somewhere else and kill some other kid?"

"She'd have to start from scratch, wouldn't she? You said she gets her power from interaction with humans; maybe she wouldn't have the strength without Jack Wilson."

It seemed to me that he was grasping at straws, putting way too much faith in my own half-assed theories. "This is all guesswork," I said.

"Yes, it is. Does that mean it's not worth trying?"

"I suppose not. But I don't know whether Mel's going to want to do it. She doesn't like traveling much. What's in it for her?"

"Saving a kid's life isn't enough?"

"*Maybe* saving a *theoretical* kid's life probably isn't."

"She doesn't owe you a favor? Seemed like when I talked to her before she was pretty determined not to let anything bad happen to you."

I resented the way he said that. "She doesn't owe me anything," I protested. "We're just friends."

"She seemed awful protective of you."

"She doesn't *have* a lot of friends."

"What about those congressmen?"

"They're not exactly *friends*," I said. "More like clients." I didn't really want to explain how Mel earned a living; Skees might not have jurisdiction in Maryland, but he still wasn't likely to look kindly on what amounted to extortion.

"Clients?"

I suddenly realized what that must sound like. "Not like *that*," I said.

Mel had actually thought about becoming a dominatrix once, or at least she'd talked about it, but she didn't have any idea how to go about it. Besides, it seemed likely most potential customers were more interested in feeling obedient than terrified, and she just plain didn't want to. It wasn't her idea of fun.

As for any other sort of prostitution, call girls' clients aren't looking to be scared. They're more likely to be doing the scaring.

"All right, whatever," Skees said. "Do you think you could invite her out here to give Jenny a little talk?"

"It's a long drive," I said.

That startled him. "Drive? I figured she'd fly, same as you did."

I closed my eyes. "Detective," I said, "she doesn't fly. You've talked to her. You know the effect she has over the phone; it isn't very different in person, and she can't turn it off. You really want *that* sealed in a plane with a hundred strangers for a couple of hours?"

"Oh," he said, blinking. "I guess not."

I didn't mention that Mel *had* tried it once, just once, after Mrs. Reinholt cursed her. She hadn't actually gotten as far as the plane. The security line had been on the verge of screaming panic, children on all sides had been crying, and travelers who didn't like flying had been canceling their trips or just turning around and going home, when she reached the first TSA agent. The guard first tried to pull her aside, and then broke down crying.

Mel decided that enough was enough, and that starting a panic in mid-flight was likely to get a lot of people killed. She cashed in her ticket and left.

"Listen, Detective," I said. "I know you don't want any other kids to get hurt, and neither do I, but I really don't think there's much we can do about it. These night-things are out there, and they always have been. They're just part of the world. If they could go on wild rampages, slaughtering dozens of people, I think we'd have heard about it. I figure they do kill people occasionally, people like Audrey Reinholt and Andrew McPhee, but that it's rare, and it's unavoidable, like being struck by lightning or eaten by sharks. I don't think we can stop it. I'll call Mel if you want, but I don't think it'll do any good. And I'll answer your questions, but I don't think I can help, either. I just want to go home. I've done my part here."

"Have you? But Jenny's still out there."

I shook my head. "Sorry, Detective, but Jenny's not my problem. If I thought I could do something to stop her, I would, but I can't. I'm not doing any good here, and I need to go home."

Maybe that sounds heartless, but really, what could I do? If I stayed, I wouldn't be able to do any good, and if Jenny did kill more kids, I'd practically have my nose rubbed in it. I'd have to sit there and listen to her gloat about how much she had loved those kids, and how they'd loved her. Maybe running away wasn't the most admirable option, but it seemed like the most realistic. I was going to be haunted by my memories of Andrew McPhee's blood soaking Jack and Jenny as it was; I didn't need to add any other kids' blood to my nightmares.

I wanted to help, really I did, but I couldn't. If I stayed I'd just be giving Detective Skees false hope; he'd think I was his wedge, his key into the spirit world, when all I was was a peephole.

"But you *dreamed* about this," Skees said. "Isn't there a *reason* for that? Doesn't that make it your problem?"

I shook my head. "I dreamed about *Jack*," I said. "Not about Jenny eating other kids. And my dreams have always been about someone that's going to change *my* life, not about things that happen to other people."

"So has Jack Wilson changed your life?"

That question stopped me for a second.

"I don't know," I said. "Not yet. Not really. He got me here, but that's not it – I didn't dream about *you*." That maybe wasn't entirely true, since Skees had been in a couple of my dreams, but I thought it was close enough. The dreams hadn't been *about* him, they'd been about Jack.

"Then stick around, and give us a hand, and I'll arrange for you to talk to Jack again. Alone, if necessary. Maybe you can figure out why you were dreaming about him."

I was tempted, but I shook my head. "I'm probably going to get fired as it is. I can't afford to stay much longer; the hotel and car would eat my savings."

"Money's the problem?"

"Well, yeah."

He frowned. "I can probably pry loose some discretionary money – maybe not a full consultant's fee, but I think I can call you a confidential informant."

That hadn't occurred to me. "Seriously?" I asked.

"Not a lot. Maybe a couple of hundred."

"That'd help," I conceded. "And if you're serious about keeping me around, maybe you could talk to my boss – we'd need to be careful about that, I told him this was a family emergency."

I don't know why I was agreeing; even as I said it, I knew I couldn't do any good, and that my presence would just be a distraction.

"It *is* a family emergency, even if it's not *your* family."

"Well, yeah..."

"Call your friend Mel, if it's not too late..."

"It's not," I said, interrupting.

"Good. Ask her if she'll make the drive. Then we'll visit the hospital and see if we can find Jenny and check out what she's up to, and tomorrow you can have a talk with Jack Wilson, and maybe figure out why you dreamed about him."

"And the money?"

"I'll see what I can do."

I considered that for a moment. I looked Skees in the eye, and while I couldn't read much there, he seemed sincere.

"All right," I said. "Give me a phone."

Chapter Nineteen

By the time I had brought Mel up to speed and asked her if she'd like to come to Lexington to try to scare away a ghost, it was almost midnight. By the time I had gotten over my shaking and convinced Skees that "I'll think about it" was the best answer we were going to get, it was well after. I thought that meant the hospital visit would wait, but Skees said no.

"You can't see ghosts by daylight, can you?"

"No," I admitted.

"Then we go now. I'm not waiting until tomorrow night."

I was too exhausted to argue. I caught a very short nap in the car on the way over, but it was only a few blocks from the police station to the hospital garage on South Limestone, and there wasn't any traffic at that hour to slow us up.

Skees talked us past the front desk, past hospital security, and past the two cops still guarding the possible crime scene, and got us to the late Andrew McPhee's room.

I hadn't been in there before; other people had gotten there first when the screaming started, and hadn't let me through the door. I looked around.

It was a normal hospital room, pretty much – a single. The last time I stayed in a hospital I was in a semi-private room, which meant I shared it with an old man with a tube in his throat, and I'd thought that was still the standard, but this room only had one bed, and more fancy equipment than mine had. It smelled of disinfectant, the bed was stripped, and the floor had obviously been scrubbed recently, but other than that, there wasn't any sign that a kid had been horribly murdered there a few hours earlier.

Jenny wasn't in the room. I told Skees as much.

"You're sure?" he asked.

"Detective, it's not exactly hard to tell. She's a grown woman, or at least she looks like one, and to me she's just as visible at this hour as *you* are. If she were in here, I'd see her."

"She couldn't hide?"

"Maybe she *could*, but why would she?"

He didn't have an answer, and I continued, "The last place I saw her wasn't in here, anyway. It was that staff lounge, or whatever it is, where Jack and I were held."

"Show me."

I showed him. Jenny wasn't there, either.

"Now what?" I asked.

"We look around a little," the detective said.

So we walked up and down a few corridors, and I didn't see Jenny, but eventually I did see something vaguely humanoid, crouching in a corner.

It definitely wasn't Jenny; it was grayish-brown and indistinct, as if I was seeing it from the corner of my eye even when I stared directly at it, and it didn't look female. It held something shiny and knifelike. I didn't remember seeing it there before, but that didn't mean anything.

Ordinarily I ignored the night-things as best I could, but we wanted to find Jenny, and this one might have seen her. I decided to try something. I gestured for Skees to wait, and then I walked toward it, trying to look as if I couldn't see it.

It raised its head as I approached; it didn't have much of a face, just darker patches where eyes should have been, and a hole for a mouth. That was disconcerting, but it could have been worse. I was relieved to not see fangs or teeth.

Of course, it did have that knife. If it *was* a knife; it was blurry, just a streak of silvery light maybe a foot long, that the thing was holding clutched in its right hand, as if the light reflecting from a knife-blade was there, but the blade itself wasn't.

For all I know, that's exactly what it was. Maybe it was a memory of a knife, or a belief in a knife. After all, if ghost-Jenny could turn herself into a lonely mother's guilty fantasy, why couldn't this thing carry the memory of a knife?

"I see you," I said, stopping and looking directly at it.

The thing froze.

"I know you're there. I can see you."

It stared at me with those dark spots that weren't eyes, but it didn't say anything.

It didn't attack me, either, which was good.

None of the monsters and night-things I saw had seriously tried to hurt me since high school, but I still worried about it sometimes. Most of them seemed harmless, but I could never be sure; after all, the thing that got Mrs. Reinholt hadn't looked all that very different from some of the ones I still saw regularly.

And some did try to scare me. Some of them succeeded, too.

This one didn't try anything. It just squatted there in the hospital corridor, looking at me.

"I'm looking for Jenny," I said. "The ghost woman who ate that kid earlier."

Something shifted slightly in its rudimentary face.

"You know who I'm talking about," I said, hoping I was right. "I don't know whether you can talk, but you can point, can't you?"

It was still just looking at me, and I still couldn't see eyes or a mouth, but it felt as if I could read something in its expression, and what I read was more or less, "Why should I tell you?"

"If you tell me something I can do for you in exchange, something harmless, I'll do it," I said. "And I'll leave you alone. I don't know who you are, or *what* you are, or what you want, but I can probably find some way to make your existence less pleasant if I have to."

It considered that, then raised the knife and pointed down a corridor – not the one we were in, but another branch, off to the right.

I glanced back over my shoulder.

Skees was watching me. I suppose to him I appeared to be talking to nothing, to the empty air.

He didn't say a word, though; he just watched.

"Thank you," I said to the knife-wielder. "I owe you a favor."

It nodded, and a shiver ran across my shoulder blades. I hoped I hadn't just committed myself to doing something horrible.

Right now, though, I had a direction. "This way," I told Skees.

The corridor was empty, the doors along either side mostly closed; the few that were open gave into empty rooms. I walked slowly along the passage, looking and listening for some sign of Jenny's presence.

I didn't see or hear *her*, but I heard a child's voice say something – I couldn't be sure of the words through the closed door, but it might have been, "You poor thing!"

"There," I said, pointing.

Skees nodded, and opened the door.

It was a room almost exactly like Andrew McPhee's, but this one had a girl, perhaps eight years old, in it, sitting up in bed and staring at us. She was thin and pale, with an IV line in her arm. The light at the head of her bed was on, but the ceiling lights were off.

She had a very faint oddness about her, as if the light on her wasn't quite the same as the light in the rest of the room. It wasn't anywhere near as intense as Jack's, not even the same order of magnitude, but she had it, ever so slightly.

And standing beside the bed, standing over her, was a black-haired, pale-skinned woman with mismatched eyes and hands. Her dress was still streaked with dark red, but most of it was white again. She was glaring furiously at me; I could feel her anger – and just a twinge of hunger.

"Hey, honey," Skees said. "Sorry to bother you, but we needed to check on something."

"Are you a doctor?" the girl asked.

"No, sweetie, I'm a policeman," Skees said, looking around.

"She's here," I said.

Skees threw me a quick glance, then scanned the room. "Where?"

"Right by the bed," I said.

The little girl looked at me, then at Jenny. Any doubts I might have had vanished; the kid could definitely see the monster.

The younger man can see me. The older one can't. The anger had faded a little, and when she spoke to the girl the hunger seemed stronger.

Or maybe it wasn't exactly hunger; it was almost lust.

The girl didn't say anything, but turned her eyes back toward me.

"I don't see it," Skees said. "I somehow thought I would, despite what you said. You sure it's there?"

"Oh, she's there, all right," I said, as Jenny glowered at me.

Go away. The anger was back, and now had a trace of desperation.

"Do *you* see it, honey?" Skees asked. "The ghost-woman?"

"My name isn't Honey," the little girl said. "It's Lisette Babcock."

Startled, Skees said, "I'm sorry, Miss Babcock. No offense meant. But can you see anyone else here, besides you, me, and Mr. Kraft?"

She stared straight at him, but didn't answer.

"She can see it," I said. "I think she sees Jenny just fine."

"I don't think you should be in my room," Lisette said.

"The call button for the nurse is right there," I replied.

"I know that! I'm not stupid."

"No, I'm sure you aren't," I said. "And I'm guessing you've been in and out of hospitals a lot, and know perfectly well how to call the nurse. Go ahead and call, if you don't think we should be in here. I'm sorry we had to bother you, but that ghost you're talking to – did you know she killed a kid earlier tonight?"

Lisette gave Jenny an uncertain glance.

The anger became incandescent fury. *Go away! Leave us alone!*

I ignored Jenny's desperate shout. "A boy named Andrew McPhee," I said. "That's his blood on her dress. She tore him to pieces."

"How can a ghost hurt anyone?" Lisette demanded. "It's not solid."

I shrugged. "Who knows anything about ghosts, really? *I* don't know why some of them can hurt people and some can't, but that's the way it is. *This* one, that calls herself Jenny Derdiarian, can only hurt kids who trust her. She can't touch grown-ups at all, or kids who can't see her, but what she does is she tricks kids into thinking she loves them, and that they love her, and then she talks them into feeding her. Except what she eats is human flesh."

Shut up shut up shut up!

Lisette gave Jenny a startled glance, then made a face. "She eats *people*?"

"That's right. She does. She ate a big piece of Andrew McPhee tonight, but I think she's already getting hungry again, so she came here to start convincing *you* to feed her. She's figured out that kids who are really sick, who think they might die soon anyway, are more likely to agree to feed her."

"That's *gross!*"

I nodded. "It really is."

The ghost glared at me. *I'll kill you, I'll destroy you, I'll ruin you!*

Lisette looked at me, then back at Jenny.

The ghost saw that look, and turned back to the child, anger giving way to eagerness. *He lies! I love you, I love children!*

"Ask her where that dried blood on her dress came from."

"It *is* blood? I wasn't sure I was seeing it right."

It's my blood! Mine!

"It's Andrew's."

"Is that true?" Lisette asked Detective Skees.

"I can't see her," Skees admitted. "I don't know what's on her dress. But Andrew McPhee was killed here in this hospital earlier tonight, and pieces of him are missing. So far, every time I've been able to check something Mr. Kraft told me, it was true. He says he can see ghosts, and it sounds like you can, too."

"I never did before," Lisette said. "But I can see Jenny. She's been here talking to me for hours, telling me about her children and stuff."

That was interesting – could Jenny *make* kids see her now? Maybe eating poor Andrew had made her more powerful, more dangerous. Lisette definitely had that strangeness that meant she could see the spirit world, but had she always had it, or was that something Jenny had done to her? There were multiple mysteries here.

But that wasn't what I needed to tell Lisette. "She told you that she locked them in their rooms until they starved to death?" I said. I shook my head. "That didn't happen." I remembered what the real Jenny Derdiarian had told me about the whole fantasy. "I mean, think about it," I continued. "If you were locked in your room for days and days, wouldn't you find a way to break a window and climb out, or a way to call for help? Wouldn't your friends or your teachers notice something was wrong and send someone to check on you? It takes weeks to starve to death! And if they *starved*, where were they getting water? They'd die of thirst first! Did they have water in their rooms?"

You lie you lie you lie! Shut up shut up! Her rage almost visible, Jenny turned away from the bed and came charging at me, hands raised, fingers curled into claws.

I stepped back. I knew she couldn't hurt me, or I *thought* I did, but still, it looked as if a grown woman was about to attack me. My brain may have known she wasn't real, but my eyes and feet didn't.

And sure enough, her right hand just seemed to disappear before it touched me, I couldn't feel it any more than I could feel a shadow – but her *left* hand, the little brown hand that looked like Andrew's, actually hit me.

It wasn't like a human hand; it was cold, and felt more like a gust of wind than like living flesh, but the nails clawed my cheek, and I felt scratches. It stung.

I was too astonished to react at first, but Lisette screamed, clapping her hands to her mouth, her eyes fixed on my face.

Skees moved, his hand reaching under his jacket and bringing out a gun I didn't know he had, but he didn't know where to point it; he kept the muzzle toward the ceiling as he looked around for a target.

He couldn't see Jenny, couldn't see her flailing furiously at me, but he did see my face.

"Oh, my God," he said.

By this time I'd brought up my own hands to defend myself, but I couldn't get a grip on Jenny's wrist, and she was still clawing at my face with her left hand. It hurt; it felt as if someone had taken coarse sandpaper to my cheek.

Die die die! she shrieked.

Lisette burst into tears. "Stop it!" she shouted.

Skees still couldn't see Jenny, but he could see me, and he could see that something was happening to me. He pushed himself in front of me, shielding me; he raised the gun, but still couldn't see anything to point it at. He looked around, trying to find some visible sign of my attacker.

Mostly, though, he simply blocked me, the back of his head close against my injured cheek. For Jenny to claw me again, she would have to go through Ben Skees.

She didn't. She stopped attacking me; she stepped back –

And she wasn't there anymore.

"She's gone," I said

"She what?" Skees said.

"She's gone," I repeated. "She disappeared." I looked over his shoulder at the girl in the bed. "Are you okay, Lisette?" I called.

"No," she said, between sobs.

"What do you mean, she disappeared?" Skees demanded, as he stepped away from me and tucked his gun away again.

"She disappeared. Vanished. Poof. She's a *ghost*, remember? Or something like one."

"They can do that?" He produced a big white handkerchief from somewhere, like someone in an old movie. Nobody I knew back home still carried one, but apparently in Kentucky the plainclothes cops did.

"Yeah, I guess they can," I said, accepting the handkerchief. I pressed it to my injured face. "I didn't know that before."

I hadn't known that Jenny could hurt me like that, either.

"So is she gone for good?" Skees asked.

"I very much doubt it." Then I pushed past him to the bedside. "I'm sorry, Lisette. Is there anything we can do?"

She swallowed a sob and looked up at me. "You're bleeding," she said.

"I am?" I took the handkerchief from my cheek and looked at it.

It was soaked in blood. Not just a few streaks; soaked.

"She's definitely getting stronger," I said.

That was when the nurse showed up.

Chapter Twenty

It took about half an hour to straighten things out. Hospital security was pretty antsy after the McPhee boy's death, and finding me and Detective Skees in a room with a crying kid did not exactly look like business as usual, especially not with half my face scratched raw. A police badge helped, but it still took a few calls before they decided not to cuff us and call the cops – *other* cops.

They did patch up my face. I got a quick look in a mirror before the bandages went on, and wished I hadn't; it looked like hamburger. Which is a cliché, but it was also true.

Or maybe it was more like cube steak. Nasty, either way.

Finally, though, we were back in Skees' car, and he was giving me a lift back to my motel room – my rental car was still in the hotel garage, but I was too exhausted to drive. I could pick it up in the morning; if that didn't work, worst case scenario was that I would turn in the keys and tell the rental company where I left it.

Except my phone was still in it; I'd called Mel on Skees' cell, not my own. Well, I told myself I'd retrieve it later.

"You chased it away," Skees said suddenly, as we slowed to a stop at a light.

"What?" I'd been thinking about cars and phones, not child-eating monsters.

"You chased the ghost away,." he said.

"I think it was Lisette's crying more than anything I did," I said. "Or you shielding me."

"Whatever. It's gone."

"She'll be back," I said. "I didn't hurt her."

"Yeah, but you drove it off. That means you can do it again."

"No, it doesn't," I said. "I got lucky – Lisette Babcock's a tough kid who actually listened to me. And we found them before Jenny had had time to really get her hooks in. And Jenny's getting stronger." I reached up to touch the bandages – one thing about getting hurt in a hospital, you get thoroughly patched up. "Next time she might tear my head off."

I wished I didn't mean that literally.

Skees didn't argue with that. "But you talked Lisette out of cooperating. We couldn't do that with Jack."

"She'd had months to talk Jack around," I said. "Lisette, she'd only had hours. If that."

"So if we find its victims soon enough, we can talk them out of danger."

"Maybe," I said. "For now. But the ghoul's a lot stronger than it used to be, and it may be getting even tougher. It may not need its victims' cooperation much longer."

"Still, you can keep it at bay for awhile, right?"

"Maybe. If I can find it."

"How'd you find it tonight? You seemed to know which way to go – you stood there talking to yourself for a bit, then you went straight to it. How did you do that?"

"I asked another ghost," I said.

Skees didn't answer that right away; he focused on his driving as we drove past the closed, dark shops on North Limestone, heading out toward the motel.

Then he said, "There were other ghosts there?"

"Yes," I said.

"You hadn't mentioned that before."

"You hadn't asked."

"Seems like you might have *volunteered* that little tidbit."

"Why? I see these night creatures all over the place, Detective; I told you that. There's nothing special about the hospital one way or the other on that."

"Okay, fine. You talked to this one, and it told you where to find Jenny?"

"It pointed. I don't think it could talk."

"But it understood you."

"Oh, sure! Lots of them understand English, even if they don't say anything."

Skees was silent again, for about four blocks.

"Is there any reason you can't learn all *kinds* of useful things with these talents of yours?" he asked at last.

"I don't know," I said.

"Could you find Jenny again the same way?"

"I don't know," I said again.

After that he was quiet for the rest of the drive, but at the motel, as I was climbing out of the car, he turned and said, "You should stick around. I'll pay you out of the informant fund to play ghost-hunter, and to find Jenny and shoo her away regularly."

"Pay how much?" I asked; I was always tempted by the prospect of money. Then I waved my hand. "No, what am I thinking? I'm not staying around here, I'm going back to Maryland."

"Why? You didn't seem to care much about your job there."

"It's my home," I said. "I have friends and family there."

"You see them often?"

"Not often enough," I said warily. "Not as often as I see those night-things around the place. That's not the point. Maryland's my home."

"This wouldn't be forever," he said. "Just until Jenny gives up. Or until the money runs out."

"She may *never* give up," I said. "She's not human. She's more or less a walking obsession."

"Then make her walk away, and be obsessed somewhere else."

I shook my head. "I can't make her do anything. It was that little girl who chased her away." I hesitated, and then added, "And other kids might not *want* to chase her away, even if they knew what she's after. Jack took her to the hospital because he thought there were kids there who were going to die anyway, right? Well, some of them *are*. Some of them are in pain and scared and might just want it to be *over*, and if they didn't actually see what she did to the McPhee kid, getting eaten might seem better than dying slowly from cancer or whatever other horrible disease they might have. In fact, I'm not sure it *isn't* better."

Skees was silent for a moment after that, until we turned into the hotel parking lot.

"It's feeding a monster," he said.

"Yeah," I said. "I know. But if it stays a monster that *only* eats volunteers..."

"It's still a monster."

"I know."

He stopped the car, and I got out. "Good night, Detective," I said.

The night clerk looked up as I walked through the lobby, and tried not to stare at the bandages on my face. I ignored her.

When I got to my room I thought for a moment about calling Mel again, since I knew she'd still be up, then remembered I'd have to use the room phone – mine was still in the rental car. "Screw it," I said, and fell onto the bed.

I was awakened by the phone ringing.

I frowned, half-awake and still muzzy, and picked up the receiver. I made a noise that didn't resemble "Hello" as much as I'd hoped it would.

"Mr. Kraft?"

It was Skees. I glanced at the window and saw daylight, plenty of daylight, so I knew he wasn't calling to take me ghost-hunting. "What?" I said.

"You need to get your phone back."

"What?" I said again, but this time not sounding annoyed at being awakened so much as baffled.

"Your friend, Ms. de Cheverley, tried to call you last night. Several times. When you didn't answer, she got worried and called me, instead."

"Oh," I said. That couldn't have been much fun. Talking to Mel when she's happy is bad enough; if she's angry or upset it's a nightmare, almost literally. "Sorry."

"I promised her you were fine, and would call her as soon as possible. Please don't make a liar out of me."

I turned over and looked at the clock – 9:30. "I won't," I said. "But I can't call her this early. She won't be up."

"I think she might," Skees said. "She's on her way here. Said she would drive all night."

"Oh, crap," I said. I sat up.

Mel likes fast cars. She could probably make that drive a lot more quickly than Skees realized. "Does she know where I am?"

"Yeah, I gave her the name of the hotel." Before I could ask the obvious next question, he continued, "I said you could use some sleep."

"Thanks." I ran a hand through my hair, wondering how long I had before she showed up, and just how much chaos would follow her arrival. I hoped she hadn't hurt anyone on the drive from Maryland; her presence tended to make people in nearby vehicles swerve or slam on the brakes in panic. That was why she mostly drove late at night, when there were fewer cars on the road and she could keep her distance.

It struck me that Skees had actually dared to tell Mel something she probably didn't want to hear. The man had nerve. I mean, *I* could do that, but I was Mel's friend, and I'd been dealing with the curse for eight years; I had experience. Skees didn't.

"I can send a man to drive you to the hospital garage," Skees said.

"No, don't bother," I said. My guess was that by the time I could get my phone, Mel would be at the motel looking for me, and I didn't want to keep her waiting. "Thanks anyway. I'll get there on my own."

"I wouldn't put it off."

"I won't. Thanks."

"You wanted to talk to Jack Wilson today, right?"

"If I can, yeah."

"I'll arrange it. Get your phone back, and I'll be in touch."

"Thanks."

He broke the connection, and I hung up.

I sat staring at the phone for a moment, then shuddered and headed for the shower.

I managed to get showered, more or less shaved, and dressed, and was about to head down to the lobby when the phone rang again. I answered it, bracing myself, expecting to hear Mel's voice.

I didn't. "Mr. Kraft? This is the front desk. There's a lady here to see you."

I could hear who it was in the clerk's tone – he was obviously struggling to sound professional, and not quite managing it. "Tell her I'll be right down," I said, and hung up. No point in delaying. I grabbed my room key and headed out.

When I stepped out of the elevator the scene in the lobby was not as bad as I'd anticipated. The front desk was deserted, the couches empty; the only person in sight was Mel.

Melisandra de Cheverley was standing in the middle of the lobby, waiting for me – and if you've never met her, you have no idea how ominous that really was, knowing she was there for *me*. The waves of dread radiating from her were almost tangible, like bands of shadow washing across the room.

She was wearing an ankle-length black dress, as usual; this one had a velvet bodice, laced up corset-fashion, and the full skirt appeared to be silk. Her curling, waist-length brown hair was pulled back in a ponytail to reveal glittering diamond earrings. A black leather shoulder-purse hung below her left arm. She had gone relatively light on the make-up, just a little blue eyeliner, and was not wearing any jewelry beyond the earrings, one ring, and her Rolex. Her skin was even paler than I remembered; her nocturnal habits probably had a lot to do with that.

This was her traveling clothes, not her full Queen of Despair regalia, but even so, it should have looked completely out of place in the sunny hotel lobby.

It didn't. Instead she made the sunlight look out of place. Although I knew nothing had actually physically changed, the lobby seemed to reshape itself around her, going from a bland business environment to an emotional wasteland, a concrete and plastic death chamber, with her at its center, like a spider in her web.

Where other people with psychic talents seemed to be somehow detached from the world around them, Mel's essence was soaking out of her into her surroundings, making them part of *her*.

"Hi," I said.

She had been smiling when I stepped from the elevator, but the smile vanished. "Greg! My God, what happened to your face?" She started toward me.

I jerked back involuntarily. "It looks worse than it is," I said. It came out as a hoarse whisper. I had wanted to say something about over-enthusiastic hospital personnel, and the ravages my morning shower had inflicted on the bandages, but the words caught in my throat.

Her hand reached out, and I backed up against the elevator doors as she touched the bandages. "This ghost-woman did that?"

"Yes," I breathed, trying not to tremble.

"I didn't think they could hurt you."

"Neither did I."

"Greg, don't panic. Please."

That was all the warning she gave me before she threw her arms around me and hugged me.

I don't think I've ever been so scared in my life. Part of me, the rational part, knew I was perfectly safe, standing in the lobby of a cheap hotel while a friend embraced me, but a deeper, more visceral part *knew* that I was dying, that death incarnate had come for me and wrapped her arms around me to suck the life out of me, to devour my soul.

My eyes widened, my mouth opened, and my breath stopped, but I didn't scream or faint; I tried to hug her back, my arms shaking as they encircled her shoulders.

"I don't want to lose you," she said, as she pressed her head against my chest. Her hair was warm and soft and reminded me of blood and burnt flesh; the pressure of her arms seemed about to crush me. She smelled of death and horror; the scent of her shampoo was like embalming fluid. "You're all I have left," she said.

I couldn't answer. Even if I had been able to breathe, I couldn't find words.

I knew what she meant; I was the only one who still treated her as the person she used to be instead of the thing she had become. She had a big house, a nice car, plenty of money, political connections, all of them acquired through what amounted to extortion, but except for me she had no friends, only victims. Her family wouldn't talk to her. Her parents had disowned her, and her sister was terrified of her – she claimed to think that Mel was involved in organized crime.

They didn't believe in curses. Even when they saw what had become of her, they were convinced that Mel had changed on her own, that it was her behavior that made her so frightening.

At least, that was what they said.

Mel's other old friends hadn't needed to make up excuses; they just said she'd changed, and they'd moved on.

I couldn't do that. I knew the curse was real. I knew what Mrs. Reinholt had done to Mel, and to me. And I had always liked her.

But that didn't make it easy to be embraced by fear in human form, by a walking incarnation of death and despair.

She released me and stepped back, then looked at my face. She had been smiling again, but the smile vanished.

I don't know exactly what she saw, but it wasn't just the bandages. Something must have shown in my eyes, or perhaps I had gone pale. The skin of my face felt as if it were stretched impossibly tight over my jaw and cheekbones.

"I'm sorry," she said.

"Don't be," I said, forcing the words out. "Not your fault."

"Of course it is. I didn't need to hug you." Her voice turned bitter, and I didn't think it was the curse. "I didn't need to come at all."

"I'm glad you did," I lied.

"It's sweet of you to say so," she said. She reached into her purse and pulled out a brown prescription bottle. "Here," she said. "Xanax. I'm told it helps."

I didn't bother asking how she'd gotten it. I accepted the bottle, but I put it in my pocket without opening it.

"I can manage," I said.

"Well, we'll see," she replied. "Come on, let's give these people their hotel back. I want you to show me where this killer ghost hangs out."

I nodded, and followed her out to her car.

It was unbelievably tempting to turn and run, flee back to my room, do whatever it took to get away from her; the thought of being closed up in a car with her was so terrifying I was afraid I'd be sick. I couldn't do that, though, not to Mel.

I was all she had left.

Chapter Twenty-One

Mel drove while I played navigator, and I gave her the grand tour of the Wilsons' neighborhood, including the big tulip poplar, and of the area around the U.K. Health Center.

Surprisingly, it wasn't all that bad riding with her. Being that close for that long, it wasn't possible to stay panicky; instead it settled into dread and despair, and with a little practice I was able to turn that into something like resignation and keep my fear under control – it never went away, didn't really decrease, but I could accept it. I just sat there in a state of abject quivering terror, waiting for it to be over.

I've heard that people who know they're going to die soon sometimes accept it, and become weirdly calm. I think that's what it felt like.

She didn't talk, which helped.

Driving through the city in broad daylight was... interesting. Or it would have been if I'd been capable of coherent thought, anyway; it was interesting in retrospect. Other drivers got out of our way; the cars behind us hung well back. Sudden swerves were common, but always directed away from us, so we were never endangered. The slightest slowing on Mel's part would set brakes squealing behind us. I don't think we caused any actual collisions, but it was close.

We stopped in the hospital garage and got my phone out of the rental car. Mel waited while I checked in with Skees and brought him up to date.

"Good," he said. "We've set up your meeting with Jack."

"Thank you."

"You... Ms. de Cheverley won't be accompanying you, will she?"

I glanced over at Mel, which was like looking into the abyss. "Did you want to meet Jack this afternoon?" I asked her.

She shook her head. "I need some sleep," she said.

I tried not to look relieved. "I don't think so," I said into the phone.

"You'll be talking to him at Youth Services, on Cisco Road."

"Okay, I can find it," I said. I had my GPS. "When do I need to be there?"

"Any time; Jack's schedule is pretty flexible today. He's being evaluated. Again."

"Thanks." I closed the phone and put it away, then turned to Mel. "I'll see you tonight?"

"Oh, indeed you will, dear boy. I'm looking forward to doing some ghost-hunting."

"We may not find it," I warned her.

"It'll be fun to try. I'll give you a call." She waved, and slid back into the BMW.

I watched her go, waited until the lingering sense of dread faded and the wave of trembling had passed, then climbed into the rental and booted up the GPS.

Cisco Road turned out to be fairly close by; I headed down Limestone a couple of blocks, then cut west for a mile or two past the harness track, and it was two left turns away. It was a quiet residential street with a school and a couple of other things mixed in among a bunch of tidy little houses, and one of the things mixed in was the Division of Youth Services.

I'd seen the inside in my dreams, so I was able to find my way around, but it still took awhile to find the right people and get it confirmed that I was allowed to be there. Then I got to wait in a nice non-threatening room, lots of calming colors and soft textures, until Jack finished talking to whoever he was talking to.

Finally, though, I found myself sitting across a small table from him. He looked very small there, and his eye-patch didn't make him look dashing or piratical, just smaller and damaged. His psychic aura, if you want to call it that, was stronger than ever – he looked as if he was about to drop out of our reality entirely.

And I thought I could feel something, as if Jack had begun to radiate his emotions the same way Jenny did. I knew that under his calm, withdrawn appearance he was furiously angry.

"Hello, Jack," I said.

"Hello, Mr. Kraft," he replied warily. "What happened to your face?"

"Got a few scratches. How're you doing?"

He shrugged.

"I don't suppose you've been entirely open with these people."

He grimaced. "Not entirely," he admitted.

"I was wondering whether there was anything you wanted to say that you hadn't been able to tell anyone."

"Like what?"

"Like, about Jenny."

He looked at me silently for a moment, then said, "What about her?"

That rage I sensed in him was closer to the surface now.

"You tell me," I said.

"You saw her."

"Yeah, I did."

"She killed Andrew, she ate his heart, and it didn't bring her back to life." The anger was beginning to leak into his voice now.

"She was never alive to begin with, Jack," I said, as calmly as I could. I probably sounded like every annoying, superior adult he'd ever dealt with, but I couldn't think of a better way to get through to him. "She's not really a ghost at all, she's... I don't know, something else. But the real Jenny Derdiarian is still alive; so are her kids. They live in Clark County. The Jenny you know isn't a ghost; she was never human in the first place."

"Seriously?" He looked me in the eye.

I met his look straight on. "Yeah, seriously."

"So she lied about *everything*." His gaze dropped, and he stared with his one good eye at his hands, folded on the table, and at the scar tissue where his missing finger used to be.

"Pretty much, yeah."

"Bitch," he said quietly.

I wasn't going to argue with that assessment.

"What a *bitch*," he said, more emphatically, looking up from his hands, and the rage burst out of him. There was no longer any question that he was radiating his emotions on some psychic wavelength that I could feel. "I loved her, I fed her my *own finger*, and it was all *lies*? *All* lies?"

"Yeah." I tried to ignore the waves of fury. Jack was trying to hold in his anger, I could sense that, and I didn't want him to know how much I felt it. I didn't want him to think I was invading his privacy.

"She's not a ghost?"

"If you mean a dead person, then she's not a ghost."

"Can she die, then? If she's not *already* dead, can she die?"

"I don't know," I said.

"I hope she can," he said, and the anger was suddenly controlled again. "I want her dead. I want her *dead*. I keep remembering what she did to Andrew, and wishing I could do that to her."

I had been so attentive to that emotional undercurrent that his words caught me off-guard. I said, "Do what?"

"Rip her to pieces." He spoke through clenched teeth. "Tear her heart out and eat it. Chop off her hand and rip out her throat, the way she did to Andrew."

"You can't," I said. "I do know that much. There may be a way to kill things like her, but you can't do it like that. I've tried stabbing them; I even hit one with a car once. It doesn't hurt them."

"Are you sure? Because I really want to tear her apart. I keep thinking about it, imagining how it would feel." He bared his teeth and flexed his remaining nine fingers. "I know I'm not strong enough to rip apart a real person, but she isn't a real person. Are you sure I can't?"

"Pretty sure," I said. I was also pretty sure that it wasn't healthy for a twelve-year-old kid to be thinking like that, or feeling such anger, but I didn't say so. I was watching him closely, trying to figure out what to say – and why he was so important. Why had I dreamed about him? If it was just because he was going to lead me to Jenny, why hadn't I dreamed about Jenny herself, or about Ben Skees, or Andrew McPhee? Was it just because Jack could see the night-things?

Or did it have something to do with his burgeoning psychic ability? He hadn't been this... this *powerful* before. He hadn't been projecting emotions before.

"You should stay away from her," I added. "She's dangerous."

"She's a good liar," he acknowledged.

"No, I mean she's *dangerous*," I said. I pointed to the bandages. "She was the one who scratched me."

That caught his interest, distracted him from his anger, and he stared at my bloodied, patched face. "I thought she couldn't hurt anyone without permission."

"Maybe she couldn't before, but she can now. At least me. She didn't scratch Detective Skees, but she did a job on my face."

"She did that?" His eyes were fixed on the bandages.

I nodded.

"She said she couldn't eat me or Andrew without our permission."

I shrugged. "Maybe she couldn't. I don't know. But she was the one who clawed me up. I think she used Andrew's hand to do it."

He frowned. "She killed Andrew. He was a good kid, and she killed him."

"Yeah, I know." I hesitated, then said, "But he was really sick, wasn't he? Going to die soon?" I hoped to ease his rage a little by reminding him of extenuating circumstances.

"He said he was," Jack acknowledged. "He was the sickest kid I could find. But he wanted to help her, and she killed him for *nothing*." He looked me in the eye, and it was as if a little bit of Hell was staring at me from behind that black eye-patch. "I want to rip her apart and take my eye back."

"That won't do Andrew any good," I said.

"It'll make *me* feel better."

"Maybe," I said. "Maybe not. These things don't always work out the way we expect."

"Yeah," he said bitterly, looking down at his hands again. "I saw that."

That oddness, that out-of-place look, was definitely much stronger; Jack hardly seemed to be in the same room I was. He was almost glowing now. I didn't know whether that reflected his mental state, whether his anger was fueling it, or whether his psychic abilities, whatever they were, were suddenly blossoming, or whether it was just something about the indirect lighting in that room.

Right now, though, he was less connected to the everyday world than anyone I had seen since high school – since Mrs. Reinholt died.

Maybe that power was what had triggered the dreams. Maybe my theory was wrong, and dreams didn't always mean that the person I dreamed about was going to change my life. Maybe sometimes it just meant I was going to meet someone with really, *really* strong... whatever it was. It's not an aura, in the usual sense, and most of the people who had it didn't consider themselves gifted or psychic; it's just an otherness.

But Jack had more of it now than I'd ever seen in anyone other than Mrs. Reinholt. He'd always had it strongly, but not *this* strongly. I didn't know whether the increase was some side-effect of Andrew's death, or because he'd broken contact with Jenny, or because he was so very angry, but it was unmistakable.

I didn't know what it meant, either. Mrs. Reinholt had been a witch; was Jack growing up to be a warlock? Was he going to do something supernatural, something magical? Was *that* why I was there?

And what *kind* of magic? Right now he seemed more inclined toward black magic than toward bluebirds and fairy dust.

"Bitch," he said again, staring at his fingers. Then he looked up at me. "If you figure out a way to kill her, I hope you use it."

"We'll see," I said.

Then I sat there stupidly, trying to think what else to ask him. Other than Jenny, we didn't have much of anything in common.

"Can you see the other night creatures?" I blurted. "Or just Jenny?"

He grimaced. "I see others sometimes – at least, I guess I still do. After I started talking to Jenny I stopped paying attention to the others. You see them?"

"All the time."

"In the daytime, too?"

"No," I corrected myself. "I meant, I see lots of them every night, but I only see them at night."

He nodded. "Same here, I guess."

"Does anyone else in your family see them?"

"Katie could see Jenny, at least a little, but that's all."

"Any idea why? Why you, I mean?"

He shook his head. "I wondered about that. I don't know."

"You're sure your parents can't see them? I mean, you don't seem to get along with them real well; any chance they were keeping that secret?"

"No." He drew the single syllable out into a derisive little melody. "My parents don't see anything they don't want to see. Jenny stood on our front lawn once, right in front of them, and they never noticed."

I looked at him, trying to think what else I could ask him. This kid was the wild card that might change everything – or might mean nothing; I didn't really know how my dreams worked. Just because the half-dozen previous cycles of dreaming had all been about people who turned my life into something new, that didn't mean this round was.

That *look* he had, though, worried me. *Was* he going to be a warlock? Was he going to curse me, or take away my dreams and visions? Was he going to cure Mel, maybe, so that we could stand to spend more time together?

Somehow, I didn't think we could be that lucky. For all I knew, his appearance meant that he was going to explode. It couldn't hurt to ask, though.

At least, I hoped it couldn't.

"Jack," I said, "have you ever tried to work magic?"

He looked up from his hands and met my two eyes with his one. "You mean other than feeding my friends to that lying bitch?"

"Other than that."

He shook his head. "Not really. I wouldn't know how."

So it was still a mystery. Maybe I could do a little fishing, and see what came up.

"Was there anything you wanted to ask me?" I said.

He considered that for a moment, then shook his head. "Not unless you know how to kill a ghost."

"Is that *all* you care about?"

His head jerked up, and his anger poured from him in waves. "Right now, it is," he said, almost shouting. "She *tricked* me! She betrayed me! You said she was a monster, and you were completely right, and she tried to make *me* into a monster, too. I want her *dead*."

"I don't think she's really alive in the first place, not the way we are," I said.

"Then I want her *destroyed*! Do you know how to do that?"

"No, I don't."

"Then what good are you?" He folded his arms and turned away.

I suppose I could have stayed and tried to coax him into opening up some more, but really, why bother? And his fury was wearing; it frightened me a little. Not in the visceral, unreasoning way Mel's curse did, but in a more cerebral fashion – I couldn't guess what he might do, what he might be capable of. I stood up.

"Thanks for talking to me," I said.

"Thanks for trying to warn me," he said, then added bitterly, "Not that it did any good."

"You were under her spell," I said.

"I was stupid," he muttered.

"You wanted to help."

"I was *stupid*."

I sighed. "Maybe you were. We all are sometimes. Good luck, Jack. Take care of yourself."

"If you find a way to hurt her, will you tell me?"

That caught me off-guard, though it shouldn't have.

I could have just said that I would, but Jack had been lied to enough – he deserved an honest answer, and I wasn't sure what I would do. Letting him avenge himself might be satisfying, but would it be justice? Would it harm Jack, as well as Jenny?

"I don't know," I said. "It depends. We'll see."

"Okay."

And that was that. I left the room and told the social worker I was done.

Chapter Twenty-Two

For the rest of that afternoon I didn't do anything important. I talked to Ben Skees, and drove around Lexington a little, and learned my way around the hospital. I looked in on Lisette Babcock, who was doing just fine, all things considered. She had leukemia – it's the most common childhood cancer – but unlike Andrew McPhee, she was responding well to treatment and was expected to make a full recovery.

I guessed that Jenny hadn't realized that. Jack had done his research in choosing Andrew; Jenny appeared to have targeted Lisette as simply the nearest sick kid staying overnight.

With that information I tried to guess who might be next on Jenny's list. It would have been easier if the staff had been allowed to talk to me, but they took patient confidentiality seriously. Lisette was chattier, but didn't know very much.

Still, I came up with the names and room numbers of four kids I thought looked like possibilities.

Then I got myself dinner at a downtown bar – the first one I looked at was full of U.K. frat rats, but the second I found was quieter, and turned out to serve pretty good food.

I walked around a bit after I ate, then headed back to the hospital. I'd just reached the door when my phone started playing "Money for Nothing." Mel was up and ready to go.

It was a nice evening; I decided to wait for her on the sidewalk on Limestone. I watched the college students walking past, and while I was waiting I called Ben Skees, who said he'd join us.

The three of us were going ghost-hunting.

I wondered whether it would work. Could Mel really use the curse to drive Jenny away for good?

Could I *find* Jenny, so we'd have a chance to test it?

There was also the detail that walking the Queen of Despair through a cancer ward was probably not going to do wonders for the hospital's survival rate. Mel knew the effects she had in theory, she had had plenty of opportunity to observe them, but she had never actually *felt* what it was like to have her around, and I worried that she might underestimate the damage her presence would do.

But the damage Jenny would do was pretty serious, too. If Mel could drive her away, that was worth a little risk.

I'd been standing there perhaps ten minutes when Mel's BMW cruised past; she saw me and waved before heading into the garage.

By the time she emerged to meet me Ben Skees had arrived, as well; he didn't bother with the garage, but parked on a service road, in a space labeled "Emergency Vehicles Only." We shook hands, and then turned as Mel walked up.

She was wearing jeans and a peasant blouse, about as innocuous an outfit as possible, but it didn't help – she still looked like oncoming doom. Behind her the skies seemed to darken, and the street scene turned into a nightmare landscape of concrete, brick, and steel.

How a beautiful young woman who stood maybe five foot three and meant no one any harm could be so threatening was inexplicable, but undeniable.

"Oh, my God," Detective Skees said at the sight of her.

She heard him, of course; she's always had good ears, and once the sun had set the traffic had diminished to practically nothing. She smiled – a smile that would have been harmless, probably even cheerful and appealing, in a photo, but that was a vicious, sardonic thing in person, not because she intended it to be, but because everything about her conjured up terror and despair. "If I were on duty," she said gaily, "I'd say something about your God being no help to you here."

Skees went white. He didn't reply.

She gave him a glance, then turned to me. "Hello, Greg. No hug this time, I promise."

"Hello, Mel." I managed a wretched imitation of an answering smile.

"I take it this is the famous Detective Skees?" She pointed.

"Yes."

"He seems to be at a loss for words. That's one of the more common reactions to meeting me. I prefer it to the ones who babble hysterically, let alone the screamers, but it does make conversation difficult."

Skees started to say something, but couldn't get the words out.

On some level I knew she was teasing him, being playful, at least partly, but neither he nor I could respond in kind in her oppressive presence. "He probably didn't realize how powerful the effect would be in person," I said. It was a struggle for me to say even that much, but I couldn't let the curse win.

"He did pretty well on the phone," Mel said approvingly. "Good for you, Detective." She smiled at him.

I was fairly sure that it was meant kindly, but I also knew it looked as if she was about to tear his throat out with her teeth.

Skees managed a strangled cough.

"So, Greg," she said, turning back to me. "Have you found this ghost you want me to exorcize?"

I shook my head. "Not yet," I said. "But it's been hanging around this hospital, and it preys on sick children. I've got four likely victims to check on." The thought of Jenny roused enough anger, countering the fear, that my voice was steady.

Mel's smile vanished. "You want to bring me near children?"

She didn't put any special emphasis or anger in her words, but she didn't need to. I blinked and stepped back.

"I don't know any other way to get you near Jenny," I said.

"I'm not sure this is a good idea after all." She cast a look at Skees that I hope never to experience directly. "But I'm here, so I guess we might as well give it a shot. How do you want to work it?"

Brakes squealed; Mel ignored it, but Skees and I both threw quick glances at the terrified driver. In my present state of mind I was half-certain that the car in question was about to jump the curb and run us down, and half-convinced that would be a good thing.

"You might as well come in with us," Skees said hoarsely, startling Mel and me. "You're just as dangerous out here."

Mel grimaced. "Words of wisdom," she said. "Have I told you, Greg, that the local police in Sandy Spring tell me there hasn't been a single accident on the road approaching my house since I moved in, but they average about one a week heading away? Seems as if some people are in a big hurry to get off Doctor Bird Road."

"I'm sorry to hear it," I said.

She shrugged. "No deaths, luckily. Just minor injuries. At least so far."

I shuddered. "That's good."

"So, we go in," she said. "Lead the way."

I led the way.

Skees did well enough until we got to the elevator, where he suddenly decided he would take the stairs. I didn't blame him, especially since we were only going up one floor.

I had a friendship to maintain, though, so I rode up with Mel, then led the way to the first kid's room without waiting for Skees.

I didn't worry about whether he could find us; I knew he was bright enough to realize that if he always went in the scariest direction, he'd eventually find Mel.

I glimpsed a couple of night-things here and there in the hallways and open rooms, but I didn't see Jenny. The first kid's room was apparently hosting a little family reunion – both parents were there, and a few other adults who might have been aunts or uncles, or maybe grandparents. I stuck my head in and looked around.

No Jenny. No ghosts or ghoulies.

The man I took for the girl's father turned to glare at me, but the glare turned to something else as Mel came up behind me. "Oh, God," he said. "What is it? Has something gone wrong?"

"No, no," I said. "Wrong room. Sorry if we worried you."

Mel heard me and backed off.

I could tell from her expression that she hated this, hated the effect she was having on sick kids and worried families, so I hurried on. If we kept moving it shouldn't be too bad, I thought.

The second kid was sound asleep. He looked so pitiful, lying there with an IV in his arm; for a moment I thought he might be dead, but then I knew that was the curse again. The kid was breathing; he was fine.

There were no visitors there, supernatural or otherwise. We moved on as the boy started to whimper in his sleep.

"Nightmares?" I murmured.

"Every time," Mel replied.

I nodded, and we moved on to Number Three.

Skees had caught up to us by this time, but he was watching from a relatively safe distance. I waved to him as I pushed open the unlocked door of my third candidate's room.

I heard voices, and expected to see another family group, but when I peered around the door, I only saw the kid sitting up in bed – and Jenny. She was standing at the bedside. Her dress was white again, the last trace of Andrew's blood faded away. She turned as the opening door let in light from the hall.

Go away, she said the instant she recognized me, and I could feel bitter anger.

I glanced at my list to be sure I had the name right, then said, "Trevor Atwater?"

"Yes?" The kid looked scared. He was maybe nine years old. He looked a little pale and sickly, but nowhere near death's door.

"Hi. We're going to be doing something in here in a moment, and it's probably going to be seriously frightening, but we will *not* hurt you, I promise. Bear with us, please."

"What?"

"This woman you're talking to," I said, pointing at Jenny. "You know she's not a real person, right?"

"I don't know what you're talking about," Trevor said, with an uncertain glance in Jenny's general direction. I suddenly realized he couldn't see her clearly.

Go away! Jenny repeated, more strongly this time.

I turned to my companions in the hallway. "Detective," I called, "we may need you to make a quick snatch and grab to get the kid out. And Mel, she's here; get your mojo ready."

"It's always ready, Greg," she said. "You know that." The faint note of annoyance in her voice made my stomach clench and my hands tremble, but I ignored it and glared at Jenny as Mel stepped into the room.

"What's..." Trevor began as he saw someone at the door. Then he got a look at Mel and burst into tears.

Jenny looked at him, at his uncontrollable sobbing, then turned to glare at Mel and me. *Leave me alone!*

"Leave these kids alone," I retorted

"Where is she?" Mel asked.

I pointed. "Right there by the bed," I said.

There was a pause that I suppose was Mel looking for Jenny; I didn't turn, didn't look at Mel, because I knew that if I looked at her I might start blubbering as badly as Trevor. Then Mel spoke.

"Begone, unclean spirit!" she said, and she put everything she had into it. I felt my knees weaken, and Trevor screamed in terror. "Leave this place, and do not return. You are not welcome here."

Trevor, it's all right. I'm here. I'll save you. The anger was gone, replaced by concern.

If she was even slightly troubled by Mel's presence, she hid it well. She was obviously far more distressed by Trevor's tears than by Mel's little act.

"Jenny Derdiarian, I cast you out!"

Don't pay them any attention. I'm not going anywhere. Her voice, if you can call it that, was completely calm.

Trevor had stopped wailing, and was instead whimpering, his eyes shut tight and tears squeezing out. His hands were clenched into shaking fists.

"It's not working," I said. "She isn't bothered."

"You're sure?" Mel asked.

"Yes."

"Well, isn't *that* a bitch," Mel said, and this time I didn't think I was imagining the anger. "I finally find someone who isn't scared of me, and I can't see or hear her."

I laughed nervously, as much to keep from screaming or crying as because I thought she was being funny. "Jenny," I said, "get out of here."

I love you, Trevor. Don't let them lie to you.

"She doesn't love you," I said. "She wants to *eat* you. She wants to rip out your heart and eat it."

"Go 'way!" Trevor managed to say through his tears.

I started to tell Mel to back off, let the kid recover, but she had anticipated me; I could feel the fear fading, and light spilled in from the hallway unobstructed.

"She doesn't love you, Trevor. She's a monster."

"Who are *you*?" he demanded. "What happened to your face?"

"My name's Greg Kraft," I told him. "I'm... I'm a psychic, here to protect you. And that thing that calls itself Jenny clawed up my face."

"Who was... what..." He glanced in the direction of the door.

"That was Melisandra de Cheverley," I said. "We thought she might be able to chase away the monster."

Trevor whimpered and wiped snot from his nose with the back of his hand. "What *is* she?"

I grimaced. "That's hard to explain. I know she's scary, but honestly, she'd never hurt you."

He looked at me in disbelief. "How do you *know*?"

"We went to school together."

You should go. Now. The concern was starting to fade back to anger.

I ignored Jenny, and spoke only to Trevor. "Listen, I'm really sorry we frightened you, but we were trying to help. You know how chemotherapy works, right?"

"What?"

"Chemo. You have leukemia; someone must have explained this. Chemo is poison, but if you're lucky, it's poison that kills the cancer faster than it kills *you*, right?"

He looked worried – not from the after-effects of Mel's visit, but a new and different worry. "That's not... they didn't explain it that way."

"Oh." I hoped I hadn't just made everything worse. "Well, that's more or less the idea. We were trying to use Ms. De Cheverley like chemotherapy. We knew she'd scare you, but we were hoping she would scare the monster even more, and drive it away."

You can't scare me, Jenny said. *I love Trevor, and I won't leave him.*

I glanced at her, then back to the kid. "Can you hear her?" I asked. "Or see her?"

"I... go away."

I shook my head. "Not quite yet. Can you see her?"

"Sort of. It's like... like she's a reflection, or something. Or standing in the dark, like there was a spotlight on her that made her darker instead of lighter."

I thought that was a pretty interesting description.

I'm right here, Trev. You can see me if you try.

"I don't hear her, but I know what she said anyway."

I nodded. "Yeah, it's like that for me, too. I can see her just as if she were real, but her voice is like that for me. Have you ever seen any other... things like her?"

"You mean ghosts? No."

"Not ghosts. She's not a ghost."

I am.

"She isn't?"

"No. She says she is, but she's not. She's more like a demon. She's just pretending to be a ghost to make you trust her. The real Jenny Derdiarian is alive and well. It's like identity theft – this thing stole her name."

What? I am Jenny Derdiarian! I could feel her outrage.

I glared at her. "No, you aren't." I turned back to Trevor. "Look, I'm really sorry about all this. This thing is a monster that eats children, but it's not strong enough yet to eat anyone who resists, so it's come here to this hospital because it thinks that some of the kids here are so sick they'd rather been eaten than die slowly from their cancer. But it can't tell how sick you really are; it doesn't know any more than anyone else, and less than your doctors. Don't let it fool you."

Don't listen to him!

"I don't – " He looked uncertain. "How do you know?"

"I've been following it and doing research since mid-August," I told him. A shadow caught my eye, and I turned to see Ben Skees standing in the doorway listening. I ignored him and stepped closer to the bed. "It spent a long time trying to get a boy named Jack Wilson, and bit off one of his fingers, but he wouldn't let it kill him. When it gave up on Jack, it went after a boy named Andrew McPhee, here in the hospital, and it killed him."

"I heard about Andy," Trevor whispered.

"It killed him. Tore him apart."

I loved him! I spared him pain.

"It tried to get Lisette Babcock, but she chased it away. That was when it did this." I pointed to the bandages.

You had no right!

"Now it's after you. We were hoping Ms. de Cheverley could chase it away for good, and that didn't work, but *you* can chase it away, and keep it from bothering you. Just tell it to leave you alone."

I love you, Trevor. Please.

"Go away," he said. "*All* of you."

Trevor, please.

"Go away!"

I said, "I'm going – but see this guy in the door? He's a cop, Detective Skees. If you need help, if the monster won't leave, or if it comes back, you can get someone to call him. He knows what's going on, and he'll believe you. Detective Skees, okay?" I paused, hoping he would nod or say something, but when he didn't I said, "Goodbye, Trevor. You take care. Don't let it get to you."

I'll stay with you, Jenny said. *I love you.*

"Go away! You, too!"

I love you. Don't listen to them.

"Get out!" He started crying again. I didn't blame him; I felt like crying myself, and I was a healthy adult, not a sick kid.

Please, I love you...

He wasn't listening.

I turned, and joined Ben Skees in the corridor.

Chapter Twenty-Three

I didn't see Mel. Skees noticed me looking around, and said, "She went out to the garage, where she wouldn't upset as many people."

I nodded. "I'm sorry it didn't work," I said.

He grimaced. "Thanks for not adding 'I told you so.'"

I shrugged. "It wasn't a bad idea."

"She gave it a good try. Thank her for me."

I nodded.

"Is it still in there?"

I started to say yes, but then Jenny was there in the hallway with us, glaring at me with her one bright eye and her one dark one. Her anger was like sunburn on my face.

You lied to him, she said.

"I did not," I retorted. I looked at Skees. "She's here."

You lied. You said I wasn't Jenny Derdiarian.

"You aren't. You're just an obsession she used to have, one she got over but that took on a life of its own."

I am Jenny. I killed my babies, I starved them to death.

"Jenny's kids are alive and well. I met Jason."

Jason is dead!

"Jason's fine."

He's dead! I loved him, so he's dead!

"What are you talking about?" Skees asked.

"She's claiming to be Jenny Derdiarian."

"Didn't she always?"

"Yeah, but she says I lied to Trevor."

You did lie.

"I did not!"

I'm Jenny. I know I am.

"No, you aren't. You're a thing – not human, not a ghost, just a thing that stole an unhappy piece of Jenny's imagination."

No! She came at me, claws outstretched, and I backed away – I had a suspicion she could scratch me right through the bandages.

I'm Jenny!

Skees stepped between us. He couldn't see Jenny, but he must have guessed, from the way I moved, what was happening.

She stopped, and spat at him like a cat; he didn't hear it, didn't see it. He just stood there, and I pressed up behind him, grateful for his presence.

Jenny glared at me with her mismatched eyes, then turned away.

And she was gone.

"Wow," I said, a little unsteadily, stepping away from Skees. "She really doesn't like being reminded she isn't what she claims to be."

"Maybe we can use that," Skees said, turning around.

I looked at him. "You mean bring her face to face with the original Jenny Derdiarian?"

"Yeah, that's what I was thinking."

I considered that for a moment. I'd wondered about the possibility myself. We didn't really know what it would accomplish, if anything – there were a lot of unknowns involved. It *might* do some good, though. It might dislodge the false Jenny's obsessions with dead children.

I was still thinking when Skees said, "You know, this whole thing – it *looks* like a fake."

"What?"

"You and the ghost. To me, it looks like you're arguing with empty air. I don't see a thing, not a goddam flicker, not a shadow, nothing. *You* say you see it, and the kids say *they* do, but I can't see anything at all. I tried squinting, or looking out of the corner of my eye – nothing." He shook his head. "It's hard to believe. And if it wasn't biting pieces off kids, I *wouldn't* believe it."

"I don't blame you," I said. "I wish I didn't *have* to believe it." I touched the bandages. "By the way, thank you – she was coming at me again when you got between us."

"You're welcome." Skees looked at his watch. "It's only about nine," he said. "Think you can find this thing again tonight?"

"I don't know," I said. "Why?"

"I was wondering about getting the Derdiarian woman here tonight."

"Seems a little late. It's a half-hour drive from Winchester."

"At least. But it might be worth asking."

I shrugged. "I guess."

"You've got her number, and she knows you – think you could talk to her?"

"I guess," I said again.

We found a quiet corner of the waiting area by the nurses' station, and I called. I didn't really know what to tell her; I mean, how do you invite someone to help hunt her own ghost? I reminded her of what we'd talked about, fumbled around a little, then said, "Here, I think Detective Skees would like to talk to you." I handed him the phone.

He gave me a dirty look as he accepted it, then said, "Ms. Derdiarian? Yes, I'm Detective Benjamin Skees, with the Lexington-Fayette police department. I realize it's late, and that you aren't directly involved in this, but we have evidence that someone here is pretending to be you, and we think it might be helpful if you could come out here and confirm your identity, maybe talk to a few people about it."

I didn't hear her answer, but Skees answered, "It'd be a big help if you could come *tonight*, ma'am."

A brief pause, and then, "You can bring your husband if you like, ma'am, or anyone else you want; it's entirely up to you. In fact, the imposter's been saying a few things – it might be good if you could bring your kids."

He listened.

"No, ma'am, this isn't an official request," he continued. "I don't have the authority to make one even if I wanted to, what with you being in Clark County and not Fayette. You aren't in any sort of trouble at all, and we don't have any legal basis for calling you a witness, so it's just a friendly request, completely unofficial."

That got a quick answer, apparently.

"Thank you, ma'am. We're at the University of Kentucky Health Center, the Chandler Hospital on South Limestone. You can't miss it. I'll be waiting for you out front. In plainclothes."

She must have had more to say, because he didn't say another word for a few minutes, just made occasional noises of agreement. Finally, though, he snapped the phone shut and handed it back.

"Thanks," he said. "She'll be here in an hour, give or take."

"Is she bringing her family?"

"Maybe her husband. She wasn't sure. No kids."

I nodded. "I'll look around, see if I can find ghost-Jenny," I said. "And this time I won't chase her off."

"Right." He indicated his own phone. "I'll call you when she gets here."

I nodded, and we split up.

I didn't start looking for Jenny right away, though; first I called Mel.

After greetings and mutual assurances that Jenny hadn't hurt either of us, Mel said, "That was weird."

"What?" I couldn't help envisioning various horrors that might prompt that reaction.

"Trying to exorcize a ghost I couldn't see. She was really there?"

"Oh, she was there, all right." I shuddered.

"I couldn't see a thing."

"She was there."

"I believe you. But she wasn't scared of me?" She sounded almost wistful.

"Not at all."

"Would've been nice to get some use out of this damned curse. I mean, besides the stuff I do all the time."

"Yeah," I said. "At least you can use yours to make a living."

"If you call this living. So, now what? Want to go out on the town?"

"No." I stopped and swallowed; it never felt good to refuse Mel anything. Then I explained, "Skees has something else he wants to try. He wants to see how ghost-Jenny reacts to meeting real Jenny."

"Oh, interesting idea! But why should she do anything special?"

"She won't admit she isn't really Jenny's ghost. We're hoping seeing Jenny alive will shatter her conviction, and maybe that will break her obsession with killing children."

"Maybe live Jenny will re-absorb ghost Jenny."

I hadn't thought of that. "Maybe," I said.

"Can I help? Or at least watch?"

"I don't think so," I said, with a very uncomfortable mixture of reluctance and relief. "It wouldn't be fair to live Jenny."

"Yeah, that's true. Not that life is fair, but why make it worse, right? I'll stay clear."

"Thank you. I'm sorry, Mel."

"Take care, Greg." Then she cut the connection.

I closed my phone, put it in my pocket, then turned and started the hunt for Jenny. I was fairly sure she would still be around. I still had my original list of four names, and they were still good, so I decided to start with those.

She wasn't in the fourth kid's room – at least, I didn't find any trace of her. I went back to the room with the whole family, and found that the gathering had broken up; only the parents and the patient were still there. The patient was sound asleep; her parents were over by the wall, whispering to each other. They stopped to stare at me when I stuck my head in.

I ignored them and looked for Jenny. I didn't see her.

The parents were glaring at me. "May I help you?" the father asked.

"Lost my phone," I said. "Any chance I left it in here?"

They, too, glanced around.

"Don't see it," he said.

"Thanks anyway," I said. "If you come across it, give it to the nurses' station, would you? Thanks."

Then I popped back out and tried Door Number Two again, where the kid was still asleep. Not easily troubled, that one.

I hesitated after that, unsure what to do next, but I decided to take a quick look in Trevor's to room, see if he had any suggestions.

He was there, propped up in bed – and so was she. The ghost-creature was back. They had both turned to stare at the sound of the door.

Go away, she demanded.

"I'll go when I'm good and ready," I said. "What have you been telling this kid?"

Go away!

Apparently she had decided the time for courtesy was past.

"It's not your room," I retorted.

"It's mine," Trevor said. "She can stay if she wants."

"That's up to you."

He didn't look as sure of himself as his words implied. "It is?"

"Sure. It's your room, and as I said before, we don't think she can hurt you unless you let her."

"But you... you brought that scary lady to chase her away."

"Yeah, we did, and we'd rather she did go away, for good. She eats kids. She killed Andy McPhee. Not everyone is strong enough to resist her; she can be pretty persuasive. We don't think that's someone who should be hanging around hospitals, and if we had a way to make her go away forever, we'd use it. But we don't, so as long as she's going to be around here, your room's as good a place for her as any."

He gave her a nervous look. "She really *ate* him?"

"Part of him."

I loved him. He was in pain.

"Is that true?"

I shrugged. "I wouldn't know. I didn't get a chance to talk to him." I looked from Jenny to Trevor and back. "So she came back, and you let her?"

He looked scared, as if he expected me to be furious with him. "Yes," he said. "She said you'd lied, that she loved me and wanted to help."

"I don't *think* I told you anything that wasn't true," I said.

You lied! Go away!

"Are we back to that again?"

"He can stay," Trevor told her. "At least for now."

"Thank you."

Trev, I love you. He doesn't. I just want to make the pain stop.

"I'm not in any pain right now," Trevor told her.

Judging by his expression that wasn't completely true, but it was good enough. *I'll be here when you're ready*, she said.

"Good," I said. "I'd be glad if you hung around, Jenny. In fact, there's someone I'd like you to meet."

Trevor, who hadn't exactly been heavily tanned to begin with, went pale. "Another one? Like that lady?" he whispered.

"No," I reassured him quickly. "Not like her. Not scary. Just someone I met recently who knows Jenny very well."

"Really? Who is it?"

I glanced at the monster. "I'd like it to be a surprise."

Jack. It must be Jack.

"Maybe."

"Who's Jack?"

"The boy who brought her to the hospital," I explained. "He lives near her old home. They've known each other for months."

He didn't love me. He said he did, but he didn't.

"That means he wouldn't let her eat him," I explained to Trevor. "Or not all of him, anyway; she did eat a finger and an eye." I pointed to her face. "I don't know if you can see it, but her eyes don't match, and that's because one of them was Jack's."

"She... she ate his *eye?*"

I nodded. "The left one."

I was so hungry, and he loved me so much! But then he stopped loving me, and I came here instead.

"That's one way of looking at it, I suppose."

Trevor did not appear happy as he glanced back and forth between Jenny and me. I wondered which of us looked scarier, with my face covered in bloody bandages.

"You'll notice she's not denying it," I said, after a moment.

Trevor turned away from us both. I thought he might be crying, or struggling not to.

Trevor, I love you. She moved closer and leaned over him, her long hair draping across his shoulder.

"I don't go around telling kids I barely know that I love them," I said, "but I don't mean you any harm. I'm here because we're worried about what Jenny might do, to you and other kids, and we're trying to find a way to get rid of her."

Trevor buried his face in his pillow, then raised it just enough to say, "You brought the scary lady here."

"Yes, we did," I agreed. "Madame de Cheverley is an old friend of mine, and she's very, very scary. We thought maybe she could scare Jenny into going away forever. It didn't work. I'm sorry."

"She scared *me*."

"Of course. She scares *me*, and I'm her best friend. She scares *everybody*. I think the fact that she *didn't* scare Jenny is the best proof I've seen yet that Jenny's not anything remotely human."

I was human once.

"No, you weren't. You just think you were."

I was!

"No. You really weren't."

How can you know? I was! I had a home, and three children...

"Ashley, Sarah, and Jason. I know.

...and I killed them, and became a ghost, and I must wander the Earth until I can make it right by helping other children I love.

"Is that really how you think it works?"

She was sitting on the edge of the bed now, stroking Trevor's hair, and had apparently stopped listening to me; she didn't answer.

Trevor didn't, either. For a moment I was afraid she had somehow managed to smother him, but I realized I could see that he was still breathing.

He had fallen asleep.

I could understand that; he was a sick little boy, it was getting late, and he'd had a very busy, exciting day. I didn't see any reason to wake him.

I settled onto a blue-cushioned visitor's chair and smiled at Jenny. "Looks like it's just the two of us for now," I said.

Go away.

I snorted. "I'm not going away. You can't make me go, any more than I can make *you* go." I smiled. "Looks like we're stuck with each other for the moment. Why don't you tell me a little bit about yourself?"

She looked at me suspiciously with those mismatched eyes of hers. *Why?*

"Because I'm curious – and hey, maybe you can convince me to go away and leave you alone after all."

Oh?

"Maybe. So let's get to know each other, shall we? Tell me, how did you die?"

Chapter Twenty-Four

We talked for almost half an hour before my phone finally sang to me. I didn't learn much new, though. The monster had only very vague memories of anything at all about Jenny's actual life – she didn't remember her parents, or her husband, or much of anything other than killing her children, and wanting to eat babies but not being allowed to. She claimed to have died quietly in her sleep under the big tulip poplar, while waiting for the authorities to come and take her away. When she woke up her body was gone, and she was a ghost.

I didn't argue with any of that; she believed it all fervently. I didn't want to anger her; the scratches on my face still stung. I was relieved she'd been willing to talk, instead of going straight to the claws; I guessed it was because she didn't want to look scary in front of Trevor.

I didn't know why she was getting stronger, but she obviously was. Maybe she was feeding off the attention the kids gave her, or maybe it came from the flesh she'd eaten – it had been her left hand, Andrew's hand, that could hurt me, not her original, unaltered right one. She definitely seemed to be getting more solid, more *real*, as she added pieces like that.

Trevor didn't have any innate psychic talent, so far as I could see – he looked like any other kid, very much a part of the real, everyday world, with no trace of that strange not-belonging that Jack and other people who could see the night-things had – but he could hear Jenny, and see her a little. He said he hadn't seen any other supernatural creatures, just her. And Lisette Babcock – well, I hadn't had a chance to talk to her much, and she'd had a faint glimmer of the talent, but I didn't think she was very prone to hauntings, either.

So Jenny was definitely a genuine threat, and I understood why Ben Skees was trying everything he could think of to get rid of her, but I didn't see how any of it could work. Mel hadn't frightened her at all. Trevor had ordered her out of his room, but she had come back. *I* couldn't chase her away anymore.

I didn't think anything human would be able to stop her.

I didn't think she would always need her victim's consent, either.

I understood what Skees had in mind, bringing the real Jenny Derdiarian here; he wanted to convince the monster that it wasn't Jenny, it hadn't starved its children to death, and it had no reason to eat children. I thought this scheme of his was like something from the original "Star Trek," where the brave Captain Kirk would talk an unstoppable killer computer into destroying itself by showing it its own internal contradictions.

And I didn't believe for a minute that it would work. This Jenny-thing wasn't a computer, it was a monster. It didn't need to be logical; eating children because it had killed its own made no logical sense in the first place. There was nothing rational about it; it was a collection of obsessions, not a computer program.

Not that computers actually work anything like they did in old Hollywood shows in the first place.

Still, I didn't see that it was likely to do any harm to get the two Jennys together, and maybe it *would* help somehow. Maybe Jenny would re-absorb her old obsessions – which would kind of suck for her, but at least *she* wouldn't actually eat any kids.

Or if she did, something could be done about it.

I'd thought that through several times by the time Detective Skees called to tell me that he and the real Jenny were on the way in.

I told him where we were, and settled down to wait.

The Jenny monster, meanwhile, was leaning over Trevor, smiling down at him lovingly, her hair brushing against his cheek. She wasn't interested in me, or my phone calls; she was there because Trevor was, and because Trevor had not sent her away permanently. She seemed almost happy – though I could feel a growing hunger.

If we were going to get rid of her, I thought the best way had nothing to do with trying to chase her away ourselves. My advice would be to tell all the kids about her. *All* the kids. If *they* all told her to leave, she would leave.

Well... probably.

The door swung open and Ben Skees looked in. I held a finger to my lips and pointed to the sleeping Trevor.

Skees nodded, and stepped into the room.

Behind him came Jenny Derdiarian, the *real* Jenny Derdiarian, looking around curiously.

"Mr. Kraft," she whispered. Then she looked at Trevor. "Is this your son?"

I shook my head. "Never saw him before today," I whispered back. "But the thing that claims to be your ghost is here." I pointed at the thing leaning over the bed.

Jenny looked around. "Where?" she asked.

I sighed. "Right there by the bed," I said. "You can't see it?" Where the monster had absorbed a part of her I'd thought there might be some connection that would allow her to see it, but apparently that wasn't the case.

"No." She gave Skees a quick look, then stared at the bed, as if she thought that if she stared hard enough, she could see her doppelganger.

"It's there," I told her.

She focused on a spot to one side, not on ghost-Jenny, but I didn't see any point in correcting her. "Now what?" I asked Skees.

"What's the ghost doing?" he said. "How's she reacting?"

"Reacting?" I grimaced. "She's not reacting. She's ignoring us. She's only interested in Trevor."

"What's she doing?"

"She's leaning over the bed, stroking Trevor's cheek," I said. "Not that he can feel it."

"Does she know we're here?"

"Hey, Jenny," I called to the monster.

Go away.

"I thought we were past that. I mean, we've been talking for the last hour."

You'll wake him. Go away.

I glanced at Trevor, who had indeed stirred. "It won't kill him," I said. "Look, there's someone here I want you to meet."

Go away, all of you.

"She knows you're here," I said.

"Has she noticed Ms. Derdiarian?" Skees asked.

"Not that I can see. She's fixated on kids; all her attention's on Trevor."

"Can you get her to *look* at Ms. Derdiarian?"

"Detective, right now she just keeps telling us all to go away. She doesn't *care* about us, not unless we interfere with her contact with the kids. *I* can't get her to do anything."

"What if the kid talked to Ms. Derdiarian?"

"She'd notice *that*," I said.

With that, Skees crossed to the bed and put a hand on Trevor's arm.

The boy's eyes opened, and he made a questioning noise.

"Hey," Skees said gently. "There's someone I'd like you to meet." He turned and beckoned to the real Jenny.

"Who are you?" Trevor asked, looking up at the detective and ignoring the approaching woman.

"My name's Skees. I'm a policeman." He stepped back and gestured for Jenny to take his place. "And this is Jenny Derdiarian."

Trevor blinked up at her for a moment, then snapped his head over to look at ghost-Jenny, then back to the real Jenny.

"You are?" he asked. "I mean, I think... I can't see her very well, and you maybe look a little like her, but you're... you aren't as thin, and your hair's different..." His voice trailed off.

"Not as thin as who?" Jenny asked.

I'm Jenny! the monster insisted.

"As her," Trevor said, pointing. "The ghost."

"I don't see any ghost," Jenny said, looking around.

Trevor stared at her. "She's right there."

"I can't see anyone there."

Trevor looked back and forth between the two Jennys. He looked scared. He pushed himself up into a half-sitting position.

"I don't understand," he said.

I decided it was time I stepped in. "I told you it wasn't a ghost," I said. "It *thinks* it is, because it stole its memories from this woman fifteen years ago, but it's not. She's alive and well."

"Stole her memories?"

No! I'm Jenny. I've always been Jenny. I died fifteen years ago.

"As near as I can tell, yeah," I said. "That whole thing about killing her kids was just something Ms. Derdiarian..." I threw her a quick glance, remembered I was talking to a nine-year-old, and changed the word I was about to use. "...worried about. It never really happened. Her kids are fine. They're all grown up now."

They're gone, lost lost lost, all dead.

"They're alive and well."

"She..." He leaned on one elbow to look at the monster. "She lied?"

No no no. They lie. Not me.

"I think she believes it," I said. "But it's not true."

There's no other Jenny.

"She's right here," I said, pointing at her.

That's just a fat old woman, that's not Jenny, that's not me.

I turned. "Ms. Derdiarian, tell Trevor who you are."

"I'm Jenny Derdiarian," she said. "I'm Ashley's mother, and Sarah's, and Jason's. And they're all healthy and alive. I'd never hurt them."

Lies lies lies.

Trevor stared up at Ms. Derdiarian, then turned to look at the monster.

"Wow," he said. "That's really weird."

"Hey, ghost," Skees said, looking over the monster's head. "You see? You aren't real!"

I'm Jenny, they lie, my poor babies died and I love you, Trevor.

"So if she's not a ghost, what *is* she?"

"We don't know exactly," I said. "A monster of some kind."

"Trevor, is it?" the original Jenny asked.

"Uh huh."

"You really see a... a ghost of me? What does it look like?"

Trevor looked at her, then at the false Jenny. "Well, I can't see her clearly, it's like she's all blurry, but her face looks a lot like yours, only skinnier. Her hair's the same color, but it's long and straight. She's real thin, and she's wearing a white dress that just kind of hangs on her – it's too big for someone so bony."

"She's right there?" She reached out, and the monster flinched back, away from the hand that would have... touched her? Passed through her?

Go away!

"Yeah. You can't see her at all?"

"No."

For a moment, we all paused. Jenny Derdiarian, Ben Skees, and I were standing around the bed, the ghoul was crouching beside it glaring up at us, and Trevor was sitting up, enjoying the attention.

"Well," I said to Skees. "Now what?"

"She's still here? She hasn't... I don't know, faded away?"

"Nope. She's a bit pissed that we're here hassling her, but she's still here, as much as ever. She says we're lying, and that she's the real Jenny, and we should all go away."

Yes! Leave us alone!

"*I* think you're the real one," Trevor told the human Jenny.

"Well, of course I am," Jenny said, startled.

"So where did the other one come from?"

Jenny looked from Trevor to me, then to Ben Skees, then back to Trevor. "It's like Mr. Kraft says," she said. "I used to... to worry about my kids all the time, so much I thought there was something wrong with me. Then one day I sat down under a big tree and took a nap, and when I woke up I wasn't worried any more. I thought God had blessed me, that He'd answered my prayers and taken my worries away, but it seems that somehow all those worries had gone into this... whatever it is that you and Mr. Kraft can see, and we can't." She looked at... well, from my point of view she was looking at the back of the monster's neck, but to her she must have been looking at empty air.

"So your worries just came loose and turned into her?" Trevor asked.

"I suppose maybe they did," Jenny said. "I don't really know." She studied the area where she thought the Jenny-thing was – which was about half the monster, and half empty air. "You know, when I was younger I used to think I saw ghosts sometimes, so I thought maybe I'd be able to see this one, but for me there's nothing there at all. There are just the four of us here. I don't see or hear anything, I don't feel any cold spot or any of the other stuff that they say goes with a haunting. You *really* see her?"

"Yeah," Trevor said, wonderingly. "She's *right there*." He pointed at the false Jenny's face.

The monster stared hungrily at the boy's finger; its mouth opened, and razor-sharp teeth gleamed in the dull fluorescent light.

Trevor snatched his hand back and tucked it under his other arm.

So hungry, the thing moaned. *So very, very hungry. Can't I have a bite, Trevor, honey?*

"No!" he shrieked. "Get away from me!"

"What's it doing?" Skees said, reaching under his jacket. He didn't actually draw a gun, but for a moment I thought he would.

Please please please, I love you so, I love you... It leaned down closer to the boy.

"Don't touch me!"

"It wants to bite off that finger," I said.

"Make it go away!" Trevor said, shrinking down into the bed.

"We can't," I said. "We've been trying to find a way, but we can't. That was why we brought Madame de Cheverley here, and why Ms. Derdirarian is here, but it isn't working. But *you* can send her away, I think."

Don't, please, Trevor, I love you.

"I don't love *you*," he said, on the verge of tears.

Please, I'm so hungry, so hungry!

"No!" He turned and buried his face in his pillow. "Go away!"

Trevor, honey...

"You aren't real! You're just a bunch of worries! *Hungry* worries!"

Please, I love you. I'm the real Jenny.

"If you're real, then talk about something else," Trevor said, his voice muffled by the pillow. "Something besides me or your kids. Tell me what TV shows you like, or where you grew up. You can't, can you?"

I wondered whether maybe he hadn't been as asleep as we thought when Jenny and I were talking.

That doesn't matter – I love you.

"You aren't real. You're *stupid*. Mr. Kraft was right, you're a monster, a *stupid* monster. Go away!"

Trevor, please.

"Go away!" He pulled the pillow over his head.

The monster stared at him for a moment, then glared at me with her mismatched eyes. *You did this*, she said. *You drove him away from me.* Her left hand lashed out, fingers curled into claws.

I tried to duck away, but I wasn't fast enough; I felt her nails scratching me, passing through the bandages as if they weren't there and continuing on across the bridge of my nose. I stepped back, my own hands coming up to protect my face. Skees saw what was happening, but this time he was too far away to intervene. He took a step closer.

But he didn't need to. She was gone.

Chapter Twenty-Five

After a moment of awkward silence, I said, "She's gone. What do you say we get out of here and let Trevor get some sleep?"

"What happened?" Jenny asked. "What happened to your face? You're bleeding!"

"I'll tell you later," I said, dabbing at my nose. "Can we please go?"

"Come on," Skees said.

We went. I paused in the doorway long enough to call, "Good night, Trevor. I'm sorry about all this."

He made a muffled noise from beneath the pillow.

"Come on," Skees said. "Let's get those scratches looked at."

We headed down the hall to the nurses' station, where they took one look at me and got out a bottle of antiseptic and another batch of bandages.

Two minutes later I was sitting on a metal chair while a nurse tended to my wounds and Jenny Derdiarian asked an endless string of questions about what was going on.

"I couldn't see a thing!" she exclaimed.

"I wish *I* couldn't," I said. "Maybe if I couldn't see her, she couldn't scratch me."

"I'm sorry to drag you out here at this hour for nothing, Ms. Derdiarian," Skees said. "I really thought that if she saw you, it would break her pattern somehow."

"I don't think anything's going to break her pattern," I said. "All she *is* is a walking, talking bunch of obsessions. Trevor was right about that – she isn't real, she's just Jenny's worries, gotten out and roaming around loose."

"I would never have really hurt anyone, though!" Jenny protested.

"No, because you're a human being. She isn't. You restrain yourself because you know better; she doesn't." I looked at her. "Could you really see ghosts before you... before she took away your obsessions?"

"I thought so. My parents always said I was imagining it, and my first husband said I was lying, but I really did think I saw them. There was an old woman that used to kneel on the sidewalk..."

"I've seen her," I interrupted. "She's still there."

"But I can't see her! I can't see any of them anymore, not even my *own* ghost."

"They aren't really ghosts," I said. "And maybe you can't see them anymore because she took that, too, along with your obsessions."

Jenny shook her head. "You're probably right," she said. "Honestly, 90% of the time I can't say I miss them."

I looked at her, at how perfectly she fit into her surroundings, how there wasn't the slightest trace of that psychic strangeness, that photoshop effect. Her psychic abilities, if that's what they were, were definitely gone – but they had definitely been real once, or she wouldn't have known about the old woman on the sidewalk.

They had gone when the false Jenny came along and carried away the obsessions with food and children and death.

Or maybe...

I didn't have any evidence, but I had a hypothesis. Maybe the false Jenny *was* her psychic power, thrown out on its own. Maybe she had somehow unconsciously used it to pull the obsessions out of her.

Detective Skees had wanted her pull those obsessions back into herself, and it hadn't worked – the separation was complete, and without her lost talents she couldn't even see her other self.

But if it had been her own psychic abilities that pulled the obsessions out of her in the first place, maybe *other* people's psychic abilities could affect them, as well.

And Jack Wilson's power had reached an intensity where he almost seemed to glow.

"I need to talk to Jack again," I said.

"What? Why?" Skees asked.

"I still don't know why I dreamed about him," I said. That wasn't anything like the complete truth, but it ought to be good enough.

It was.

"I'll see if I can set it up for you," Skees said. "You'll see if you can come up with more ideas for stopping that thing?"

"I'll try," I said, touching my new bandages. "I don't want it running around loose any more than you do."

He nodded.

After that we split up; Skees escorted Jenny Derdiarian back out to her car, and I gave Mel a call. She met me in the garage, and we went out for a drink.

That was not a happy occasion for the bar we chose. Within ten minutes of our arrival every other customer was gone, and the bartender's hands were trembling so much that she spilled half my beer. She didn't *dare* spill any of Mel's screwdriver, but she needed about five minutes to get it to us. If I hadn't been so miserable and frightened just because Mel was there, it would have depressed me.

It *did* depress Mel. We finished our drinks, and I gave her as detailed an account of what had happened in Trevor's room as I could, but after that she wasn't smiling or talking. We paid our tab and got ready to go.

"Listen, Greg," she said as she slid off her barstool. "I'm not doing any good here. I'm going to head home."

"When?" I asked, trying not to sound eager.

"Now," she replied. "Tonight."

"It's a long drive."

"I'll manage."

I tried to think of something intelligent to say, something that wouldn't offend the Dark Lady, but all I could come up with was, "Okay."

"I could give you a lift."

I thought about that. I was tempted. It would save me the airfare and get me home sooner – but it would mean spending several hours in a car with the Queen of Despair. I didn't think I could face that. Staying near her as long as I already had was wearing me out.

Besides, while Mel might be done in Lexington, I wasn't. The Jenny monster was still there, and I was the only adult who could see it. I didn't know what I could do, but I wasn't quite ready to give up and go home yet. It was close – if someone other than Mel had offered me a ride, or if Skees had told me he didn't need me anymore, or that he couldn't pay me, I'd probably have left. But there was no other ride, Skees seemed to want me around, and there was that promise of a little money from the police slush fund.

Further, I still didn't know why I had dreamed about Jack, or what was to become of him, and I wanted to see if he might be able to do something useful with that psychic power of his. I wanted to talk to him again, to at least give it a try.

"Thanks," I said, "but no."

"Don't want to spend that long cooped up with me?" She smiled wryly. "Well, I can't say I blame you."

She *was* depressed, I thought. "I need to stay and talk to Jack Wilson." I didn't want to explain my idea; I was afraid it would sound stupid.

Besides, talking to Mel I was afraid of *everything*.

"Suit yourself," she said, starting toward the door.

I watched her go, and called "Goodbye!" after her.

And that was that. She headed back to Maryland, and I took my rental car back to the motel.

I didn't sleep very well; those scratches hurt, and that kept me awake. Eventually, though, morning came.

I wondered how Trevor was doing. Had he managed to sleep? Had the fake Jenny come back again, to beg him to feed her?

I hoped not.

I got breakfast in the hotel, uninterrupted by any policemen. It was after ten, and I'd worked my way through the local paper, the Herald-Leader, when my phone rang.

I answered, and Skees told me that I could talk to Jack again, but he was home with his parents, so it would be at their house. A social worker would be present.

"That's fine," I said.

"Can you be there around 3:00, then?" he asked.

"Sure," I replied.

I spent the next couple of hours doing nothing much – a little driving, a little reading. When I pulled up in front of the Wilson house at 2:55, Skees was waiting on the front lawn with a woman he introduced as Angie Ballard, from Youth and Family Services.

"I'm afraid I don't really understand why you're here, Mr. Kraft," she said, before we'd even finished shaking hands. She was visibly trying not to stare at my bandaged face.

I glanced at Skees, but he didn't give me any useful cues. "I've taken an interest in Jack, that's all," I said. "I was the one who found him the night he lost his eye."

"We're hoping Mr. Kraft can coax some more information about that out of Jack," Skees said. "It's still an open investigation. Jack seems to trust Mr. Kraft."

"If this is an interrogation, Detective Skees, perhaps a lawyer should be present."

"I'm not a cop," I said, "and it's not an interrogation. I just want to talk to him again, Ms. Ballard. I feel as if there must be some *reason* our paths crossed the way they did – some higher purpose. I'm hoping that Jack can maybe put me on the right track to figure out a little more about that purpose."

She clearly didn't like the idea. She frowned.

It was Skees who spoke, though. "Angie, Jack and his parents have all agreed to let Mr. Kraft have his chat. You'll be there to stop it if anything's out of line."

The frown stayed, but she stepped aside. "Go ahead, then."

I marched up the steps and rang the bell, and Emily Wilson opened the door so quickly that she must have been waiting just inside.

"Hello, Mr. Kraft," she said. She didn't have Angie Ballard's control, and did stare at my bandages.

"Hi, Mrs. Wilson," I said. "How are you? How's Katie?"

That apparently caught her off-guard, that I would ask after Katie rather than Jack. She looked downright astonished, but recovered in a second or two and said, "She's fine, thank you. We're both fine."

"Is she still mad at Jack?"

Emily looked at Angie Ballard and Ben Skees before answering, "A little."

I didn't turn to see their expressions, or whether they'd given her any signals. I just nodded. "I would be, too. May I come in?"

"Sure, come on in." She ushered me in.

The interior was exactly as I'd seen it in my dreams; the door opened into a little foyer at the foot of the stairs, with the undersized living room to the right, and a passageway heading toward the back of the house on the left. I tried not to look as if I'd seen it before as I followed her back to the family room, where Jack was sprawled on the couch in front of the TV, his eye-patch pushed up almost off his ruined socket – he had slid down the upholstery, and the cord that went around his head and held the patch in place had been pulled up against the rough fabric.

I almost stopped dead when I saw him, but managed to keep moving. "Hey, Jack," I said.

He looked up, and his face seemed to shimmer. That psychic aura, or whatever it was, had grown much more intense; he seemed distorted, bright, the colors of his face and hair and hands all strange and wrong. When he moved it almost seemed as if there were lingering after-images. The black eye-patch was like a hole in that vivid face.

I had never seen anything like it. It had intensified visibly in just a day.

And he was still radiating anger.

"Hey," he said. "Did you get scratched up some more?"

"A little," I said. I turned to Emily, and gestured at the chair next to Jack's end of the couch. "May I?"

"Oh, of course! Can I get you something to drink?"

"A soda would be nice," I said. "A Coke, if you have it."

She bustled off to the kitchen, and I sat down. Angie Ballard perched herself carefully on the chair at the other end of the couch, while Ben Skees took up a post by the door, leaning against the frame with his arms folded across his chest.

"You wanted to talk to me?" Jack said.

"Yeah, I did. About Jenny."

He looked up at me, not moving from his comfortable slouch. "Have you figured out some way I can kill the bitch?"

Angie Ballard blinked, startled; I was looking at Jack, but I could see her from the corner of my eye.

"I don't know," I said.

He stared at me. I stared back.

After a moment, he said, "You didn't say no."

"That's right," I acknowledged. "I didn't."

He sat upright, his one good eye fixed on me. "You think you might have a way?"

"Mr. Kraft..." Ballard began.

"Jenny's his imaginary tormentor," I said. "She's invisible. She's not a real person. I'm not planning a murder."

"How do you know that?"

"We spoke at the hospital. Right, Jack?"

"That's right." He glanced at Ballard, then turned back to me. "So what's your idea?"

"Hang on." I turned to Ballard. "Look, this is going to sound crazy, but it's part of this sort of game we were playing after he lost his eye. Bear with me, okay? I really think this could be helpful."

"Are you a psychologist, Mr. Kraft?"

"No, I'm a sales associate at a home supply store, but give this a chance, okay?"

She looked at Skees, who was being studiously uninvolved. She frowned. "Go on," she said.

Just then Emily returned with a glass of soda; I accepted it while Jack and the others watched in stony silence. She looked around, aware of the atmosphere in the room, and said brightly, "Would anyone else like a drink? I could put some coffee on."

"That would be lovely, Mrs. Wilson," Ballard said.

Emily smiled and hurried back to the kitchen.

"Can she hear us?" I asked Jack.

He shrugged. "If she wants to. She's good at not hearing things, though."

I remembered the very first dream I had, where Emily had sat silently while her husband berated their children. "I bet," I said.

"Mr. Kraft, I don't think that's an appropriate..." Ballard began.

"Yeah, yeah, I'm sorry," I interrupted, holding up a hand. This would have been easier without her there, but I wasn't about to let her presence stop me. I set my drink on the endtable and said,

"Jack, you said you kept imagining yourself chopping Jenny up, didn't you?"

He looked at Ballard, considering, then acknowledged, "Yeah, I said that."

"Are you still doing that?"

"Oh, yeah. All the time." His fists clenched, and the anger I felt from him intensified. I could almost see the images myself – Jack's hands pulling the ghost apart. "I want to rip her to pieces, chop off her head and her hands, and tear out her heart."

Ballard looked seriously troubled, but this time she didn't say anything.

"I know someone who used to have a really horrible obsession like that," I said.

"Yeah?" Jack didn't really sound very interested. I think he was too busy picturing himself killing the ghoul.

"Yeah. A woman with three young children. She kept imagining herself locking them in their rooms until they starved to death."

That got his attention. "Yeah?"

"Yup. She was constantly picturing it, in elaborate detail."

He stared at me, waiting for me to continue. When I didn't, he demanded, "So did she really do it?"

"No, no. She never hurt them. What happened – well, somehow the obsession took on a life of its own. It climbed right out of her, as if it was a ghost, or a demon that had possessed her. It got out and never came back."

Jack clearly knew exactly what I was talking about. He glanced at Ballard, then looked back at me. "How?" he demanded. "How'd she do that?"

"I don't know. But my idea was, I wondered if maybe *your* obsession might do the same thing."

He slumped back a little. "What good would *that* do?"

"Well, I know you want to kill Jenny, but you can't, because she's... imaginary. Right?"

"Yeah, so?"

"So if *your* obsession... came loose, then it would be imaginary too, right?"

"You think it..." He blinked his one eye. "Would that work? Could it kill her?"

"I don't know," I admitted. "I told you when you asked me if I had figured it out – I don't know. But I think it might. *We* can't touch her, but maybe you could make something that can."

I could see Ballard getting antsy, sitting there listening to what must sound like pretty twisted nonsense. I didn't look directly at her; that would only encourage her to say something.

I could just barely see Skees; he was listening intently.

"How?" Jack repeated.

"I don't know. I was hoping you could figure it out, maybe. Just... I don't know, reject wanting to kill her? Push it away?"

He thought for a moment, then shook his head. "I don't know how," he said.

I had been afraid of that. Jenny Derdiarian hadn't known how she did it; it just happened. And it had happened after months, maybe years, of fantasizing – she said she didn't remember when the starvation idea had first come to her, but she had been through *at least* seven or eight months of constant obsessing before it split off. Jack had only wanted to kill the monster for a couple of days.

But that – that *aura* of his was so strong!

"Can't you think of some way?"

"No!" He slumped back on the couch again. "No. I can't. It's... it's not a *ghost*, it's just this thought stuck in my head. How can I make anything out of it? That's just crazy."

"*Try*, Jack," I said. "You know what Jenny's like. You know what she did to Andrew McPhee. This may be the only way to stop her."

"But it's crazy! It's nuts. It's just an idea, okay? What am I supposed to do, pull it out of me like a magician pulling a rabbit out of a hat?" He plucked at his sleeve. "I can't do it. There's nothing there to get a hold of."

"There is, though! I can almost see it. It would be real if you could just find some way to pull it free."

"Well, I can't," he said angrily. He held out his arms. "Maybe *you* can."

I reached out, thinking that maybe I could pretend to help him, and that would make whatever mental connection he needed to believe in it and make it happen, and my hands touched his forearms, and I *felt* it.

It was like an electric shock. I almost snatched my hands back, but at the last instant I stopped myself, and closed my fingers around his arms.

That energy surged and buzzed in my grip; it was the weirdest thing I had ever felt, but at the same time I recognized it. It was the same thing I had felt when the Jenny monster attacked me and clawed my face, but woven through a boy's arms instead of having its own existence, an existence shaped into fingernails.

"Do you feel that?" I asked.

"Feel what?" He looked down. "I feel your hands, if that's what you mean."

"No, I meant that... that..." I didn't have a word for it. It wasn't really energy; it was something else. Ectoplasm, maybe. I could feel it, but I couldn't describe it. I curled my fingers, expecting it to slip through them. I wanted to know what that would feel like.

It didn't slip. It tugged and struggled; I had hooked it.

I could see it now; that unnatural brightness that had made Jack so strange-looking was pulling up from his flesh, caught on my own fingers. His arms looked like a sort of double exposure, the normal, dull skin of his wrists beneath the bright, distorted substance I was tearing loose.

I pulled harder, releasing his wrists – his *physical* wrists. I still held his psychic, magical, ectoplasmic, whatever-they-were wrists

The stuff more or less held its shape, which meant it was coming free of his arms for their entire length. The hands were exposed now, hands that were much bigger than Jack's own, a grown man's hands with long, thick fingers that ended in curving black claws. The arms were thickening as I watched. I could feel their desire to grab, to tear, to destroy.

And Jack could see them now, as well. His eyes widened. "Holy crap," he said.

"What are you *doing*?" Ballard demanded.

I rose awkwardly from my chair, getting myself in a position to pull farther. Jack's shoulders separated into a grown man's broad, heavily-muscled pair and a boy's narrow ones, and a second face lifted itself out of his, a face with a heavy tan and prominent cheekbones and a dark stubble, wearing an eye-patch that was more like a movie pirate's than like the modern one Jack wore; the elastic band was replaced with a black leather bootlace. Anger poured from the man like smoke from smudge-pot.

Then the ghost pulled free of Jack completely, and stood there in the Wilsons' family room, grinning at me. He had fangs, or perhaps tusks, in his lower jaw, and his uncovered eye seemed to glow, but otherwise he looked human enough. He wasn't very tall for a grown man, scarcely taller than Jack himself, but he was broad, and built like a weightlifter.

"What happened?" Jack asked.

"That's what I want to know," Ballard said. She had risen and was standing next to Jack, who had fallen back, sprawled on the couch, looking a little dazed. Ben Skees had left his place by the door and was standing behind the social worker.

I was standing now myself, standing face to face with the creature I had pulled out of Jack's body. I stared at its face for a moment, then realized I was still holding its wrists. I released them.

It vanished instantly.

I suddenly found myself staring at Angie Ballard's worried face. I could see Ben Skees over her left shoulder, and Jack on the couch to her right.

Jack's aura was gone. That detachment from his surroundings was completely gone. I could no longer sense his emotions. Except for the eye-patch and missing finger, he was just an ordinary twelve-year-old boy

There was no trace of the ghost I had pulled out of him.

And I knew that *this* was why I had dreamed about him. *This* was how he was going to change my life. He was the one who showed me I could do this strange new thing, freeing ghosts from their creators.

This was the fourth addition to my education that Mrs. Reinholt had given me. The dreams, the apparitions, the psychics – and this.

I just didn't know what it meant.

Chapter Twenty-Six

The three of them, Jack Wilson and Angie Ballard and Ben Skees, were staring back at me, awaiting answers, and I had no idea what to say. I didn't understand what had just happened.

"What the heck did you do?" Jack asked.

"I don't know," I said. I looked at him. "What did you see?"

"I didn't *see* anything at all," he said. "You did some weird stuff with your fingers, then you stood up and waved your arms around. That's all."

He hadn't seen the ghost? That was interesting. But then, I had apparently pulled his psychic abilities right out of him. "Then why are you asking what I did?"

"Because... because I feel different."

"Different how?" Ballard asked.

"Different... kind of good, actually." He looked down at his hands. "I'm not as angry anymore." He looked back up at me, his one eye wide. "You did it, didn't you? You pulled it out of me."

"Pulled what out?" Ballard asked.

Jack looked puzzled. "Whatever it was that was bothering me. The anger. About the ghost. About Jenny."

Just then Emily Wilson reappeared in the kitchen door. "Coffee's ready," she said.

That reminded me of my own beverage. I picked it up and took a gulp, then said, "I should probably be going."

"Already?" Emily glanced at her son. "But I thought you wanted to talk to Jack."

"I think I've found out everything I needed to know," I said. "I don't want to be any bother." I set my glass back down. "I need to go."

It wasn't that I wanted to be rude, or that I didn't like the cola; it's that reaction was starting to set in, and I was trembling. If I hadn't put that glass down I would have spilled it, or dropped it.

I had just done something *weird*, pulling that creature out of Jack, and it had taken something out of me, as well. It felt as if I had just touched... *something*. Another world, maybe. An aspect of reality that I hadn't known existed. My brain didn't want to accept what I had just seen, and my body was not handling it all that well, either.

I think Skees saw that. Ballard's attention was on Jack, as it should be, and Emily was too far away to really see what was happening. Besides, as Jack would have pointed out, she was very good at not seeing things she didn't want to see.

"I'll walk you to your car," Skees said.

I nodded; I wasn't sure I could keep my voice steady if I said anything more. I headed for the door.

Neither of the women tried to stop me, or to accompany us; they stood and watched as we walked out of the house.

Jack lay sprawled on the couch, not speaking, looking slightly dazed – and far calmer than I had ever seen him before. He didn't move, either, as Skees and I departed.

Once we were out the door we went down the front steps together, and down the walk, but halfway across the lawn Skees grabbed my arm and stopped me.

"Are you all right?" he asked.

"No," I said.

"What happened in there?" he demanded.

"I'm not entirely sure," I replied. I looked back at the house. "I did something I've never done before, something really strange."

"Like what?"

I took a few seconds to gather my thoughts, then said, "You know how we think the monster that calls itself Jenny somehow came from Jenny Derdiarian? That one day her obsessive little fantasy just came loose and took on a life of its own?"

"Yeah, I heard you explain that. So?"

"Well, Jack's been dreaming of killing Jenny for what she did to him. He said he couldn't stop thinking about it. So just now I pulled Jack's obsessive little fantasy out of him, and gave it a life of its own."

Skees cocked his head. "You did what?"

"I pulled it out of him."

"How did you do *that*?"

"I don't *know*," I said. "I had no idea I could do that. Mrs. Reinholt said once, when I was complaining about what she'd done to me, that she'd given me more than I knew – maybe that's what she meant."

Skees frowned. "You gave it a life of its own – what does that *mean*?"

"That means it's a new ghost. I saw it. It's like a grown-up version of Jack, the way he'd like to be – big and strong and bad-ass."

Skees' expression hardened. "And he was obsessed with revenge killing? So you've just set *another* one of those monsters loose? You think that was a good idea?"

"Well, yeah," I said. "Not that I did it entirely on purpose, or knew it was going to happen, but yeah, it's more or less what I was hoping for."

"Turning another monster loose?" He looked angrier than I'd ever seen him.

I tried to explain. "Detective, there are ghosts all over the place. There's one that crouches on the sidewalk right over there every night." I pointed. "There are half a dozen prowling the hospital. One more won't do any harm."

He looked where I pointed, saw nothing, and turned back to me. "I'm still not getting it, Mr. Kraft. You said this new one was a bad-ass killer."

"This one isn't obsessed with killing *kids*," I said. "It's *Jack's* obsession, not Jenny's. And he was obsessed with killing *Jenny*. For what she did to him and Andrew."

The anger turned thoughtful. "The *ghost* Jenny, not Jenny Derdiarian?"

"Jack never met the real Jenny."

"Does this ghost know that?"

"I don't think the ghost knows anything Jack didn't. How could it?"

"Mr. Kraft, I don't know how *any* of this works. Do you?"

"Not really," I admitted.

"So you think this new Jack ghost will kill the Jenny ghost? That it can do that?"

"I'm hoping so, yeah."

He looked me in the eye for a moment, then asked, "It doesn't bother you, setting up someone to be killed?"

"It's not *someone*," I protested. "It's an inhuman, child-killing monster. It's a bundle of appetites and obsessions, not a living being."

"So you're sending a kid's dream to kill it. A *kid's* dream."

"Yeah," I said defiantly. I lifted my chin. "Yeah, I am."

"It doesn't bother you, using a kid?"

I shook my head. "Detective, it isn't *Jack* that's going to kill anyone. In fact, if this works the way I think it does, Jack doesn't even *want* to kill anyone anymore. *That's* what I pulled out of him. I yanked out all his anger, his obsession with Jenny, his psychic abilities. Now he can go back to being a kid."

"Psychic abilities? *What* psychic abilities?"

"He could see Jenny, couldn't he? *That* psychic ability. I pulled that out to make the ghost."

Skees clearly didn't understand that, but I didn't know how to explain it.

"And this new thing, it'll kill the ghost Jenny?"

"I hope so."

"So how will you know if it worked?"

I shrugged. "Maybe I won't," I said. "We'll just have to wait and see."

"You said you pulled this ghost out of him. Where did it go? Can you see it now?"

I shook my head. "It vanished," I said. "It's still daylight; I can't see ghosts in daylight. Once it was completely separate from Jack, and I let go of it, it disappeared."

"And you don't know where it went."

"That's right."

He glared at me for a moment, while I stared back, as calmly as I could manage. Finally he said, "Fine. Then go. Go back to Maryland if you want; seems like you've done everything you can here." His expression softened slightly as he added, "No point in getting you clawed up anymore."

"Thanks," I said. "I was planning to try for a flight for tomorrow morning. We can settle up my consultant's bill later."

He smiled at that. For a moment I thought he was going to offer his hand to shake, and I think he thought he was, too, but he didn't. I nodded farewell, and went back to my rental car.

I sat in the driver's seat for a few minutes, catching my breath and thinking about what had just happened. I had *pulled an apparition right out of a living person.*

That was *weird.*

It was apparently something that sometimes happened spontaneously, the way it had to Jenny Derdiarian, but I could *make* it happen.

A possibility occurred to me. Did this mean that *all* the ghosts and night-creatures I saw came from people? Were they *all* unwanted obsessions and fantasies that had gotten loose somehow?

And if Jenny's experience was typical, the people they came from didn't just lose their obsessions; they also lost the ability to see the things lurking in the night.

Maybe *everybody* was born with the ability to see the creatures, but most people lost it early on, when they had some sort of *idée fixe* get loose. Maybe that was why so few adults still had the knack. Maybe that was where all those blurry little night-creatures came from, the harmless ones that didn't look human – kids too young to have a clear image of themselves might have generated those.

Or maybe I was making stuff up, and reading too much into it. This theory of mine might explain ghosts, and even vampires and werewolves – I could imagine people being obsessed with sucking blood, or with turning into wolves – but it didn't explain Mrs. Reinholt, or what she did to me, or to Mel.

Eventually I got my thoughts into some sort of order, got my hands steady and my stomach calm, and started the car. I turned the car around and headed carefully back to my motel. I didn't go straight to my room; instead I got the desk staff to help me book a flight home; I couldn't get a direct flight, but there was one the next morning at 10:55 a.m., changing planes in Charlotte. It cost more than I liked, but I didn't have very much choice.

Thinking about that money got me wondering whether there might be some way to use my newly-discovered talent to make money, the way Mel had used her curse. Maybe set myself up as a sort of freelance exorcist?

That had real possibilities, I thought. Maybe I could finally *use* my abilities, instead of being trapped by them.

And as for Mel, I wondered whether I might be able to tear that curse right out of her.

I went back to my room and called her, or tried to. She hung up on me; she was still in bed, recovering from the long drive home.

I wondered whether the Jack ghost had found the Jenny ghost and killed her yet. Did they even exist by daylight? I knew I couldn't see them, but were they still there?

I went out for dinner eventually, a burger place on New Circle Road – I'm used to eating alone, but that doesn't mean I enjoy it enough to go to anywhere fancier than a burger joint, especially when I have bandages covering half my face, inviting stares. I'd picked up a copy of USA Today at the motel, and took my time reading it. By the time I walked back out to my car the sun was out of sight in the west, and the sky's sunset colors were starting to fade.

I settled into the driver's seat, and reached to put the key in the ignition, when I suddenly realized I wasn't alone in the car. Someone was sitting in the passenger seat next to me.

I started, and dropped the keys. I straightened up, whacking my wrist on the steering wheel, and turned to see a tusked, one-eyed face grinning at me.

I stared at it for a moment, taking it in. I hadn't had a chance to really look at the ghost Jack before it vanished, but now I had all the time I needed.

It was definitely Jack Wilson's face, but in exaggerated, tough-guy caricature. The nose was longer, the jaw stronger, the brows thicker, and of course there was that coarse brown stubble, and the tusks, or fangs, or whatever you would call them. The eye-patch was a rough wad of black cotton, like a black bandage, held in place with a black leather string, and the intact eye was inhumanly bright, the enlarged white almost glowing.

The thing was wearing the same dull-red plaid shirt that the real Jack had been wearing, the same cheap blue jeans, but its shoulders were broad, its thighs bulging with muscle, its hands as big as dinner plates.

That makes it sound like a cartoon, but believe me, there wasn't anything funny or cartoonish about it. It looked genuinely dangerous.

It didn't speak; it just sat there, smiling at me.

"What do *you* want?" I finally asked.

Take me to her.

So it could talk the same way that the Jenny monster could – I didn't so much hear it as remember what it had said.

I didn't answer immediately, and it added, *Gonna kill the bitch.*

"What do you need *me* for?"

Can't drive. Don't know where she is. You do. Take me to her.

I glanced around. "How'd you find me here?" I said.

Been waiting in this car all afternoon. Come on, take me to her.

I bent down, never taking my eyes off it, and retrieved the keys.

I was having second thoughts. Yes, this was what I'd intended all along, to set one ghost against the other, but suddenly I wasn't sure that was such a good idea. That thing looked mean, and it *was* a killer, or wanted to be. I had shrugged off Skees' doubts, but now I wondered whether he might have had a point. *Had* I created another monster?

What would it do to get at Jenny?

What would it do *after* it found her?

Come on. Gonna kill the bitch.

I started the car.

Jenny was a murderer; she had ripped Andrew McPhee apart. She had torn out Jack's eye and bitten off his finger. Now I was going to bring a bigger, meaner monster to punish her for that. This was ugly, and I was sure it was going to get uglier, but in the end, wasn't it the right thing? I shifted the car into drive and headed it out of the parking lot.

I drove slowly and carefully, taking Winchester Road into downtown.

When I passed Strader, where I would have turned if I were going back to the Wilsons, I was tempted to make a little detour – the ghost wouldn't know the difference, would it? And it would have been interesting, I thought, to see how he and Jack reacted to each other.

But I didn't. One glance at the thing, and feel of the bandages on my face, convinced me I didn't want to do anything that might annoy my passenger. I drove straight to the hospital, following Winchester to Midland to Main, then turning south from Main Street onto Limestone.

It was full dark by the time I pulled the car into a space in the garage and turned off the engine. The creature beside me seemed completely real and solid – not that it had ever been particularly ghostly; from the instant it first reappeared, it had been entirely opaque and three-dimensional. Still, it had acquired a certain definition that hadn't been as pronounced at first.

I didn't rush to open the car door; I hoped the thing might take it from here without my help. I looked at it.

Take me to her, it said.

I swallowed, unbuckled, and got out of the car. "This way," I said.

I led it into the hospital; I didn't know what else to do. I didn't know which room Jenny would be in, if she was there at all, and I told it that.

Find her, it said. *Take me to her.*

So I led it in.

I went to Trevor's room first – or rather, the room Trevor had been in the night before. He'd been moved.

I tried Lisette's room; she wasn't there, either. I asked at the nurses' station, and was informed that she'd gone home with her family, a few days earlier than originally planned – the McPhee boy's death had triggered some changes in routine.

It was strange, talking to them with that big one-eyed ghost at my elbow, hanging on every word. I was constantly aware of his presence, I could almost *smell* him, but I could tell that the nurses couldn't see him at all.

I thanked them, and walked away. They probably thought I was leaving, but I doubled back; I still had other possibilities to check.

And one of them paid off. The boy I'd seen sleeping with the IV in his arm, Jesus Martinez, was still there. He looked asleep this time, as well, but he wasn't alone.

Jenny was there, leaning over him, gently stroking his head with one hand; I had the impression that if she had a human voice, she would have been crooning wordlessly.

I was about to say something, I'm not sure what, when the new creature, the one-eyed ghost, surged past me.

Die, bitch! Die, die, die!

Jenny looked up, astonished; the long hair fell back from her face, exposing the one bright eye and the one dark one. The sight seemed to further enrage the false Jack, if that was possible; he grabbed her throat with both hands and snatched her off the bed.

Jack? I could hear her surprise – or remember hearing it, at any rate.

I hadn't expected her to recognize her attacker.

Die die die die!

Then it tore her head off.

Chapter Twenty-Seven

There wasn't any blood. Even though I knew it wasn't human, I had expected blood. There should have been a veritable *fountain* of blood.

There wasn't. Instead there was a sort of scattering of darkness, little bits of blackness drifting off in various directions, unaffected by gravity, and then vanishing, like negative-image flames blinking out. The Jenny thing's head seemed to dissolve into black smoke, then fade away to nothing – mostly.

One bit didn't fade, and the new monster's hand closed on it, and yanked it free. It shoved the captured object up under its eye-patch.

Then it tore off the eye-patch and flung it aside.

While it did that, Jenny's headless body had remained crouched on the edge of the bed. It hadn't collapsed when decapitated; it hadn't moved at all.

Little Jesus screamed; his eyes, closed a moment before, were wide open, staring at the ruins of Jenny's neck. He flung his arms wide, pressed back against the bed.

"It's okay!" I called, gesturing desperately. "It won't hurt you! It can't!"

I wished I was sure of that.

Once it had recovered Jack's stolen eye, the vengeful ghost reached for what was left of Jenny and tried to tear off an arm. Jenny was struggling now; a shadowy image of her head was reappearing, and she was trying to push her attacker away.

Jesus screamed again, and I ran in. I scooped him out of the bed, slung him over one shoulder, then grabbed the IV stand with my other hand and pulled it along as I rushed him out of the room.

As I had expected, two nurses were running toward us, drawn by the screams. "Here," I said, handing them the terrified boy.

"Get a wheelchair," one of them ordered the other as she accepted the child.

Jesus wasn't screaming anymore, just whimpering. I watched just long enough to be sure the nurse could carry him, then turned and stepped back into the room.

Jack and Jenny were clawing at each other, tearing strips of ectoplasmic flesh from one another, scattering that powdery blackness everywhere. Jenny was putting up a fight, and the shadow of her head was still there, but Jack was clearly getting the better of it.

He got his teeth around one of her wrists, and bit down hard; a child's hand, solid and real, fell to the floor, and red blood spattered. I felt a pressure in my head, as if Jenny was screaming.

Then Jack picked her up in those big hands of his, shaking her as if she were a naughty child, and thrust her other arm into his mouth, in horrific imitation of Goya's painting of Saturn devouring his children. The resemblance was so close I suspected Jack had seen the painting somewhere. The monster bit down again, and more of that darkness spread.

After that it wasn't a fight anymore, it was a hideous combination of a massacre and a meal, and the false Jack, no longer one-eyed, seemed to grow larger as I watched him devour what remained of the child-killing monster. Every so often bits of red, torn flesh appeared amid the darkness, and tumbled free.

When it was done there was nothing left of Jenny; there was only Jack.

Jack, and the remnants of Andrew McPhee.

The ghost-Jack turned to face me, an expression of supreme satisfaction on its face. Where before it had been Jack's height, barely up to my shoulder, now it towered over me.

The bitch is dead.

"Yeah," I said. "I saw that."

I got her.

"Yeah." I looked at Andrew's scattered remains and struggled not to vomit. "Can we go somewhere else, please?"

Sure. Lead the way.

I turned and got out of that room, away from the smell of blood. "Nurse!" I called. "You need to get someone in here. Call security. And a doctor."

"What?" She had gotten Jesus Martinez into a wheelchair, straightened out his IV line, and calmed him down – he still looked shocked and miserable, but he wasn't screaming or moaning. He might have been crying quietly; I couldn't be sure from where I stood.

"There's something in there – something bad," I said, pointing.

She gave the other nurse, who was holding the wheelchair, a quick glance, then straightened up and bustled toward me.

I stepped out of her way, then turned and walked quickly away. I didn't want to hang around; I didn't want to be involved in the discovery of what was left of poor little Andrew.

The hulking ghost followed close behind me.

I heard the nurse gasp; I didn't look back. I kept walking.

When we were two corners away, I turned and asked the ghost, "So, you've done it. Now what?"

I hoped that it was satisfied, that it was done, that it would fade away now that its purpose was served, but I feared I was wrong. What if it went after Jack's other enemies? What if it went after his parents, who had neglected and belittled him?

Gotta kill the bitch, it said.

I blinked. I hadn't expected that. "You just did," I said.

Yeah, well, gotta do it again. Take me to her.

"I can't," I said. "I don't know where she is anymore."

Don't tell me that. Take me to her.

"I can't! I swear, I don't know where she's gone!"

Take me to her! It clenched its fists and loomed over me threateningly.

I heard running footsteps in the distance, heavy footsteps – probably security guards, not nurses. I heard voices. "I... okay, look, I don't know where she is right now," I said. "You wait here, and I'll go find out."

Gotta kill the bitch.

"Yeah, you bet," I said. "Just stay right where you are, and I'll be right back."

It hesitated, then said, *Okay.* There was something of the twelve-year-old boy in that, despite its broad shoulders, beard stubble, and fearsome face.

I nodded. "Right there," I said, pointing at the floor. "Don't you move until I get back!"

Then I turned and hurried away.

I didn't start running until I was out the door onto the sidewalk, but then I bolted as if my life depended on it. Which, for all I knew, it did.

I'd thought that when it had killed Jenny it would just vanish; its purpose for existence would have been fulfilled. I thought it could just fade away harmlessly.

That was stupid. After eight years of watching the night-creatures obsessively, endlessly, and pointlessly repeating themselves, why had I thought anything could satisfy one and make it go away? They did the same things over and over; they were *never* satisfied.

I got the rental car out of the garage as quickly as I could, tires squealing as I made the turn onto Limestone. I didn't head straight back to the motel; I'd come out of the garage pointing the wrong way, and I didn't want to take the time to get turned around. I wanted to put some distance between that thing and myself.

Maybe it seems crazy to be so scared of it, since all it wanted was to kill Jenny, and I bore no resemblance to a skinny ghost in a white dress, but I had those scratches on my face to remind me that sometimes, when a ghost got strong enough, it could hurt people other than its actual target. More specifically, it could hurt *me*. Maybe my ability to see the night-things gave me an edge in some ways, but it also apparently made me vulnerable to them.

I did not want to be around when Jack's ghost got frustrated and angry because it couldn't find the monster it had already devoured.

I took South Limestone all the way out to New Circle Road; somewhere in there it changed name to Nicholasville Road, but I didn't pay any attention. I got on New Circle, headed west – this part of it was limited-access highway, instead of being old-fashioned urban sprawl like the stretch north of Winchester Road, so I was able to give the car some gas and put some miles behind me.

The drive let me calm down, and by the time I got back to the motel I was in control again. I called Ben Skees.

"Ding, dong, the bitch is dead," I told him, feeling more than a bit giddy. "Jack's ghost ripped it to bits. Some of those bits came from Andrew McPhee – had you heard about that yet?"

"I'm off duty," he said coldly. "Hadn't heard squat."

The possibility that he might be off duty hadn't even occurred to me. "Oh," I said. "Sorry."

Then I gave him an account of my evening, from the moment I got in my car at the Burger and Shake right up until I called his cell. He listened.

When I was done, he said, "So you left this monster standing in a hospital corridor?"

"Yeah, I did," I admitted.

"You think that was a good idea?"

"Well, yeah, I kind of do," I said, irked. "It isn't going to hurt anyone. The only thing it wants to hurt is already dead, and I don't think it *can* hurt anyone human, except maybe me. This one isn't interested in finding suicidal kids to eat, Detective; it wants to *avenge* them. If anything, I think it might be beneficial – if any other predatory ghost-women turn up, it'll dispose of them."

"I don't like just leaving it there."

"I don't see much of a choice." I sighed. "Look, I didn't know this was going to happen; I thought when it had done what it was created to do it would quietly fade away, or pop like a soap bubble. I was wrong."

"I may have told you I didn't think creating it was a good idea."

"You made your opinion known, yeah. But did you have a better idea? Jenny's gone, Detective; I consider that a plus, and I'll bet the parents of Trevor Atwater and Jesus Martinez and Lisette Babcock agree with me. The McPhees, well, I'm sorry about them, but what could I do?"

"Maybe," he grudgingly said.

"One thing, though – I don't know what would happen if it met Jack. And maybe his father. You might want to suggest to his family that if they ever need to take him to a hospital, they choose a different one."

"Um."

"I'll call Jenny Derdiarian myself."

"Yeah," he said. "You do that."

He hung up.

I called Jenny Derdiarian myself.

I didn't go into a lot of detail; in fact, I went into as little detail as I could. I just told her that we'd found a way to dispose of her doppelganger, and that we'd had to leave our device active, and while it might not be a danger to her, she was the one person in the world it might mistake for its target.

"It won't come after you," I said. "It's very stupid, doesn't know where you live, doesn't know you exist at all. If it *sees* you, though – well, I wouldn't risk it."

"I appreciate the warning, Mr. Kraft," she said.

And my third and final call, of course, was to Mel.

I desperately wanted to talk to a friend at that point, someone who wouldn't be angry that I hadn't found a tidier way to deal with Jenny, someone I didn't need to warn away from the U.K. Health Center, someone who knew me and would take my good intentions as a given. Mel should have been that person.

But Melisandra de Cheverly was the Dark Lady, the Queen of Despair, Mistress of Fear. Nothing she could say could be comforting or reassuring; her best attempts at sympathy scared me half to death.

But she was all I had, and she tried hard to be the friend I needed, and when the trembling had stopped I was grateful for that.

I went to bed, hoping I wouldn't dream about what I had seen that day, and hoping that I wouldn't dream about anyone new.

I didn't need any more big changes in my life right then.

And I didn't get them.

Epilogue

I caught the 10:55 flight without any trouble, and got home without incident.

I'd lost my job. No surprise. Mr. Sanchez was apologetic about it, at any rate. He said that if the economy had been better they might have kept me on, but they'd been looking to cut staff anyway, and my sudden mysterious absence had provided a good excuse.

Mel drove down from Sandy Spring a few days later, to see whether I could pull the curse out of her the way I had pulled the ghost out of Jack Wilson. I couldn't.

I couldn't change my own psychic abilities, either. I tried.

Ben Skees called me once, just to chat. There hadn't been any more incidents at the hospital after the body parts turned up, but that gory little evening had been enough to trigger two lawsuits and five resignations. If the thing that I'd left in the corridor was still there, it was invisible and silent.

Jenny Derdiarian was fine; the destruction of her counterpart hadn't troubled her at all.

Angie Ballard thought I was some sort of con man, a quack pretending to be a child psychologist, and had debated filing charges of some kind, but decided, in the end, not to bother. She wanted it known, though, that if she ever saw me again she wouldn't be as tolerant.

And Jack Wilson was doing okay. He was a surly, withdrawn child, but he was doing better. No more disappearances, paying more attention in school, treating his kid sister better. No anger issues. He didn't dwell on what had happened; he barely seemed to remember it. His father seemed to have been chastened by the whole thing, and was reported by the neighbors to be doing much less yelling these days.

All in all, it had turned out reasonably well, even if Skees had to list the attacks on Jack Wilson as unsolved and leave a few hundred parents nervous about the mysterious lunatic who had maimed the Wilson boy.

I landed a new job over in Silver Spring – retail again, but it paid the rent. Just barely.

I started planning out ways to use my newfound talent. Finally, I could not only *see* the spirit world, I could *do* something about it. It was only a very limited something, but still, it was *something*.

And night after night, I watched the creatures in the streets and parks, saw them plummet from rooftops and throw themselves under buses, saw them try hopelessly to attack women, and I wished I couldn't see them.

But now, at least, I had a few clues about what they were, and maybe someday I could change their world.

- end -

About the Author:

Lawrence Watt-Evans has been a full-time writer for more than thirty years, with more than forty novels and well over a hundred short stories to his credit. He served two terms as president of the Horror Writers' Association, and won the Silver Hammer award for service to HWA. His story "Why I Left Harry's All-Night Hamburgers" won the 1988 Hugo for short story, as well as the Asimov's Readers Award. He lives in Takoma Park, Maryland, with his wife and an overweight cat.

His website is at www.watt-evans.com.

Made in the USA
Lexington, KY
18 October 2011